Poetic

Fiona Forsyth

Copyright © Fiona Forsyth 2023.

The right of Fiona Forsyth to be identified as the author of this work has been asserted by her in accordance with the Copyright, Designs and Patents Act, 1988.

First published in 2023 by Sharpe Books.

To the margarita girls, who taught Ovid how to party

POETIC JUSTICE

Prologue

Volsinii, Italy, 10 BCE

My mother killed my father before I was born. The goddess has confirmed this to me.

In a dream I had when I was twelve, my mother changed before my eyes into the goddess Hecate, and I fell to my knees at once. The goddess had the usual three heads and at her heels was an engaging black puppy, its ears ragged and lopsided and its mouth panting in a grin. I knew I shouldn't, but I wanted to stroke the puppy and even began to hold out my hand before I remembered who was in front of me.

"You are very full of yourself, Sabina, aren't you?"

"Yes, Lady," I replied honestly.

"I have plans for you, girl. Listen to your mother rather than your teachers. Ask her why she killed your father. Your education is all very fine, but you will live your life as your mother's daughter."

When I told my mother of this dream the next morning, and asked her why she had killed my father, she merely said, "It is time," and took me to the little temple of the goddess.

I had been to this temple before: it was on the outskirts of the town of Volsinii where we lived. It was very old, built by the Etruscans before Rome took over their lands. Inside was a statue of the goddess and an old priestess, and with no ceremony, my mother said, "It's happened," and pushed me forward. "Tell her your dream, Sabina."

I told the priestess of my dream and she smiled at me. Over my head, she asked my mother, "What education is she getting?"

"She is in a school run on the Strabo estate for local children," said my mother. "The supervisor recommended her."

The priestess nodded.

"Keep her in this school and bring her here every month. We shall teach her about the Lady."

She finally looked at me.

"You are fortunate, Sabina. First you have been chosen for education by Strabo, a man who will be powerful at Rome, and being in his patronage will benefit you and your mother. But Hecate has chosen you for training in her arts, and that will always come first. Do you understand?"

I did understand. I had understood from the moment the goddess spoke to me that I was hers for the rest of my life.

"She told me to ask my mother why she killed my father," I said.

"Your mother will tell you at home," said the priestess. "I will stay here and arrange for an appropriate offering to the goddess." I remembered the black puppy from my dream.

In this way my service to Rome and Hecate began.

My father? Oh, he was killed by my mother of course – have you not been paying attention?

POETIC JUSTICE

Chapter 1

JANUARY 9CE
Tomis on the Black Sea, January 15
FESTIVAL OF CARMENTA

Marcus Avitius, Security Advisor to the Governor of Moesia, had picked up a ship heading north to Tomis. The winter was not as harsh as usual, so the River Danube had not iced over and the local tribes had been kept penned into the inland areas quite satisfactorily. Avitius had wintered along the coast, checking on the tiny garrisons in each town, and now he was looking forward to a gentle spring in Tomis, making sure the Governor was up to date. He'd be there until late summer, he reckoned, and then he would be sent — well, the gods know where. But preparing the province for incursions from the hungry tribes across the river would probably figure quite highly. Avitius leaned against the ship's side and gazed at the grey sea ahead, almost surprised at how keen he was to see Tomis again.

His new job was working out well in every respect. It had to be better than serving in Spain or Germany — especially Germany, thought Avitius, who had heard stories of the dark forests and mad natives. Avitius himself had served in Spain and Macedonia, by no means easy billets, but he was now focussed on the months ahead. Two years ago, when the bureaucracy in Rome had noticed that he had done many more than his twenty years in the Eagles, he had retired and had taken up a post as Security Advisor to the Governor of the young province of Moesia. There was work to do wherever one served Rome, and Avitius was a traditional man who believed in duty and loyalty. He had come a long way from the Subura in Rome, had travelled all over the empire, and now he was considering settling somewhere here on the Black Sea coast. Yes, there were harsh winters, but the summers were fine, and despite some local unrest it was a quiet place. He had no dependents, no obligations, some land and a business. In short, he had his life in order: he was determined that this time he would settle. Well, maybe after just a few more years.

The ship made its cautious way towards the harbour — there were winters when one could not sail up and down this coast because of the ice, and the Greek cities that overlooked the shore could find themselves cut off. Avitius watched as the little town of Tomis did its trick of seeming to slide down the snowy hill to meet him. Then he was past the two natural curving headlands and home.

He wasn't due to meet up with his boss for a couple of days, so he could set his quarters straight — he had no doubt that someone had stored all the detritus of bureaucracy in his room over the winter — and still have time to remake his acquaintance with the bar he owned, The Lyre of Apollo. He huddled down into his old winter cloak and waited for the docking process to be complete, looking with professional curiosity at the handful of passengers grouped on the deck. They were all men, young to middle-aged, dressed for comfort and warmth. More traders, no doubt, or craftsmen hired in by Tomis' ambitious town council. Avitius hoped they would do something about the sewers. A Roman always valued the local water and waste systems. He turned back towards the land and looked for the roof of the little Temple to Neptune that lay on the ridge above the harbour. That would be his first stop once he had made it to land. Never neglect the god who rules the seas.

The Lyre of Apollo had been a bar without anything to recommend it when he had first set eyes on it, and two years ago Avitius could not have told anyone why he liked it, except that it was very well-situated on a crossroads near the small marketplace that was the focus of town life. He had used his retirement lump sum to buy it and brought in a husband-and-wife team to run it. The wife had the ambition, the husband chose the wine and Avitius enjoyed owning it because between them the pair ensured that the place was always clean, served good food and had a supply of "special" wines for favoured customers, such as himself. And the landlady was his sister.

POETIC JUSTICE

He was greeted with enthusiasm by both Vitia and Macer as he ducked his head under the lintel.

"Where have you been?" demanded Vitia, with the rude familiarity of a little sister. She didn't wait for an answer, gave him a hug, and went on with, "I know, being busy and important, sit down and I'll get you something to eat. Sit there, by the brazier, you look starved and frozen," and he was settled into a corner, warmed and welcome. He smiled. He liked coming home.

"Where's your bags?" called out Vitia as she rummaged around behind the counter.

"I sent them to Headquarters," he said. "I didn't want to take up a room here."

"Always room for you," said his brother-in-law appearing at his side with a tray. "Here, see what you make of this."

Macer sat on the other side of the table, sharing the warmth of the little brazier, and poured a cup of wine for each of them. They saluted one another and tasted, before Macer added water to each cup, the ritual as easy and welcoming as the inn itself. Avitius, drank, relaxed, stretched out his legs and sighed as the wine slid down.

"This is good. Where did you get it?"

"From a place in Bithynia, one of the towns on the coast of the Black Sea. Nice easy journey so the wine doesn't suffer," said Macer, a man who had turned his passion into his work and loved his life.

"You worry too much about your wine," said Avitius, settling in for a well-worn argument.

Vitia brought over his bread and stew and took a cup of wine herself.

"Never mind the wine," she said, sipping. "What is the news?"

Avitius shrugged. "Same old. A milder winter means not so many raids from the tribes. The river not freezing helps. By next winter, the Governor will have the coastal patrol working more smoothly, and he plans to reinforce the inland forts. Just what you'd expect."

"The Getans aren't that much bother," said Macer easily. "Not this far east anyway. You soon get used to their Greek. I'm not getting any chatter about the Dacians either."

"Our locals are decent enough people," added Vitia. "I've had some lovely animal furs off them for bedcovers in winter. I bought one for you of course — you won't go cold tonight, brother."

"What about the town?" asked Avitius. "Any wild doings while I was away?"

"Nothing wild," said Macer. "This is Tomis."

***

The letter arrived in the imperial post this time, and I was impressed. It was on a folded and sealed wax tablet, which was also unusual, and I eyed the courier carefully. He knew what I was thinking.

"Open it now, carefully, and you will find instructions," he said.

I broke the seal to find a single sentence scratched on one side of the tablet and a small silver charm pressed into the wax on the other.

"Show this to the courier," read the instruction. I kept a finger on the little silver charm to ensure it did not fall from its wax cradle and turned the tablet to show the courier. He nodded and dug around under his cloak until he drew out a leather cord on which hung a similar charm – a small silver sword with a pommel.

"It's a new idea from the boss, a way we can recognise each other," he said. "Let me just show you something."

He carefully prised her sword from the wax and turned it over, pointing out a tiny letter P engraved on the back. "P for Praetorian. Keep it safe and don't tell anyone about it – not even the Governor."

I snorted with laughter. "The Governor and I are not exactly friends."

"Good," said the courier. "He is my next stop though, and I must be quick. You have this as well," and he handed over a small leather tube. Then, with a courteous nod he was gone.

I tucked the tube under my arm as I closed the wax tablet and went back into the house, straight to my study where a lit brazier was next to the desk, with Phoebe carefully tending it. I dismissed

POETIC JUSTICE

Phoebe and settled at my desk. The document tube was filled with a thick papyrus roll, and one loose sheet wrapped around the roll. The sheet carried my instructions and as I read the goddess rose inside me, whispering with excitement.

I was exactly where she intended me to be, ready to carry out her will.

From Aelius Sejanus in Rome to Sabina in Tomis, greetings
You will have received with this letter:
1. a small silver amulet, shaped like a sword and
2. a draft of a work of poetry about the calendars and religious festivals of Rome, stolen from the poet Ovid.

The amulet is a token enabling agents of the Praetorian intelligence service to make contact in confidence. Be very discreet in its use.

The poetry is more interesting.

The poet Ovid has been exiled to Tomis by the Emperor, until further notice. Details are not to be made public, merely that it has happened. Technically, the man is not even exiled, but banished by the Emperor himself, using his personal authority. A decree of the Senate will formalise this in due course.

It is important that the man never returns to Rome. Your instructions are to note and report on his activities to me personally, via our Athens office, and to ensure that he is seen as persona non grata.

Using the draft poem included, you will carry out various antisocial activities on dates mentioned in the poem. Gradually, you are to ensure that people realise the link between these activities and the poet. I rely on your considerable abilities to think up ways of making sure this comes about.

Chapter 2

January 30
ANNIVERSARY OF THE ALTAR OF AUGUSTAN PEACE

After the tussle to get the cat to swallow, I held it until it fell unconscious, then laid it, still wrapped in sacking, on the floor at my feet. Over it, I whispered the prayer, "Hecate of the underworld, in blood and ashes, I bind my enemies," then turned back to the desk. The papyrus unrolled easily after all its recent handling, and I reread the lines of verse I had picked out, whispering them to myself as the cat's breathing slowed.

My song has led us to the altar of Peace, the second day from the month's end.

Priests, throw incense on the fire at the festival of Peace,

And sacrifice a white animal, sprinkling its head with wine....

A small gasp at my feet brought my attention, and I bent to look carefully. The cat was unconscious, despite the glint of yellow that seemed to look up at me from half-closed eyes. The creature would be dead soon. I turned back to the poem and whispered, "Hecate of the Underworld, in blood and ashes, I bind my enemies."

In the hour before dawn, I slipped through the streets to the alley behind the temple, carrying a lamp and the sacking with its pitiful contents. Over and over, in my head I intoned, "Hecate of the Underworld, in blood and ashes, I bind my enemies."

***

When the attendant of the Temple of Jupiter, Juno and Minerva smelt the smoke of burning, he automatically checked inside the temple, but, no, the odour definitely came from outside, a smell of scorched flesh and something richer and sweeter — incense. Gods above, what was going on? The man huddled himself into an old blanket and set off on a circuit of his precious temple, crunching through shallow drifts of snow and grumbling to himself about the lack of respect shown by the temple's neighbours. When he turned the corner and saw the small smoking bonfire right up against the temple's back wall, he was outraged. Who had dared? It was practically sacrilege. He drew nearer, and the smell intensified, overcooked meat and — herbs? He sniffed cautiously and there it was, the familiar odour of sage. He peered at the fire which was already dying down in a puddle of melted snow and saw a blackened little shape. With distaste he realised that it was an animal, a small cat. There were quite a few cats in Tomis nowadays, so he hoped somebody was not missing a precious pet. The sacrilege outraged him once more and he gathered up an armful of snow and used it to dowse the fire. He noticed several tufts of black fur scattered around the fire and felt slightly sick.

"Keep going," he told himself firmly, "make sure that it is properly out, and then go and tell someone. And get rid of the smell."

People were going to come to the temple for an official sacrifice soon and they weren't going to be pleased to smell burned cat.

***

Avitius had put his office in Tomis back to rights, updated the Governor and written up every report conceivable. He was now back in the normal day-to-day of a quiet winter in Tomis. The dead cat behind the Temple was the most exciting thing that had happened since he got back, so when he took his seat in The Lyre of Apollo that evening, he was not surprised to be the focus of many stares.

His brother-in-law was as swift as always in serving him but stayed to share the jug and pump him. Macer leaned forward as he poured and said quietly, "I hear the big sacrifice was nearly buggered up this morning."

"The big sacrifice?"

Macer gave him a wise look but decided to play along. "Anniversary of the Altar of Peace, and orders from Rome were to put on a show, am I right? Unfortunately, Tomis' grand civic sacrifice came complete with the persistent whiff of burned cat. People are already saying it's an omen of a disaster, so how much do you bet that we'll have some sort of military defeat announced soon?"

"You're a superstitious idiot. There aren't any military defeats when the legions are in winter camp," said Avitius comfortably. "It's January."

"When we first came here, you said that's when the barbarians across the river like to attack," pointed out Macer.

"Only when it ices over," said Avitius. "Anyway, that doesn't count as a military disaster. Tell me about this cat. Do we know who did it? What are people saying?" and he waited for the story.

Throughout Tomis, the tale of the burned cat was told at bars of all sorts, from the large and organised River View Inn outside the walls to Hermes' Place, a small hostelry specialising in plain cooking and even plainer wine. Nothing ever happened in Tomis, so this sacrilege (behind the temple itself, and on the day of the solemn rites of Peace!) was inflated as the evening went on. One very drunk merchant from Bithynia told anyone who would listen that this was the beginning of a major conspiracy of someone-or-other, probably the Dacians. Or the Thracians. Or maybe the Germans had sent agents to stir up the Black Sea cities... When the bar's owner, Hermes, patted his customer on the back and said, "And why would the Germans want to burn a cat then?" the Bithynian's eloquence vanished. Some sort of religious nutter, was the general view by the end of the evening.

***

I sing to the Moon, the goddess,
who walks between sky and sea and land
through the street of the Tombs
on blood and sage and bay leaves.
I offer the barley, the bay and sage,
the flesh and bone and hair,
the blood and the burning.
I sing to you, sweet light of the Moon,
Dread darkness of Hecate.

It went well. The last day of the month, always special as endings are special. And Rome's great ritual of Peace shown for what it is, an empty piece of pageantry. I have never felt Roman, even when I lived in Italy, even though my father was a citizen. My mother once told me that citizenship is of little use for a woman. She isn't quite right, I think, but since the age of twelve, I have been Hecate's.

POETIC JUSTICE

Chapter 3

Tomis, February 1
FESTIVAL OF JUNO THE SAVIOUR

Avitius spent some of his precious free time helping out at The Lyre of Apollo. He was given the job of painting the yard walls with a fresh coat of lime, because although it was cold it was a bright day, and his sister didn't see why not. This gave him a chance to think about the dead cat behind the temple.

Avitius had come across his share of animal abuse stories and they were never pretty, but he also had a theory that crimes like this were the outward manifestation of a mind led by demons, and often the perpetrators went onto more serious offences. Avitius knew some people were like that, though not many were in the army, or not that he'd come across anyway. But now he definitely had someone who didn't like cats in Tomis.

He sloshed more lime on to the wall, and it dripped down the walls and slowed in protest at the cold. His fingers sympathised. He was getting old.

When he was tired of painting, he put everything away methodically in the shed in the yard and went into the bar for something to eat. Macer heated some spiced wine for him and Vitia gave him a bowl of the stew of the day, and he enjoyed the feeling of warming up once more as he ate and drank.

"Did you hear that we're getting a famous visitor?," called Macer. "Rumour says he's a poet, that Ovid who wrote *The Art of Love*. And — he likes his drink. Not sure how he'll cope with being away from the big city."

"Isn't he that one who you knew when you were doing patrols in Rome, before you joined the Eagles?" asked Vitia, who had always had the gift of remembering what Avitius would rather not.

He didn't want to discuss it, but Vitia's eyes were bright and innocent and she wasn't going to be fobbed off.

"Yes, and look," he began, watching her eyebrows shoot up in triumph. "The Governor's warned me — there's something dodgy about Ovid's punishment, and I want to avoid politics. Let's keep it quiet." He changed the subject by taking a casual look around and remarking, "Have you heard any more about the dead cat? Who do people think did it?"

It didn't work.

"You thought this Ovid was all right when he was in charge of your Commission for — whatever-it-was," said Vitia.

"The Commission for Prisons and Executions," said Avitius.

"You know this bloke?" demanded Macer. "What's he like?"

"I knew him thirty years ago," said Avitius. "I was nineteen or so, he was only just older than me. He won't be the same man."

"We all feel sorry for him, of course, being exiled," said Vitia. "I like his poems, the early ones, and the *Metamorphoses*. Macer here won't let me read the *Art of Love* of course."

Macer looked embarrassed.

"Not right for a good Roman woman, that sort of smutty stuff," he muttered.

"And how would you know it's smutty?" demanded Vitia and pushed herself up. "No, don't answer that, I've got work to do. Don't get my brother too drunk."

The men settled back as she went into the small kitchen behind the bar and clattered pots noisily to prove her independent mindedness.

"Did you really tell my sister she couldn't read Ovid's poetry?" asked Avitius, knowing the answer.

"When was the last time anyone told your sister anything?" said Macer amiably. "And don't look at me, I may be legally in charge of everything, but I make sure to give her no orders."

"Have you read *The Art of Loving*?" asked Avitius curiously. Macer laughed.

"I don't read any poetry," he said. "But what I heard about it was funny, just the sort of thing the moralists would hate. When did Rome start crawling up the bum of all things virtuous?"

Avitius knew the answer to that one and did not bother to take up the discussion. He might be far away from the city, but he still served Rome and he wasn't going to be caught out bad-mouthing the regime.

POETIC JUSTICE

He stood and went over to stick his head in at the kitchen. Vitia was stirring something, a frown on her face. He waved.

"Time I was off," he said.

"When does this poet get here, then?" she called out.

Avitius shrugged. "No idea."

And left before this could be challenged.

Ovid was expected in Tomis at any moment, though the latest news was that he had decided to visit the island of Samothrace on the way into exile. The Governor had rolled his eyes and muttered at this and Avitius agreed – when the Emperor ordered you to go to Tomis, you went to Tomis, with no diversion for sight-seeing. But the upper classes tended to do things their own way.

Chapter 4

The eastern Mediterranean, February 1

Letter to his dear wife, Fabia, from Ovid — I'm not quite sure of the date, it might be February already. I'm on Samothrace, broke my journey here for a few days. But it is time for me to move on before the authorities get annoyed. Despite all the mist that seems to surround us, the nautical sort of people I meet say that the crossing to Tempyra is straightforward enough. I can't delay, really, can I?

Anyway — there is an absolutely magnificent temple sanctuary complex here and they allow anyone — man, woman, slave, free — to become an initiate in the Mysteries. So, I asked and it was an experience. I am really not sure what to make of it. I can't tell you much of course, but the sanctuary itself is beautiful beyond words. It lies on the slopes of a mountain that rises straight up almost from the cliffs of the sea. Rather cleverly, they make you toil up a hill and then enter the sanctuary from the top, so you come in on a view over the hill, the buildings, the town further down and then the sea stretching away forever into the mist. You walk down into the sanctuary, descending from the clouds almost like the gods themselves — no, that is hubristic, and I really can't afford to annoy the gods any further. So, you go unhubristically through an underwhelming entrance, skirting the theatre, and then you see the main buildings. The highlight in the daytime is a splendid statue of Nike, wings outstretched as she lands on the prow of a boat. She is caught at the precise moment when she is about to fold her wings, and the wind that bore her in flight is now plastering her dress to her body, threatening to push her off her perch. She, however, is completely balanced, concerned only with urging on the rowers to greater speed as they plough into an enemy hull. And despite all this magnificence, when it is the night you barely notice her! I can't say much more except that the drink they give you is powerful and I wasn't entirely sure I enjoyed that particular part of the experience…

POETIC JUSTICE

But back to my sign. The Mother Goddess has granted me protection as I cross the sea, and this is the one bit of hope I have felt since leaving Rome. I can't tell you the details, but I was granted a vision when I slept after the initiation, and it was utterly convincing. Interestingly, Baucis and Philemon also underwent the rites, and Baucis was clearly very moved. She is a devout woman. Philemon never seems to be affected by anything. I am grateful of course that the two of them have been so loyal to me and they are looking after me well.

Rome and her gods seem far from me at the moment. Maybe these eastern gods will protect me, but I long to step out of our front door and turn to see the Capitol rising up with all the red-roofed temples crowning it.

I send this letter and all my love to you, your mother and the girls. I suppose Vidia is still in North Africa and may not have heard yet? I hope so. Keep Perilla far from Rome. I know the authorities will see her as only my stepdaughter, and she is protected by you and her father, but it may be safer.

In the meantime, make a list of everyone we can lobby. Which reminds me of my rather good plan – I'm going to write a series of poems, expressing my sorrow and yearning for Rome. I shall send them back to you and to various others, enough to make sure that copies circulate among all our friends. This will ensure that the Emperor will read them, so make sure that you nudge people, won't you? I'm calling the collection "Sorrows," which is appropriate and pithy. I enclose the first poem in the series with this letter.

I know what you'll say, Fabia — "You don't want to upset anyone, let things settle before you start nagging." I don't want to irritate Augustus or Livia of course, but I have friends who will approach them on my behalf. I'm counting on your father of course, after all those years of friendship with Augustus, his voice must have weight. I'm going to cultivate that nice young Germanicus too, must be a good idea now he is officially Augustus' grandson. Do you think it would be too much if I dedicate my new work, *The Calendar of Festivals*, to him? When I've finished it. Anyway, if you could have copies made of the poem I'm sending to you now, and distributed to everyone you can think, I'm sure it will make its way to the correct people.

The Governor of Macedonia is a fan of my work and has offered me an escort from Tempyra to the Black Sea coast. No doubt he will let me use the official post so you should expect this by the end of February.

And Fabia, try and restrain your mother — this is too important to let her loose on editing my poems.

My Sorrows, poem one, by Publius Ovidius Naso
 Off you go to the city, little book,
Without me, but that's all right.
No gilt edges for you, little book,
Grieving for your creator's plight.
No bright cover for you, little book
or red silk ribbon to mark the line.
Happy scrolls are coloured, little book —
You must bow to the Palatine.

POETIC JUSTICE

Chapter 5

Tomis, February 27
FESTIVAL OF THE EQUIRRIA

Outside the old town wall, the inns specialised in offering stabling, cheap rooms and horses for hire. They were used by the outsiders — the farmers around the town who had their own modest share of the Black Sea grain trade, and traders from the tribes who lived along the banks of the river. They came to Tomis to sell meat, cheese, weapons and jewellery, and bought wine, pottery and spices. Everybody knew that Moesia's history with Rome was a bloody one, but the Greek towns of the Black Sea also knew that survival lay in trade.

When the groom at the inaccurately named River View Inn awoke to the sound of hysterical neighing, his first dream-infused thought was that there was an attack on his childhood village, something which had happened nearly every year when the neighbouring village ran out of food. Then he became fearful that there was a fire in the stable. He sat up, trying to disentangle himself from the noise and his blankets, and realised he could not smell smoke, though the horses beneath him were frantic. He skittered down the ladder and ran along the row of boxes, looking for a disaster. In the stall nearest the open door, he found it. The pool of blood had already stretched across the width of the stable, and a thin shaft of early dawn daylight pierced the gloom to make the dark surface glint horribly. The smell hit him, catching the back of his throat, forcing him to stop and swallow and try to calm himself. He now knew what he would see as the stall's occupant came into view. The beautiful creature lay with its head towards him, a huge, splintered dent in its skull between the dead and long-lashed eyes that seemed to be looking right at him. The horse lay in a pool of blood, and as the groom took one creeping step nearer, he saw that the animal's throat was cut. The combination of wounds was unmistakable. He fell to his knees, unable to stand, and started to pray to Thagimasadas, Lord of Horses. At the back

17

of his mind, he registered the slight crunch under his knees and the smell of sage and bay leaf briefly stirred his nostrils.

***

The sacrificial death of the horse reached Avitius with all the swiftness that an upset business owner can muster. He had been in his office at the Headquarters, deciding whether he really was ready to advise on numbers for the new garrisons that Governor Caecina was setting up. It was his misfortune that Headquarters was the nearest official building to the River View Inn, and that the inn's owner considered himself Tomis' most important entrepreneur.

There weren't many aspects of life in Tomis that Lucius Sergius Sulla was not involved with. He owned three ships that sailed around the Black Sea collecting grain, wine and anything else he thought might sell, and traded with the local tribes inland. He also owned several businesses in and around Tomis – a couple of shops, the River View Inn and another establishment near the docks catering for the seafarers who regularly put in to Tomis. He boasted that if anyone in Tomis needed anything he was the man to approach. He was also an extremely useful source of information for the almost the whole length of the river as far as Avitius was concerned, and, no snob, he respected Sulla's willingness to co-operate with the authorities if it helped them manage the delicate peace in Moesia.

Sulla had been visiting the River View for one of his regular business meetings with the manager and had been greeted by the hysterical and blood-smeared groom as he walked into the yard. The sight of the dead horse had more than upset him — he was angry at the waste and violence, and more than a little concerned about some of the aspects of the death.

"It looked just like the animal had been sacrificed," he explained once Avitius had calmed him down. "You could see it quite plainly — the horse had been stunned and then had its throat cut. I suppose I should be thankful that it was one of my horses and did not belong to a guest. But why a horse and why in my inn?"

"Having any business problems at the moment?" asked Avitius.
Sulla frowned.

POETIC JUSTICE

"Nothing out of the ordinary," he said scratching his chin and staring thoughtfully at Avitius without really seeing him. "I mean, I usually have some sort of an argument going with someone or other but that is just the game I'm in. And I don't think this was directed at me. I'm as respectful of the gods as the next man, but I would never have thought that anyone would want to conduct a sacrifice in one of my stables. It just seems weird, you know?"

Avitius agreed that it did indeed seem weird. He asked if the horse was still in the stables, but Sulla shook his head abruptly making a little shivering movement that hunched his shoulders up to his ears.

"I had it moved as soon as I could," he said. "You have to, the other horses were going mad and I didn't want any of the guests to see what has happened. As it was, most of them know because I can't stop the slaves gossiping."

"What have you done with the body?" Avitius asked and Sulla's eyes slid away from him. The businessman shrugged again, this time carefully, as he said, "Ooh I'll think of something," and Avitius knew that the horse had already been butchered and the meat used for the gods alone knew. He decided that he would not eat at the River View Inn for a few days.

Avitius was not particularly worried about seeing the horse *in situ*. He would have gone if it had not been moved but he did not feel that actually seeing it was of great benefit. He knew that the significant point was that the horse had been a sacrifice.

And that reminded him of something.

***

I sing to the Moon, the goddess,
who walks between sky and sea and land
through the street of the tombs
on blood and sage and bay leaves.
I offer the barley, the bay and sage,
the flesh and bone and hair,
The blood and the burning.
I sing to you, sweet light of the Moon,
Dread darkness of Hecate.

The song sends echoes around the world.

I was pleased with the sacrifice. Working together, we got the horse stunned and its throat cut swiftly. We scattered the wine and the herbs and left the inn with little trouble. We had cloaks ready to hide the bloodstains, and we just climbed back over the locked gate. It wasn't a very high gate, and it was hard to see why they had bothered locking it.

This time, they have recognised that it was a sacrifice. The larger picture escapes them completely. Just as Sejanus thinks I am working for him. He does not see the world through the eyes of Hecate.

POETIC JUSTICE

Chapter 6

Tomis, March 1
BIRTHDAY OF THE GOD MARS

On the same day that his wife in Rome received his letter, the poet Ovid approached his new home, his prison, his assigned place of exile. At first he was so entranced by the glints that danced over the waves that he did not notice the town approaching. It was only when the water became choppy, lining up in rows of white-tipped teeth like a saw, that he looked up: the ship was passing between two headlands and into a circle of water, with a man-made quay ahead. The cliffs reached out of the ocean then fell behind him, cutting off his way home. He had finally arrived at Tomis.

The water in the harbour was quieter, cowed by the town perching on top of the cliff. As he looked, a single wave made a valiant attempt on the quay, hurling itself against the stone and getting slapped back in a curling fall, scattering its energy in a spray of drops. Ovid too had no energy left. Tomis had drawn him in, not with an embrace but captivity. He clung to the ship's rail, already mourning the open sea.

Behind him, Baucis and Philemon watched their master as his new home became real.

***

Menis, Archon of the Town Council of Tomis for this year, was told of the arrival as soon as the customs officer saw the name on the ship's manifest. Tomis had been awaiting the arrival of Rome's most famous living poet for a month and so Menis had everything ready. Hastily he threw on his winter cloak, and gathered a small entourage — secretary, slaves for helping with baggage, daughter, daughter's maid — before leaving the house. With any luck, their swift downhill journey would get them to the harbour in time.

Their hurried passage down the hill was spotted straight away and a crowd soon formed behind them at a respectful distance. Now all that was needed was the poet himself.

The activity at one quay identified the ship. Knots of people stood looking lost on deck and on the quay, while officials checked bags and amphorae. Sailors shuffled with impatience to be allowed to go to the line of bars that overlooked the harbour, and passengers looked around with blank faces, left in limbo until they were officially welcome to Rome's newest province. As Menis approached, heads turned and the shifting skeins of people moved apart until a space appeared in front of them and a short, middle-aged man was revealed. He was grey-haired, wore a clean, blue tunic that Menis immediately envied, and a heavy cloak. He stood with a heap of bags at his feet. Behind him stood a younger man and a woman, well-wrapped up and looking as uneasy as their master.

As soon as he saw Menis and entourage, the grey-haired man took a step forward, and then hesitated. Menis saw the uncertainty immediately and felt for Ovid — of course, the etiquette was unknown. How was a disgraced exile supposed to behave? Well, he should know straight away that the people of Tomis welcomed him, so Menis smiled, pumping out reassurance. This might turn out to be a good thing for his town, and by Zeus, he was going to make the most of it.

"Publius Ovidius Naso, you are welcome to Tomis," he said in ringing tones as he walked up to the man in the blue tunic. "I am Menis, this year's Archon, and I represent the town council. We would like to be of some small help while you stay with us."

He could hear the crowd behind him chatter excitedly, and one or two people clapped. Ovid even smiled, just a little.

"That is very kind, Menis," he said. His Greek was classical and correct, and his voice was not as mellifluous as Menis had instinctively expected.

"Just because the man is famous for his love poems," Menis chided himself silently. He made a note — don't judge a man by his poetry. He moved closer to take Ovid's hand.

"I hope you don't mind me talking in Greek, but I want as many people as possible to understand what I say to you," he said. "Most people here have some Greek. My Latin is passable, I'm told, and no doubt will get better through conversation with you. Now, the town has made a small house available for your use. I realise that after your journey you won't want a big fuss, so let me just escort you there, and I shall leave a couple of people with you for a few days to help you and your household settle in."

Ovid looked overwhelmed and Menis thought, "Oh, he wasn't expecting kindness. Poor man."

"I only have Baucis and Philemon here," said Ovid, half-turning to the couple behind him, and if his voice shook a little, only Menis heard.

"Then let's get you there quickly," he said warmly. "The walk will help you find your land legs as well. Hephaestion, would you start moving things — get a couple of porters if you need. I'm sure Ovid's people will help you." And he took charge.

***

Ovid allowed himself to be walked along the quay and up the hill overlooking the sea. He did not look around as he walked. The need to get to a house, and out of the gaze of all these people was paramount. He tried not to think of what he had seen in the few glances he had taken before Menis swept down on him, but he couldn't help a little wail inside just because the people were an unfamiliar mix. Funnily enough, the women could have walked out of any marketplace in Rome, but the men! The strange hairstyles, the beards, the tunics that looked so rough — and cloaks made of furs and animal skins, practical, of course, but hardly chic. It all rammed it home to him, brutally. He was no longer in Rome, no longer anywhere he would feel comfortable. He was at the edge of empire, in a small town he could not leave, surrounded by Greeks and Asians and barbarians from tribes he had only heard of in myths. He had even mentioned them in his poetry, oh so casually, Scythians, Thracians, Getae and Sarmatians, all without a single real thought about them. Now, all around him were harsh voices, and he had to work to understand even Menis' Greek. The accent was so strange.

"What must the man's Latin be like?" Ovid thought enjoying a spiky little sneer, before training himself back into sad acceptance of Fate. "Gods of the Capitol," he prayed, "don't let this last too long. I'm not going to be able to be polite to this mob for more than a few months."

He stretched his mouth into a smile and walked with Menis through his new home town, while the excited crowd followed at a respectful distance. At the shrine to Neptune that overlooked the harbour, they stopped so that Ovid could make an offering of wine and incense, and then they moved on. At the town's main square, tiny in comparison to the Roman Forum, Ovid could not help but note, Menis gracefully said farewell, leaving his secretary Hephaestion to lead the poet to the new home. Ovid was grateful to see that the crowd stopped following at that point.

He was almost relieved to hear Philemon mutter behind him, "I should grow a beard – look, everyone here has beards."

"Except the women," Baucis snapped.

Without turning his head, Ovid said loudly enough for them to hear, "No beards. We're Roman, not bloody Greeks."

There was a pause, then Philemon said, "Glad you said that in Latin, sir."

***

Menis persuaded the crowd to go home, and finally turned to his daughter.

"Well, Apolauste," he asked, "You managed to remain silent throughout that. Congratulations."

"Very funny, Papa," said his teenager automatically, before saying, "What do you think?"

"He is not a happy man," said her father.

"I thought he would be a lot taller," said Apolauste, adding, as she turned away to go into their house, "He's very old, isn't he? Will he die before he gets pardoned, do you think?"

POETIC JUSTICE

Chapter 7

March 2

On the day after his arrival, and slightly hung-over after an evening bar-hopping, Ovid wrote a short letter to his wife back in Rome, then decided he might as well walk around his new home, before the misery of acceptance really set in. He was familiar with the way his moods ran and knew that this general feeling of apprehension was about to descend into a prolonged bout of unhappiness. But he could try and postpone it.

He stepped out of his new front door and wondered whether to go left or right. He could remember little of the day before but knew that the journey from the harbour had been nearly all up hill to get here. Ovid had no worries about this, having lived in a city of hills all his life. He risked superstition and turned left.

Back in the house, Baucis and Philemon were a little concerned.

"Should he have an escort?" said Philemon doubtfully. In Rome, Ovid would not set out without a bag carrier or torch holder.

"Well, there's you or there's me," said his wife as she reorganised the kitchen to her liking.

"We could send one of the lads lent us by that Menis chap," said Philemon.

"They're busy," said Baucis firmly. She had set the two young slaves a lengthy list of fetching, carrying, rearranging and cleaning and did not want them distracted before she sent them back to Menis in two days' time.

Philemon shrugged and accepted his wife's superior knowledge, as he usually did. "I suppose Tomis is safe," he said. "And it's so small he can't possibly get lost."

"And you can give the privy in the yard a good clean," said Baucis. She saw Philemon about to object and said, "You'll do it properly. We have to share it with next door and we don't know what they're like yet."

"They're Greek," said Philemon. "They'll be fine."

He found a bucket and strolled off to the yard while Baucis wondered if it was too soon to call on next door's kitchen to pick up tips on markets.

***

In between the roofs of the buildings, Ovid could see the sea and a salty wind blew in his face. It was not unpleasant, but he did wonder if this breeze was a year-round occurrence. He had never lived by the sea before, except for the summers at the Bay of Naples, where he went to dance attendance on the bright, clever people who liked having a poet in their circle. And that brought back some uncomfortable memories that made him want to stop and cover his face in the middle of the street.

"The sea," he thought with determination. "I shall go down to the sea."

Most of Tomis watched the poet as he strode through the town that day. Nobody offered anything more than a nod or a smile, but he knew he was the subject of much speculation. That was what happened when the main source of your fame was a sex manual in verse.

"But it isn't a sex manual," Ovid argued to himself, his lips pursed into a cross expression. "It is a light-hearted look at attracting someone you like. I even make sure women are not left out, because I like women, unlike my wonderful Emperor with his ridiculous laws against any form of sex he hasn't personally approved…"

"He's muttering to himself," said Gorgo, the cook at Hermes' Place, as Ovid strode past without giving the little bar a glance.

"Maybe he's composing poetry?" suggested Antiope the barmaid, peering out of the front door to see the celebrity pass.

"Maybe he's mad," said Gorgo unsympathetically.

"He's older than I expected," said Antiope, and turned back to wiping down tables.

Ovid made for the harbour, occasionally hesitating before choosing a street, but generally making good progress. Progress was easy in Tomis. You went downhill from everywhere to get to the sea, and uphill to get to anywhere else. If you wanted to go inland, you headed west. But west was no good for Ovid. He was not allowed outside the town boundaries, and until he was sure he knew where these were, he wasn't going to risk it. Besides, he wanted to look out to sea.

At the edge of the quay, Ovid stood and gazed out at the harbour, tracing the route of a merchantman that made its ponderous way to the wide harbour mouth. Rocky arms reached out to protect the harbour and the ship sailed between them, on its way to adventure and risk. Ovid sent silent prayers after the ship and the journey he had just made from Rome suddenly seemed an impossibility. How in the name of all the gods had he made it here, in the middle of winter? The last three months retreated into history and became as unreal as something he had read of in a book, then dismissed. His new life was the only real life, surrounding him, pressing on him, and he felt his body brace for the onslaught.

Sulla the businessman, standing at the door of his warehouse on the hill, saw the peculiar movement of the man's body, as though he were squeezing his whole frame inwards. For a moment he wondered if Ovid was going to collapse but after a few moments, the poet stood straight, turned around and stomped back up the hill from the harbour to the town. Sulla watched him climb past and almost felt sorry for him.

At the top of the cliff overlooking the harbour Ovid marched past the street with the big baths and accompanying line of bars. He was not interested in discovering the town's sights, he was heading home, maybe via a bar. But, as he passed one of the main crossroads in Tomis, he glanced around, and at the sight of a man painting the wall of a bar, stopped and stared.

***

"She works you too hard," said a voice behind Avitius. He put down the brush carefully before turning.

The man looking at his handiwork was shorter than him and looked a lot older but it was just a year or so in reality. Ovid's brown eyes seemed smaller now they were set in wrinkles, and his hair was grey and too long.

"Morning, sir," Avitius said and held out a hand. "Good to see you. What's it been? Thirty years? Forty?"

"Avitius," said Ovid and took the proffered hand. "You bastard, I was hoping to surprise you."

"Like you did on the Aventine that time with the old woman and the bunch of carrots?"

"Ah, now you're just sweet-talking me. What's going on in Tomis then? And why are you painting what is clearly going to become my favourite bar?"

"It's my bar," said Avitius.

"Is it? Congratulations! Sounds like I need to buy you a drink and get us all up to date," said Ovid. He sounded hopeful but was not surprised when Avitius nodded at the paint pot and the spare brush lying next to it.

"Help me with this first. Just a quick coat, won't take long."

Ovid looked at the brush, shrugged and picked it up. He watched Avitius, and joined in the painting, saying, "The number of times I've walked along a street in Rome and seen someone doing this, and thought to myself, "That'll last until tomorrow morning at the most, before someone's drawn a cock on it." But buildings here don't get nearly as much graffiti I've noticed."

"You only arrived yesterday," said Avitius.

"I've walked around a bit," said Ovid, discovering that the lime wash dripped a lot, and wondering how to avoid getting it all over his tunic.

"Nobody scrawls on my bar," said Avitius.

"It really is yours? How come?" Ovid almost enjoyed the rhythmic slapping of paint on stone. It was warm work in the cool March air, and his arms grew tired quickly. "Gods, I'm unfit," he thought. He slowed down a little and hoped that Avitius wouldn't notice.

Avitius said, "I bought it with my retirement money, got my sister and her husband to come out and run it for me. I work for the Governor now."

"So I heard," said Ovid.

"You've heard? Already?"

"Yesterday evening, I went to the baths and a found a barber. Amazingly, barbers here gossip just as much as they do in Rome. I found out quite a bit about the place, then found a bar in which to drown my sorrows once I had found out about the place." Ovid shrugged. "I asked about the Governor and his staff and your name came up."

He decided not to mention that this morning he had trailed in misery down to the harbour to look at a sea he could not sail. He stepped back to admire his paintwork, and trod on the foot of a small boy, who along with several friends had been standing close behind them, watching. The boy cried out in pain, then yelled, "Latin speaker!" as he and his friends ran off.

"Latin speaker?" Ovid was bewildered. Never had he thought of his native language as an insult before.

"Aren't many of us speak Latin in Tomis as an everyday sort of thing," said Avitius. "And not everyone is happy to be part of the Empire, you'll be amazed to learn."

Ovid was still looking after the boys. An old man walking by on the other side of the road winked at him, and, comforted, Ovid put down the brush, hoping Avitius would take the hint.

"This is a nice place, Avitius. Ye gods, look at us — the last I saw of you, you were setting off for the legions with the whole of our patrol seeing you off, not to mention a very pretty young lady whose name escapes me, in absolutely floods of misery."

"I remember it well," said Avitius. "I was so hungover I could hardly walk, thanks to you and the lads. And the young lady married someone else as soon as I'd gone, according to my sister, so she didn't suffer for long."

"How long were you in the Eagles?"

Avitius paused. "Twenty-eight years. Far too long. Served with the Tenth Legion in Spain under Agrippa, moved to the Fifth in Macedonia to get my promotion. When my commander got made the Governor of Moesia, I retired, but he asked me to stay on as a Special Adviser. I bought this place, and persuaded Vitia and Macer to come out from Rome to run it, and now you're up to date."

"Twenty-eight years in the Eagles and you're still younger than me," mused Ovid. "I feel old, ex-Centurion."

"The Eagles were good to me," said Avitius. "Maybe poetry wasn't quite as good to you."

"Poetry is an exacting mistress," said Ovid solemnly. He looked at the wall. "Isn't this done now? How about that drink?"

Over Macer's wine, a Bybline find from Asia Minor, and Vitia's bread, cheese and sausage, they caught up. Ovid was surprised and touched to find that Avitius not only remembered their year together in the Commission for Prisons and Executions fondly but seemed to be able to talk to him as though he were not a disgraced exile. He ventured to say this and Avitius looked surprised.

"Surely nobody in Tomis has given you trouble?" He had dropped the "Sir" quickly, Ovid noticed and was glad for it.

"Everyone has been spectacularly nice, and the town more than generous," said Ovid gloomily. "But I feel as though I wear a huge label, you know, like the placards around a slave's neck at an auction. And everyone takes one look at me and knows I'm that man, the poet, the one who...."

"Well, painting a pub wall won't do you any harm," said Avitius. "Enough people noticed so it will be all over Tomis soon."

Ovid was surprised, then remembered the boys and the old man.

"Is there really so little going on here that I'm news?" he asked, knowing that he would have been news wherever in the Empire he was sent.

"Oh, there's lots going on in Tomis," said Macer cheerfully eavesdropping as he cleared plates. "Did you hear about our animal killings?"

"Animals?" Ovid turned back to his old friend.

"A burned cat found behind the Temple of Jupiter in January, just before all the great and good turned up for the ceremony celebrating the Altar of Augustan Peace."

"Well, that is not nice," said Ovid. "I've written about the Altar of Peace, you know. I was at the dedication ceremony of the Altar, years ago. And then went and looked at it when it was fully open, gawped at the carvings like everyone else. It's remarkable. Have you seen it?"

Avitius shook his head. "I've been back to Rome twice in the last twenty years," he said. "Didn't spend my leave visiting many altars."

POETIC JUSTICE

"The Altar of Augustan Peace," said Ovid dreamily. "It's in my new work. I'm writing a poem that will cover the whole year, calendar, festivals, stars."

"I hear you've written a lot of poems," said Avitius mildly. Ovid scowled. Macer rejoined them from the kitchen, unable to make any sort of pretence that he wasn't dying to be part of this conversation. Ovid smiled at him.

"You said animal killings plural," he said. "How many?"

"Just the two this year," said Macer.

"They might not even be connected of course," said Avitius. "There was a cat in January, then a horse was killed, funnily enough on the same day as the festival of the Equirria. You'll know all about the Equirria, eh, Calendar Boy?"

"I do indeed," said Ovid. "I always went to watch the horses racing on the Campus Martius if I was in Rome."

"And wrote about it, no doubt?"

"Of course," said Ovid.

"I don't like the feel of these killings though," said Avitius. "Do you remember that man who killed dogs on the Aventine?"

"Yes, and the whole thing was horrible," said Ovid soberly, remembering the almost inhuman creature they had finally tracked down and dragged off to the prison.

"It was," said Avitius. "But we got to him before he moved on to children."

"And his neighbours expressed complete surprise when we caught him, then said they always knew there was something wrong with him." Ovid frowned at Avitius. "Have you got someone like that here?"

"If we do, nobody is saying," said Avitius. "People like me don't get told things of course. I am a Roman."

"We have a couple of weirdies," said Macer. "The boy whose parents run the laundry is a bit strange. But no hint of him doing anything like this before."

"What do your informers say?" asked Ovid. Avitius didn't answer. "Oh, come on," said Ovid. "You've got informers, I know you have."

Avitius looked at him and sighed.

"This isn't Rome," he said. "I'm still feeling my way around."

"After how many years?" asked Ovid.

"Two," said Avitius. "But I travel, checking out the Danube forts, the coast, that sort of thing. If the River freezes over, we get invasions. And the tribes beyond the River are quite capable of getting as far as a coastal town like Tomis. You might find yourself doing a stint of duty on the wall."

"It's easy," said Macer. "We all take turns standing on top of the wall so that we see if anyone comes for us. Did mine a couple of months ago."

"I've not even noticed a wall," said Ovid.

"The wall that goes across the neck of the peninsula," said Avitius. "West of the Governor's headquarters."

"You mean the big heap of rubble with a gate in it? That's not a wall," said Ovid. "Who threw it up?"

"The Greeks about four hundred years ago," said Avitius. "It's done the job so far."

"Why anyone would want to attack this place is beyond me," said Ovid. He looked into his wine cup and saw the days stretching out ahead of him. Guard duty, for Jupiter's sake...

Avitius looked at Ovid for a long moment and saw the lines of depression that pulled down the poet's long, thin mouth. He hardened his heart. Sympathy was not what Ovid needed now. He nodded at Macer, who obediently slid off his stool and went in search of something else to do.

"A word to the wise," Avitius said very quietly so that Ovid looked up and leaned forward over the table. "Bad-mouthing this place will get you nowhere and lose you goodwill. The people here aren't what you are used to, but they're good people. Be nice."

Ovid looked stubborn.

"Too soon," thought Avitius, "but I had to say it."

"I'm going to dinner with your Archon tonight," said Ovid stiffly. "I promise I'll behave."

"Menis is all right," said Avitius. "A widower, has a teenage daughter he dotes on."

Was there a warning note there? Ovid scowled.

"Note to myself," he said bitterly. "Do not seduce the host's daughter. Well, Avitius, I think I can manage that." He drained his cup and moved his chair back.

"Thanks for the drink."

He stalked out of The Lyre of Apollo. Macer came back over and said, "Well, that went well. He looks older than I thought he would."

***

Ovid found dinner at the Archon's house a combination of excellent food and excruciating conversation. This was entirely his own fault. He had decided that he did not want to enjoy anything about Tomis, and that he would make a point of having as little as possible to do with anything within its walls. When invited to dinner, he should have refused. But Baucis said he couldn't, and even unpacked a good tunic which she checked over critically before leaving it on his bed. The tyranny of a faithful retainer and his own curiosity won, but the Ovid who arrived at Menis's house was tired and inclined to grumpiness.

Perhaps Menis should have invited more people, but out of consideration for Ovid he had arranged nothing more than a small family gathering, just himself, his daughter and his secretary.

"The poor man has had a long journey and does not need to meet the great and good of the town all at once," he had reminded his daughter. "We shall all speak Latin this once. And — Apolauste, be sensitive. The man has been sent here against his will by the Emperor, and may not be thrilled, despite the opportunity of meeting you that this gives him."

She gave him the disdainful look perfected by all sixteen-year-old girls and attacked their guest with enthusiasm over the olives and eggs.

"Why were you sent here, I mean, why Tomis?" she demanded. Despite his mood, Ovid found he appreciated her direct approach and waved away Menis' murmured apology. He replied seriously, "I don't know. I thought it would be one of the islands, but Augustus himself chose this town, presumably to make it clear that he really hates me."

The silence lasted a few heavy moments as everyone analysed what he had said.

"Well, it isn't exactly a compliment to us," complained Apolauste.

"Well," echoed Ovid. "This is hardly the sort of place I'm used to."

He could hardly believe he was saying these things, and knew he had made a great blunder, allowing himself to be pushed into rudeness rather than stay silent.

"It strikes me that it would be useful for you to know a little of our history," said Menis so smoothly Ovid knew he had to work hard to redeem himself. He thought quickly.

"I know of course that you were founded along with several other Greek cities along this coast several hundred years ago," he offered. "You were a colony established by Miletus, weren't you?"

"Indeed," and Menis' tone had relaxed a little. "Though I think we shall only trouble you with the last hundred or so years. We were taken over by Mithradates of course when he was at his height. Your general Lucullus kicked Mithradates out and we were left alone again until another of your generals Antonius Hybrida decided to make us the target of his advances and was defeated heavily."

"He was an idiot," said Ovid. He turned to Apolauste and asked politely, "If you haven't read it already, I recommend Cicero's speech in which he attempts to defend Hybrida. Unsuccessfully. The man was a brute."

She nodded but let her father continue. "That left the way for Burebista, great king of the Getae, to take us over. When he died in the same year as Julius Caesar, we lay low while the locals warred with each other: Roman generals came and went but it was a mere ten years ago that your Vinicius decided we must be permanently made part of the Empire."

Menis stopped to sip wine and Ovid wondered what in the name of all the gods he could say in answer to such a recital.

"I gather local feeling was not too positive about this," he said, and Apolauste giggled, stopped and coughed.

"I'm afraid the Romans were not well-liked for much of my youth," said Menis sounding a little less like a lecturing teacher. "We just wanted to go on as we always had, ruling ourselves, banding together with other towns to keep the more warlike tribes at bay, minding our own business."

"And now you are Rome's business," said Ovid carefully keeping his tone neutral.

"Maybe," said Apolauste. "We always knew it would happen someday but now that it's happened we don't really know how we stand, do we, Papa?" She turned at Ovid with a face of righteous criticism. "You see we aren't officially part of the Empire yet. The governors we have had so far have concentrated on the interior not the coast, because that is where all the trouble comes from. They've had to spend a long time providing support to the war on Illyricum, though I admit Caecina Severus did check up on us when it was feared that the Getae were going to attack last year." Ovid detected the echo of her father in her words.

"Apolauste is correct in that we do not know what role we are to play in the new province yet," said Menis. "In the meantime, we run the town ourselves as we always have done and maintain good relations with the Governor. When the time comes we shall be in a good position to make the most of any advantages Rome brings. I must say that it is nice to have a Roman army at our disposal in times of threat."

"Are you often attacked by local tribes?" asked Ovid.

"No, because we take good care to be on good trading terms with as many of them as possible," said Menis. "We leave stirring them up to you Romans."

Apolauste clearly started to feel sorry for Ovid at this point. She gave a polite little throat clearing sound and asked, "Did you ever meet the poet Virgil? I had a tutor last year who practically died of excitement every time we read Virgil."

"Yes, I met him" said Ovid, "but I very much doubt if he noticed me. I'd only just started letting people hear my poems when Virgil died — the two events are not connected," he added hastily as he saw her smile. "I just meant that I was too insignificant then to get close to the great man — and he was great, no doubt about that.

Didn't act like it. He always gave the impression he wasn't at ease talking about his poetry. Poor man."

"Who else did you meet?" asked Apolauste. "Horace?"

"Oh yes, Horace. Great at parties, could tire the sun with talking. You know his father was a freedman? But wherever the gods dropped him, Horace always looked as though he was happy to be there. In fact, it was as though he was perfectly confident that he had a right to be there. But what I really appreciated about him was that he was very good at making younger writers like me feel that we also deserved to be at whatever the occasion was."

"Where did you recite?"

"Anywhere," said Ovid. "At first, I was a part of Messalla Corvinus' set. He was an excellent patron of poets, would arrange readings for us, make sure we met all the right people, and sometimes there would be parties where all the fun people got together and…" he saw Menis' face and mentally edited what he was about to say. "That's where I met Tibullus, and Sulpicia who is now my mother-in-law, although of course I didn't foresee that. Ye gods, that was more than thirty years ago…"

"You've met everyone," said Apolauste, her voice lilting higher as she envisioned for a brief moment the vastness of the world that the old man in front of her had seen. She sat up excited by a sudden idea.

"You know what? You should give public lectures."

"Lectures?" Ovid could not keep the horror out of his voice.

"Well, why not?" Asked Apolauste, puzzled. She looked at her father. "Have I said something wrong?"

"No," said Menis. "It's an excellent suggestion. But not everyone is suited to lecturing."

"Well, he must be used to reciting his poetry," said Apolauste. "I don't see much difference."

"*He*," and Menis emphasised the pronoun to indicate how rude she had been to talk about their guest in such a manner, "might disagree with us. However," and he turned to Ovid, "if you were interested in offering a public reading, I am sure you would be overwhelmed at the enthusiasm. We like our poetry here."

POETIC JUSTICE

"Er... even Latin poetry?" said Ovid, wondering how he could get out of this. "Surely very few people here know Latin?"

Menis strove to keep the weariness out of his voice.

"Greek is the language of trade here, of communication, but many of us know Latin," he said. "Apart from the Roman officials, there are Romans who have moved here for various reasons. Then there are people like me who were taught it from an early age, and reached the heights of Virgil, as Apolauste has just shown. Many of the merchants have learned it to help with their trade. Even a few local tribesmen have picked up Latin, and they are very fond of their poetry, they have an excellent oral tradition. The bards are honoured highly. I think you may be surprised by Tomis."

"I can see that," said Ovid politely. He was absolutely determined that he would never be surprised by anything in Tomis.

As a stilted conversation prolonged itself, Apolauste gazed with an increasing disappointment at the guest whom she had thought would be so exciting. Instead, she saw a man approaching old age who had compensated by embracing grumpiness. She thought of the copy of *The Art of Love* that she kept hidden in a corner of her clothes chest, under a thin piece of wood that almost covered the bottom. She had read nearly all of it, intrigued by its air of sophistication. This, she had thought, was how Romans in Rome behaved, approaching love as an elaborate and entertaining game. She was half-way through Book Three with its advice to women and found it wickedly thrilling.

"While you can, while you are young — play!" the poem advised, and at sixteen, Apolauste intended to try. The poet recommended the places she should try to be seen — alas, they were places in far-off Rome, with names that spoke of heroes, princesses, excitement, glamour — the Portico of Pompey, Livia's and Octavia's arcades, and the Circus Maximus. As an intelligent and curious young woman, she had worked out the basics of sex for herself, but Ovid's poem hinted at a world where women were entitled to their own entertainment and pleasure ("I'm not saying you have to be a whore — but you won't miss what isn't worth anything") and to Apolauste, that seemed delightfully logical and fair. And the advice he gave! All the way from the practical "Try padding for a flat chest" to the sly "Each girl should know herself" before — unimaginable — describing how best a woman could display herself in bed. Apolauste felt her blush begin and resolutely turned her thoughts to the old grey man in front of her.

But Ovid was looking bored. Apolauste started listening properly to conversation once more. Her father and Ovid were talking about, of all things, provincial administration.

*Surely, if you have a Governor, you are official, a fully recognised province?"

"We have had an official Governor for two years," said Menis. "But we have not been confirmed as a province in Rome. I must admit, I didn't quite understand why not. I suppose these things take time."

"Or aren't considered very important," said Apolauste.

Ovid was despite himself, intrigued. "Rome can't tax you if you aren't a full province," he mused. "Yet, keeping the troops here is expensive."

"There is also a coastal fleet," said Menis. "Our Governor, Caecina Severus, seems decent enough. He was in Macedonia for years, knows how things are here. He is a fan of your work, isn't he?"

"I don't know," said Ovid. "Never met him."

Apolauste decided that it was time to retire and fussed with her draperies. Her maid woke up and came forward, making the flapping hand movements designed to steer a child to bed, and Apolauste made a swift but polite farewell. Ovid raised his cup to her with a small smile, relieved that he could soon make his excuses and leave.

POETIC JUSTICE

Chapter 8

March 10

If you worship Hecate, then you will be called a witch: and if you are a witch, you live on the margins of life. It sounds like a terrible thing but in fact, it gives you an excellent view of the sad little life experienced by most humans. The onlooker sees the whole battle, remember, while the participants' view is limited. Women are already pushed away from the centre by men, who pretend that politics, trade and war are all that matter, while we, relegated to the outer rings of experience, quietly get on with the scary business of making sure life continues.

I wondered if I would like Ovid when he arrived. As an exile he too had been pushed away, and in Tomis he was on the edge of Empire, far from Rome, the centre of his world. I thought that at least he celebrated his world with warmth and humour in his poetry, and he painted striking portraits of witches such as Circe and Medea. I would of course carry out my orders from Hecate, and incidentally those instructions received from Sejanus, but if Ovid was not a typical example of Roman male arrogance, then I might not enjoy killing him.

His first few days in Tomis were not promising. I enlarged my network and had him followed until I had a clear idea of his routine, and after that it was a case of making sure I had informants in the bars he frequented. I was soon under no illusions. He was a spoiled, over-educated and rather pompous Roman male, typical of his class.

***

In Hermes' Place, Ovid was regaling a bemused audience of local traders with a detailed account of the unfairness of his life, and particularly his exile. The fact that Ovid was declaiming in slurred Latin meant that he was understood by few, though he was entertaining enough to everyone.

"I was exiled to this –" Ovid looked around carefully, worked out what he was going to say and declared, "place. Exiled. Exiled prim – primarily – in the first place because I saw something" Again, he looked around, then said in a stage whisper, "Which I am not at the liberty about to speak."

"What's he on about?" Gorgo muttered to Hermes. Hermes shook his head. All the barmaids leaned on the counter in a row, enjoying the show.

At this point, everyone became fascinated by Ovid's attempts to tap the side of his Roman nose, attempts that failed every time but caused him to cross his eyes spectacularly as the finger flew past his face. The sniggering became louder, and just as Hermes was regretfully deciding that their new customer had better be escorted home, the Governor's Security Advisor came into the bar. The laughter died as everyone buried their faces in their drinks, and the girls found cups and trays to polish.

Avitius strode over to Ovid, picked him up by the back of his tunic and dragged him out of the bar.

Avitius took Ovid home and asked a sleepy Baucis to bring a basin and jug of water. He sat Ovid in the entrance hall (too small to be called an atrium) and carefully positioned his head over the basin before pouring the water over him. Then he took a seat himself and waited.

"How often in my life have I done this for someone else?" he thought.

As if guessing Avitius' thought, Ovid lifted his head and gazed blearily around before saying, "You're good at this aren't you? I bet you made a wonderful centurion."

"I did," said Avitius. "Holding squaddies' heads while they threw up was my speciality."

"Did I throw up?" asked Ovid.

"Not this time," said Avitius. "But you need to drink a lot of water before you try to sleep tonight."

Ovid pulled a face.

"Water gives me tummy troubles," he said. "Unless it's mixed with wine of course."

"Tomis has the best water I've ever come across," said Avitius. "Drink it. And as you drink, think of how you are going to stop opening your mouth and spewing every detail of your life across the town."

"I don't do that, do I?"

"The Governor will soon hear about your complaints," said Avitius. "And then he will be concerned that you pose a security threat,."

"I don't know anything that consti – constitu – oh bugger it, I know nothing that's a threat of what you said." Ovid was now feeling ill.

"You are a fool," said Avitius bluntly. "Trying to do the comic drunk routine gets you nowhere. You pick a bar, get drunk and tell anyone who will listen that you saw something so secret that the Emperor himself organised your exile. Then you drop hints. Then you pass out. The Governor will have to report back to Rome if you let slip anything in the least embarrassing to the Imperial family, you do know that don't you?"

"Yes," said Ovid. "I do know that. But I don't know how to stop myself."

"Don't drink so much, don't go out, if you do go out, take someone sober with you. It's easy," said Avitius.

"They hate me you know," said Ovid.

"Nobody hates you," said Avitius. "Drink some water and go to bed."

"They do, the Imperials, they hate me," said Ovid. "Not Augustus, not him, not really. But Livia and Tiberius. I don't know why but they hate me."

"Learn how to not say any of that in public," said Avitius, standing up. He called for Baucis and Philemon, then left as soon as he could, wishing he could believe that Ovid would follow his advice.

Chapter 9

March 15
FESTIVAL OF ANNA PERENNA

"He's hungover again,' called Baucis, as she passed through the kitchen carrying a bucket full of something smelly and repulsive. Philemon grunted as he peeled vegetables at the table.

"The veg stall had some nice onions," he said to the table, knowing Baucis was already out of earshot in the little yard at the back. "They aren't as far ahead with their veg here," he told the table. "But what they've got is nice. And cheap. Makes you realise how much we were being ripped off just for living in Rome."

The clattering of an angry bucket broke into these musings. The privy block was shared with the house next door, inhabited by a blameless old man and his blameless housekeeper but Baucis was always complaining about the smell and the state other people left it in. Philemon thought that the house was quite nice, despite its shared conveniences. Not what they had been used to in Rome, of course, but he had never expected it to be. And it was free, so they couldn't grumble. He laid the prepared vegetables in a row on the freshly scrubbed table, and wondered if he should try and lever his master out of bed, or at least get some water down him. Sighing, he gathered a tray, loaded it with some dry bread, a small dish of olive oil and a cup and jug. Baucis returned in time to see him leave and wish him luck.

"And when you are done with his lordship," she said, "the privy needs a sluice down. I don't know why next door can't aim properly or sit down, but he can't."

Philemon nodded stoically and headed for the door.

"It's nearly midday," he said in practiced quiet tones, as he set the tray on the little table next to the bed that was a twisted heap of blankets. A smell of overripe and sweaty pears hung in the air, and Philemon unshuttered the tiny window.

"I'm going to be sick," said the heap of blankets. Philemon moved a bucket next to the bed and left. He might be only a

POETIC JUSTICE

freedman, but he had some dignity and no longer felt obliged to wait for the next instalment.

***

When Menis, Archon of the council of Tomis, paid a visit to the town's most famous inhabitant, he was not surprised to be politely fobbed off at the front door by Philemon. Since the awkward dinner, he had made a point of dropping in on Ovid, concerned that the poet was not settling in. Ovid had been too unwell to see him on all but one of those occasions. Town gossip made the cause of his illness clear, for Ovid's wine supplier had never learned discretion, while the poet himself seemed bent on getting himself thrown out of every bar in the town. Shaking his head, Menis began to walk back along the road, heading for the centre of Tomis where his own house, one of the largest in town, sat in a desirable corner of the town's main square.

Ever since Ovid arrived in Tomis, Menis had felt sorry for him — and irritated with the authorities in Rome who had decided that Tomis, a perfectly nice town on the Black Sea, was sufficiently ghastly to be a place of punishment.

"Arrogant sods," thought Menis as he strode along a clean, wide street lined with shops and bars. "None of them has ever been here, nobody asked the council, they just decided that my town could be slandered without any comeback."

And they had been right. Tomis might be the most important town in Rome's newest province, but it apparently barely impinged on official consciousness back in the city that ruled the known world. Maybe he should write a letter to the Emperor, thought Menis and grinned to himself as he imagined it, the Emperor reading a letter in his study and crying out, "Jupiter, we have upset the people of Tomis! What can we do?" Yes, very likely.

In the meantime, Menis was determined that he was going to persevere with Ovid, because the man needed a friend. Pleased with himself, Menis sailed on, his mind already pondering the next thing on today's list — the town drains. Every year, he thought, every single year we have trouble with the drains. We need a way of cleaning them properly. From this he moved on to the arrangements for dinner with the new Governor and had a brilliant idea. Maybe Ovid would accept the invitation to dinner as well Menis knew that he himself spoke Latin admirably: but the poet might perk up at the thought of conversation in his native tongue with genuine Romans.

Once he reached home, he went straight to his study and pulled out the ideas for a new drain from the town's engineer. He was immediately interrupted when his daughter came in, tapping softly on the doorway's frame.

"How is our rude poet, Papa?"

"Still rude," said Menis. "Be kind, Apolauste."

***

Avitius received a message from his sister at his work, of all places. Apparently, there was a sad poet in The Lyre of Apollo. He felt exasperated with both her and Ovid, Ovid for being so obviously needy, and Vitia for using this as an excuse to get him to stop working for the day. Still, he set off. There was, he thought, always work on his desk, and if he finished it, why, then there would be more in the morning.

He joined Ovid at the usual table without making any fuss, and accepted the cup that Macer placed in front of him. His brother-in-law patted his shoulder on the way back to the bar. Whether this was for good luck, thank you, or sympathy, Avitius could not tell. He looked at Ovid carefully. The poet had not shaved for several days. His eyes were bloodshot, and his mouth turned down. He could not continue like this. Avitius sipped his wine and waited.

Suddenly Ovid spoke.

"Do you know what day it is today?" he asked.

Avitius had been writing the date on his paperwork all day. "It's the Ides — the Ides of March."

"And," said Ovid, "the festival of Anna Perenna, a deity so obscure that nobody knows her origins. But everyone in Rome takes a picnic and their favourite girl down to the banks of the Tiber. It's a break just in time for spring, when, for a few hours you can actually look for the flowers coming through."

Avitius said, "And it's the anniversary of the assassination of Caesar."

"Yes, yes, it's that too, and unfortunately nobody is going to remember it for anything else now. But Anna Perenna was such a lovely day before the assassination spoiled everything — or it was if it didn't rain."

"I remember freezing my enthusiasm off during a very unsuccessful picnic," said Avitius. "The young lady in question wore her best dress which was as thin as a miser's purse, and she got grass stains on it, for which she blamed me."

"How unfair," commiserated Ovid, "as no doubt you were only trying to keep her warm."

"And I succeeded in that," said Avitius. "But she never forgave me for the dress. Anyway, enough of idle chatter. Do you remember the first time you came on patrol with me and the boys, thirty years ago?"

"Oh yes," said Ovid. "I was terrified, especially of Cornelius, the patrol leader. He was an ex-centurion, wasn't he?"

"He claimed to have fought at Philippi," said Avitius. "Laziest man I ever met until I joined the army."

"Don't generate any paperwork!" said Ovid, in a deep bark, which was a pretty good centurion's voice, Avitius thought. "But he had some good tips too — listen to what the barkeepers tell you, because they know everyone, and they know what's going on. Next best is to find the old granny who lives on the corner and sits outside pretending to shell peas all day long. Sometimes the kids will be helpful, but you have to let them hold your sword as a reward. And they always try to run off with it."

"That's an impressive memory you have," said Avitius. "And he hated murders. 'If we find a body, it's not our job to say whether or not it's a murder. Look for the family, deliver the dearly departed, walk away.' The man was all heart."

"My first dead body was on that night," said Ovid. "The wound on the corpse's head was so horrific, I thought he'd been killed by some mad axe-murderer. It was you that pointed out the broken roof tile lying in pieces next to him."

"That was the second time you came on patrol. The first time was the man who killed his wife's parrot, so she pushed him out the window. Those were the days," said Avitius. He held up his cup and said, "Happy Anna Perenna."

"I remember being astounded when Cornelius expected us to touch dead bodies," said Ovid, lost back in a different world. Avitius stayed silent, deciding that the poet needed to talk. "I asked him if he wasn't scared of the pollution and he just said that after twenty years in the Eagles, he'd seen a lot of dead men, and a dead man doesn't harm the living."

"We just pretended the dead man was barely alive and found out where he lived so we could get him home," said Avitius. "Kinder to the family than waiting for a priest to come and mumble a few words to release the corpse."

"I think we did a good job on the whole," said Ovid. "I know that the new City Watch is probably going to be a lot better, but considering the pitiful number of men we had, we didn't do badly. And it was an interesting experience. I've never done anything like it since."

"Why did you go for the post?" asked Avitius. "Given what you went on to do, I always wondered."

"My brother died," said Ovid. "He was exactly a year older than me, and he was supposed to become a senator and make the family proud. That's why the old man had us so ridiculously well-educated. I was in Rhodes learning oratory when I was called back to Rome to fill a dead man's shoes. One of the old man's friends had a word with the Urban Praetor and lo! I became one of the Commissioners for Prisons and Executions. Ye gods on Olympus what a title. And what a job. I barely lasted the year. And I never fulfilled my family's ambitions."

"Nobody stayed any longer than they had to," said Avitius. They were silent as they remembered the people of their little squad. Cornelius the ex-centurion who knew how to avoid work, nevertheless gave Avitius a glowing reference for the Eagles. Blandus, who fancied himself the squad's funny man, lived with his old mother on the edge of the Subura and supported two widowed sisters and a gaggle of nieces and nephews. Philo was a freedman, and spent all his pay on books, to the amusement of the rest of the squad, who of course nicknamed him 'professor'.

"And I was the youngest member of the squad, the one who was always sent on errands," said Avitius.

"What was my nickname?" asked Ovid. Avitius grinned.

"'Nosy,' of course. We weren't imaginative."

"And the really sad thing is," said Ovid, "that now I look on those days as the good times."

"You're maudlin and I'm taking you home before you disgrace yourself," said Avitius, striving to keep his tone light. "Say thank you to my sister."

As they left, the night air seemed to revive Ovid, and he stood breathing in and out in the doorway.

"I like the air here," he announced. "There, did you see that? I said something nice about this place."

"Please keep talking in Latin," muttered Avitius as he grabbed Ovid's arm and steered him up the street. Could he risk leaving Ovid at the crossroads? The poet was striding out confidently but talking too loudly. "He's challenging me," thought Avitius and in a burst of irritation decided to let Ovid alone. As they approached the crossroad, he broke into Ovid's loud diatribe on the problems of small towns, in particular the lack of a good brothel, and said, "I'm staying at Headquarters tonight. Can you get yourself home without trouble?"

He did not wait for an answer but turned smartly off to the left, ears pricked for the tirade. When it came, he waved a careless hand and did not look around.

Ovid stood looking after Avitius for a moment, practising feeling injured and abandoned, then turned and went down the right-hand road towards the Market Square and another bar. Hermes' Place, run by the eponymous Hermes was small, had a very mediocre house wine, and the girls were sweet. Maybe he could persuade one of them to be nice to him.

Avitius had not abandoned Ovid completely though and thought things over on his way back to Headquarters. The poet needed a reason to stop drinking and whining, he decided, half-exasperated that Ovid had become his problem. And as he marched down the dark streets back to Headquarters, he wondered if a distraction was all that was needed. Those animal killings were still niggling him in the back of his mind. What if Ovid were given a little task? Avitius had rated Ovid's instincts highly during that year in Rome, and even if it was thirty years ago, maybe a little light detection was just the thing. It was risky though — he was going to have to warn the Governor. He entered through the main door and saw the Governor's secretary Timomarchos lying along one of the benches for visitors. The Governor must be working late. As Avitius came nearer he could hear Timomarchos' gentle snoring. The wooden door to the Governor's study was slightly open, and Avitius could see the flickering light of oil lamps. He tapped lightly on the door.

The Governor looked up and smiled as Avitius put his head around the door.

"I'd say come in but I'm just about to go," he said. "Is Timomarchos still out there?"

A mighty yawn began behind Avitius.

"Snoring like a drunk dog," said Avitius cheerfully, and the yawn became a yelp of outraged innocence.

"Don't worry, Timomarchos," called the Governor. "We'll be leaving soon, get your things together, while I just have a word with Avitius here."

Avitius said, "I'll be very brief, sir. Ovid can't be trusted to keep his mouth shut in the town's bars."

Caecina groaned and held up one hand.

"Can we talk about this tomorrow morning? I had to kick off early this morning with a sacrifice in honour of the God Julius Caesar."

"Sir," said Avitius. "I have an idea; I just need your say-so."

Avitius was quick with his explanations and the Governor was swift to nod approval. All it took was a quick, "As long as you remain officially in charge and keep an eye on him," and permission was granted. Avitius then headed back to his own room, planning his visit to Ovid in the morning, intent on his distract-a-poet plan.

POETIC JUSTICE

Chapter 10

March 16

Ovid, to his own as well as Avitius' amazement, was up when Avitius arrived at the little house. And even more amazing, he was washed, dressed and cheerfully eating breakfast.

"I need a shave," he announced. "There's a man in the marketplace who manages a respectable scrape, can we talk on the way? You look terribly serious, Avitius, as usual."

"Where did you go last night, after I left you?" asked Avitius.

"Nice little bar, called Hermes' Place, near the marketplace," said Ovid. He made no mention of his half-hearted attempts to flirt with the barmaids that had ended in ignominy.

Avitius said, "These animal killings I told you about — I'm making no progress mainly because nobody thinks it is important and I have other things to do. Would you do me a favour?"

Ovid looked up at him. "Ah, a little job for the exile? Yes, why not? Make myself useful, get me out of the house. Baucis will be thrilled. She worries about me, you know."

"Don't sneer," said Avitius.

"Token sneer only, I assure you," said Ovid. "I'm happy to help, particularly if it is brought to the Governor's attention."

"Already done," said Avitius. "He's willing for you to do some unofficial poking around."

"Why are you being so nice to me?" asked Ovid, half dramatically and half seriously.

"Couldn't say, I'm sure," said Avitius. "Maybe I'm like Baucis and just worry about you. Now — I'd like you to talk to the priests at the Temple of Jupiter and the groom who found the horse. You should also talk to old Sulla, he owns the inn, though you'll find him in his warehouse by the harbour. He doesn't have anything to tell you really, but you'll be amused by him."

"And the inn is where?"

"Go through the gate, past the shabby houses and The River View Inn is about a hundred paces down the road on the right. It's a big place — what?" Ovid had coughed meaningfully.

"Am I allowed beyond the city walls?" asked Ovid.

Avitius thought. "Yes," he said. "I say you can."

Ovid waited but Avitius did not qualify this. No warnings, no request for a guarantee or an oath. A small weight lifted from Ovid's soul. It felt good to be trusted. He stood and announced, "I'll make a start then."

***

The path that led up from the harbour of Tomis climbed the steep hill in stages, and connected rows of warehouses that rose in terraces, their openings ready to swallow up the goods constantly being unloaded. Snakes of porters wound up and down the slopes in the hours of daylight: once the sun set the lights of the bars at the top of the hill beckoned travellers and dockworkers alike.

Ovid was unlucky enough to hit a rush. He managed to get as far as the lowest row of warehouses, then was stuck, waiting for the longest procession of porters he had ever seen as they peeled off along the path he needed. He was tempted to retrace his steps to the bars but sternly told himself to be patient and enjoy the view. He found a place off to one side where there was a handy wall against which he could lean and gazed at the harbour, imagining the ship that was going to take him back to Rome once Augustus pardoned him. This developed into quite a substantial narrative and he had got as far as reading an imaginary letter in which Augustus gracefully and fulsomely apologised when he realised that the steps were now clear and he could make his way to find Lucius Sergius Sulla. Avitius had to told him enough about Sulla to intrigue him and he told himself that he was going to enjoy this. Ovid shook off his homesickness and made his way down the steps.

Lucius Sergius Sulla welcomed Ovid into his harbour office, which was a table and chair in the far corner of a warehouse right in the middle of the row. As Ovid made his way through the warehouse, he was careful not to look at the piled wares too hard. Most merchants would object to someone like him opening sacks or examining the labels on amphoras, but he was pleased to note a healthy number of wine jars, carefully stacked in specially made wooden pens. He would ask Sulla about those.

Sulla himself was the sort of person you knew would be on top of the heap at all times. He did not stand when Ovid approached and introduced himself, nor did he offer a chair. His green eyes flicked over Ovid, then round his warehouse, then to the papers on his desk constantly. But, Ovid noticed, when interested, Sulla looked at him very keenly and made no pretence that he was doing anything else. "It would be interesting to see if I could get a lie past this man," he thought, "but not now. Now is the time to be open, because I have no reason to lie and it would take too much effort."

"So why all of a sudden is there interest in my horse?" was Sulla's opening challenge. Ovid waited, sure there was more. Sulla's eyes flicked over to the rack of wine jars, then back to him.

"The Advisor came to see me last month, but nothing seems to have come of it," said Sulla. "And forgive me, but you are not part of the Governor's staff, are you?"

Ovid answered honestly.

"I am not official, no. But Avitius, though he doesn't have the time himself, thinks it worth another effort. Has the Town Council done anything?"

Sulla laughed. "They think it's up to me to sort out my own premises," he said. "And I get their point but — a horse? Never known that happen."

He sat back and looked at Ovid. Still no chair was offered.

"So why send a poet to do a soldier's job?" The tone was hostile.

"I wasn't always a poet," said Ovid. "Avitius and I worked together years ago in Rome, so I said I would have a look. Animals getting killed usually leads to something bigger."

"Nothing's bigger than a horse," said Avitius. "Or more expensive."

"Elephants are horrendously expensive," said Ovid. "But what I meant was this person might kill a man or a woman next time.'

"And the Emperor might come to Tomis himself and compensate me for the horse," said Sulla.

Ovid started again.

"Is there any reason someone would want hurt you?" he asked.

"Look," said Sulla, "If there was anyone with an obvious reason to kill my horse, then I would have found him and sorted it out. I'm not stupid enough to tell you I have no enemies, everyone has them. But only a madman hurts someone by killing their horse, and I don't know any madmen."

"Don't tell me there are no madmen in Tomis," said Ovid.

"Why?" Sulla looked at him then. "Are you hoping that there's an easy suspect here? Blame it all on the town softhead? Save all that Roman embarrassment?"

Ovid stared at him. "You are a Roman," he pointed out.

"I have Roman citizenship," said Sulla. "It's not the same thing." He chuckled at Ovid's expression. "I'm Sicilian, actually. Not Roman."

Ovid gave up.

"I'm sorry about your horse," he said. "And I would really like to track down whoever was responsible." He put on his sad face.

Sulla relented.

"Not what you were hoping for, am I? Let's talk about the horse then."

"Avitius also said you knew everyone in the town and could get hold of anything I wanted," said Ovid.

"That is true," said Sulla. "Look, if I can think of anything, I'll find you, but in the end, someone cut a horse's throat and nobody saw who did it. You won't find them. Now tell me — who is your wine supplier?"

"I'm cutting down on the wine," said Ovid quickly, canny enough to know that he must not show any interest.

Sulla smiled hugely, finally stood up and went over to the amphoras Ovid had noticed. He went through them, checking labels and humming a little to himself. Eventually, he said, "Aha!" and turned to smile at Ovid.

"I'm going to send this amphora to your house — don't worry, everyone knows where you live — and if you don't want it after you've tried it, then send it back. If you decided to keep it, bump into me again and make sure your purse is groaning."

Ovid had to agree. He had one last question.

"When you saw the horse, was there anything that struck you about the scene?"

"The scene," said Sulla thoughtfully. "Like it was a piece of theatre. The wheeled platform that comes out at the end of the tragedy, covered in dead bodies." His eyes stopped moving and lost focus, and Ovid stood very still.

"It was like a sacrifice," Sulla said. "But no garlands around the animal, nothing fancy, just the stunning blow to the head and the throat cut. It stank of blood but there was another smell. There were herbs scattered around the head, dried herbs, a sharp smell. Sage, I think."

***

"Why did I have to see Sulla?"

They were walking along the Main Street of Tomis. Ovid had suggested a bar, Avitius decided to take Ovid on a tour of Tomis instead. It was approaching midday, and the marketplace was quietening down but the street was still as busy as it ever got. The weather was kind and, dead animals apart, this spring was a happy one.

Avitius ignored this and stood looking at the main marketplace. Now that Tomis was Roman, some were conscientiously calling it the Forum, and everyone else laughed at them. It lay to the north of the street, and was a wide space filled with stalls that blocked off the official buildings that surrounded them. At the western end rose the Temple of Jupiter, Juno and Minerva, built a few years ago with a generous donation from Rome. It sent all the right signals, thought Avitius. Straight lines, piety, superiority.

"It's so clean," complained Ovid. "That's what I can't get over. The whole town — such as it is — is clean. How does that happen?"

"There are dark and smelly corners, don't worry," said Avitius. "Just like Rome."

Ovid turned with a sweeping gesture and caught the shopping of two women passing him. They gasped as packages leapt like startled cats, and one of them clutched her chest and said something unfriendly in a language Ovid did not recognise. Ovid added to the confusion by waving his hands at them ineffectively, but before he could say anything more, they were several paces away, tugging their shawls over their heads, scurrying. Avitius said, "Clumsy and unpopular – how do you do it?"

"Did she seem familiar to you?" asked Ovid. "She gave us quite a look."

"No," said Avitius. "I don't know that many people here. Not yet. I'm away too much. Tell me more about Sulla. Did you learn anything that he didn't tell me?"

"Yes," said Ovid proudly. "The horse was scattered with dried herbs."

"Someone was really trying to mimic a sacrifice," said Avitius. "Why?"

"Not quite like a sacrifice," said Ovid. "You scatter grain on an animal at a sacrifice in Rome." He stood in thought and Avitius waited, while around them the shoppers of Tomis flowed in a grudgingly divided stream. Eventually, the mutters of exasperation got through to Ovid and he turned back to Avitius.

"Let's get out of this place," he said, and they began to walk along the Main Street again, this time towards The Lyre of Apollo. "You know, for a moment I was back in Rome, thirty years ago. Do you remember the girl with the dead parrot?"

Avitius did, most unromantically.

"Killed her husband and had a protective maid. You fancied her."

"She was called Corinna, and it was such a great name, I used it in my first love poems," said Ovid.

"I did wonder about her when I read your poem about the parrot," said Avitius. "So, she was — what, your muse?"

"Well, sort of, mainly because of the name," said Ovid. "And the girl herself... she made an impression."

"You met her once and she murdered her husband," said Avitius. "She made an impression all right."

"She was my ideal woman," said Ovid.

"Did you hear me saying the bit about murdering her husband?"

"Corinna," said Ovid, and almost started to sing. "Corinna, Corinna, Corinna!"

POETIC JUSTICE

"I hope she never read your poems," said Avitius. "She won't have liked you using her name."

Ovid looked outraged. "What do you mean? Most women would love to have been a poet's inspiration, to be written into history, to be idolised and — and…" Ovid flung out his hands, "famous! Ah, here we are, time for a drink."

Avitius stood staring after him, then with a shake of his head followed the poet into The Lyre of Apollo.

Ovid stood in the middle of the bar, flung out his arms and proclaimed, "Corinna!"

"Don't shout" said Vitia sternly.

"The only Corinna I know," said Macer, as he placed cups and jugs on the counter, "is the blonde hussy in your *Amores*. Cracking poems they are. The one where she…" and he remembered that Vitia was present and fell silent.

Ovid was still feeling dramatic.

"How come," he demanded of the world, "that I have only ever met one woman called Corinna?"

They stood in a row, Macer, Vitia and her brother and watched him sadly.

Avitius said, "He really doesn't know. Explain it to him."

Vitia said slowly, "Before your poems were published, nobody was called Corinna, you know. Everyone thought you'd made the name up, because you were concealing the identity of your real-life girlfriend. That's what all the poets do, isn't it?"

Ovid stared at her. "So?"

"Well, it's a pretty name, fair enough," said Macer. "But nobody was going to call their kid Corinna after the girl in your poems were they?"

Ovid just looked puzzled. Macer sighed and went on.

"Because your Corinna was a bit of a girl, wasn't she? You wouldn't want a girl growing up being teased because she's named after someone who dyed their hair so often it fell out? Someone, who let's face it, is not exactly pure and virginal."

"What about the poem where Corinna has an abortion?" said Vitia quietly. "And it goes wrong so she almost dies? Or would you, if you were a woman, want people to think you regularly slipped away from your husband to come for an afternoon liaison with you?"

"But people wouldn't think that, would they?" said Ovid.

"Oh, the sweet innocent boy!" And Vitia turned away to go into the kitchen, her back seeming to indicate her contemptuous pity.

Macer shook his head and said practically, "Time for a cup of something. Take a seat and I'll bring it over."

Ovid crumpled onto the stool Avitius pulled out for him, and said, "People know that poetry isn't real. I mean, obviously, yes, it's real, it has meaning and messages and all that, but nobody thinks I write what actually happened, with a real woman, called Corinna — do they?"

"No, they don't," said Avitius. "But they still don't call their daughters Corinna unless they are stupid."

"I never thought of it except as pretty and unusual and something that would fit into an iambic pentameter," said Ovid. "And she — the parrot woman, the real Corinna — was so beautiful."

"She was all right," said Avitius. "I preferred the maid."

There was a silence as Ovid looked into his drink and dreamed of thirty years previously, and Avitius wondered how Ovid's brain worked. Macer came over with jugs and cups.

"I suppose the real Corinna is dead now," said Ovid.

Avitius shrugged. "What of it? She killed her husband, as you keep forgetting."

Macer stood listening, then took a stool and drew it up to the table.

"All right boys," he said. "You've got me hooked. Tell me the story. How did you meet the real Corinna and how do you know she killed her husband?"

"We were on night patrol," began Ovid and the story unfolded. The man falling into the street, the two frightened women in the top flat, and their swift disappearance once the funeral was decently over. On questioning, the neighbours had told of the violent husband and how he had even killed her parrot in a fit of anger.

POETIC JUSTICE

Macer shook his head. "Nasty," he said. "But it happens and what can you do? And let's face it, you don't know that the neighbours weren't lying or exaggerating."

"They weren't lying about the parrot," said Ovid. After talking to the neighbour, they had gone round the back of the block of flats and found a corner where the community's rubbish was heaped up. With the aid of a broken broom handle, a few gentle prods had revealed a glimpse of bright greenish-blue plumage. Infested with insects and stinking, the pathetic little corpse nevertheless had information to give as its head flopped eerily and unnaturally to one side.

"Okay so he killed the parrot," said Macer. "Maybe he hit her about. You still don't know she killed him, do you?"

Avitius shrugged and said, "She ran pretty quickly."

"But there wasn't any real proof, was there?" Ovid chimed in.

"She got away with murder," said Avitius.

"She escaped," said Ovid. "And now she lives forever in my poetry."

He barely noticed the exasperated sigh that Avitius let slip. He had had an idea for a poem, and got up and saying, "I must go home."

Macer watched him leave The Lyre of Apollo and said "It was a good story. Did you really dig through the rubbish for the parrot? Could you really tell how it had died?"

"Ghoul," said Avitius.

Chapter 11

March 17
THE LIBERALIA

Ovid had been inspired by his bout of reminiscing with Avitius and Macer the night before. It had reminded him of the excitement he had occasionally felt as he and his squad had patrolled the night streets of a far more wicked city than Tomis. The death of Corinna's husband had undoubtedly been the highlight, if you could call it that, of his year as Commissioner, but there had been a myriad of less dramatic encounters that had wormed their way into his memory. He had gone home and sat at his desk and spent the evening revising his calendar poem with an enthusiasm rarely found in the editing process. Now, despite the cool meeting with Sulla, he was encouraged, and set off early the next morning to talk to the attendant who had discovered the dead cat.

The Temple of Jupiter, Juno and Minerva was new, and familiar to any Roman, a temple you would find in every town in the Empire. It stood facing down the long axis of the marketplace and was set on a high podium so that it could look down on every other building. A flight of steps led up to the pillared entrance, plinths on either side of the stair waiting for statues to be commissioned.

"Hmmm," thought Ovid, "I'd put Augustus on the right and — let's see — maybe Tiberius, as the heir on the left?"

Except that Tiberius was only heir because all other contenders had died, and at about the same age as Ovid, he was elderly to be taking up the reins. And everyone hated him, of course. Much more popular was the young Germanicus, hero of the German wars – but Ovid shut down that line of thought quickly and strode through the marketplace to his destination.

Above the pillars that faced him, the painted pediment showed Jupiter standing in the middle where the height of the roof meant that the king of the gods did not have to stoop. Juno and Minerva stood on either side and as the roof sloped down, bowing and prostrate figures conveyed the superiority of the central deities.

POETIC JUSTICE

"Oh Rome, so unsubtle" thought Ovid as he climbed the steps.

Inside the darkness came down softly around him, tinged with incense, and serene. Ovid enjoyed the peace for a moment, then took a cautious step forward, nodding respectfully at the statues standing against the far wall. They were competent copies of Greek originals, a style that never went out of fashion, and there was no pity for humanity in their lofty expressions.

An acolyte glided forward and directed him to another acolyte who confirmed that he had indeed found the disgraceful blasphemy of the burned cat in January. Ovid invited him to sit in the sun and tell his story, and the man seemed to accept this as perfectly normal. His life as a temple attendant must have been very tedious. The two of them settled on the steps and looked out over the marketplace as they talked, a scene so ordinary neither man noticed it at all. Ovid's new friend was a freedman from Bithynia, who had been in his current role for more than ten years, and his first intention was to make it clear that he served the best temple in Tomis. He spoke of other temples with mild contempt, but really did not like the Temple of Cybele across the marketplace. He was not impressed by Cybele or her attendants and waxed lyrical.

"They all spent yesterday whipping each other, practicing for the Spring festival," he reported disdainfully. "Got to draw blood, especially if they haven't yet done the — you know — business on themselves." Ovid crossed his legs automatically.

"I thought that — er — castration wasn't actually insisted on," he said cautiously. He'd seen the priests of Cybele in Rome, of course, and knew that it was considered a great honour to emasculate oneself in service of the goddess, but the whispered wisdom had always said that only the really important priests had to be eunuchs. The rest just flogged themselves on important occasions.

"I don't think any of them in there are," said the attendant. Ovid hadn't asked his name — he should have done, to form a bond, make it easier for the man to talk. Not that this seemed a problem as they had got onto castration already.

"I'm out of practice," Ovid said to himself and aloud, "My name's Ovid, by the way. I'm a friend of Security Advisor Avitius, and because he knows I did a bit of this work years ago, he asked me to check up, make sure nothing else has happened."

The attendant nodded, and said, "Thallos of Nikaia at your service. You've only just arrived, haven't you? Enjoying Tomis so far?"

Gods above, no…

"It's a nice town," said Ovid. "Everyone's been very friendly."

Thallos nodded. "Bit of a shame that you have to find out about the cat then," he observed. "It was just before you arrived, nasty sort of thing to happen. I can't remember anything like it before. And then there was that horse got killed at the River View. Looking into that too, are you?" His brown eyes smiled at Ovid, just to let him know that Thallos of Nikaia knew what was going on.

"Well, yes, I'll be having a look there later today," said Ovid. "But I want to make it clear that this horse business was also before I arrived."

Thallos considered. "Yeah, must have been a few days before, I remember you arriving, beginning of this month. You must wonder what you've got yourself into, eh?"

"It's still quiet here, compared to Rome," said Ovid. "So, tell me about this cat."

Thallos shrugged. "Not much to tell," he said. "First thing in the morning I always sweep the steps, because the wind blows the rubbish from the market towards us overnight. You'd think that Jupiter, being the god of weather, could do something about that, wouldn't you? Anyway, as soon as I got out, I could smell burning. I followed the smell, and there it was in the alley round the back of the temple. Not very big, just a load of rubbish piled up against the wall and smouldering away."

"What was in the fire, apart from the cat, I mean?" asked Ovid.

"Well, some wine, because you could see the drips on the ground where a jar had been set down a little way away," said Thallos. "And there were herbs burnt as well, you could smell them."

Ovid looked at Thallos with respect.

POETIC JUSTICE

"You notice things, don't you?"

"Got the time to notice," said Thallos. "For example, I notice that you haven't tried to sell me your hard luck story, which does not tally with what everyone else says about you."

"I'm not drunk," said Ovid, startled into honesty.

"And you've got something to do," said Thallos. "Very wise, got to keep yourself busy. Want to see where it happened, this fire?"

They walked around the temple, and entered a narrow alley that went across the back wall, extending on both sides.

"Go that way," said Thallos pointing left, "and you come out on the Main Street, just next to a bar called Hermes' Place. Know it?"

Ovid could see the scorch marks where the fire had been, on the path and the temple wall. It had been tiny. No wonder the poor cat's body had survived.

"How long before you arrived do you reckon it had been going?"

Thallos pursed his lips and said almost at once, "Hardly any time at all. Smallest fire I ever seen, already dying out when I come round the corner. There wasn't anything to burn really, few leaves and stuff, but it was mainly cat, and cat doesn't burn that well."

"Are there many cats here?" Ovid realised he hadn't really noticed that many strays scrabbling around in the rubbish.

"Oh quite a few," said Thallos. "Temple of Isis has some, they give the kittens away to people to keep down the mice. You want one?"

Ovid opened his mouth then thought about it. "Yes, actually," he said. "We've got a little back yard and I'm guessing it won't be long before we need some way of dealing with the rodents. Temple of Isis is the place to go?"

"That's right, though they'll ask for a donation to temple funds," said Thallos.

"They always do," said Ovid solemnly. "Talking of which — here. A donation to you, with my thanks."

Thallos was pleased.

"Anything else you need to know?" he asked.

"Well, if you can figure out where the cat came from, and which direction the fire-setter went after he came back down the alley, let me know," said Ovid.

"Cat could have been from anywhere," said Thallos, "but the wine drops went back down the alley towards Hermes' Place. Of course, from there, he could have gone anywhere, and nobody notices someone walking along the street with a jar in the morning."

"But he decided not to cut across the marketplace," said Ovid. "If he knew that you swept the temple steps every day, he'd be worried about you noticing him coming from behind the temple just as the fire was beginning to make itself known. The alley to Hermes' Place was a better bet for not being seen. Interesting."

"Nasty business, killing animals," said Thallos. "And the horse was looking like a sacrifice. What do you make of that?"

"I'm relying on people like you to come up with an idea there," said Ovid.

"It'll be a religious nutter," said Thallos.

They parted on good terms, and Ovid returned home, via the Temple of Isis. A patchwork kitten with blue eyes sat on his shoulder, digging its claws into his cloak and meowing into his ear.

"You are a poet, little one," said Ovid, as the two of them entered the house. The kitten relieved itself and Baucis tutted as she gently unhooked its claws from the damp cloak. Philemon turned from mopping the floor and said, "Is that a cat?"

"Here," Baucis said as she passed the kitten back to Ovid. "I'll quickly rinse the cloak. What are we calling this little boy?"

"He's a boy? How do you know? You are amazing Baucis."

"Not really," said Baucis, already turning to take the cloak to the back of the house. "He has balls."

"Good Gods, so he does," said Ovid. "You are going to be the terror of the ladies, aren't you, boy? We'd better think of a good name for you. I know – we shall name you after Tiberius."

"The Emperor's heir?" asked Philemon. "That old man?"

"A mark of my esteem for Rome's premier general," said Ovid solemnly. "Who also has balls."

POETIC JUSTICE

"You shouldn't make jokes about high-up people like that," said Baucis, coming back into the entrance hall. "Give me that animal, and let's see if we can persuade him to grow up into something useful. We've more mice here than I'd like."

***

Ovid left Baucis and Tiberius the kitten playing with some scraps of papyrus and set off for the centre of Tomis to pick up an investigative sidekick. He had had an idea about this. Despite Avitius saying he could set foot outside the city walls, he felt strangely reluctant to test this on his own, and so he had formed a plan. He would invite Menis, leader of the town council, to come with him. After the rather unimpressive start which, Ovid knew, was down to his own ungracious behaviour, he had made an effort with Menis, sending a very polite thank you note, and a copy of his great poem of mythology, the *Metamorphoses*, for Apolauste. He knew from the conversation at dinner that she had read some of the work, and even if she had a copy of her own, a new one signed by the author would go down well with father and daughter. He hoped that this present would gain him a warm welcome when he turned up now.

He found in Menis an appreciative audience and his confidence bloomed.

"It's about a couple of incidents where animals have been found killed for no apparent reason," he began.

"The horse?" Menis said immediately. "I've already had Sulla, the owner of The River View complaining about it. I don't know what he expects me to do. I suggested he put a guard on the stables overnight and he said he wanted me to set up a Town Watch to do it for him."

"Anyone who wants to get into a stable at night to kill a horse will be able to avoid a Town Watch," said Ovid. "Your idea is much better."

Menis looked at him. "You sound as though you have some experience of this," he observed.

"When I was younger, one of the many tedious offices I held in order to prove my worth, was the Commissioner for Prisons and Executions," said Ovid. "Our main job was patrolling Rome at night and I was naive and enthusiastic enough to go out on patrol several times. It's where I met Marcus Avitius."

"He's a good man," said Menis. "Interesting that you both ended up here in Tomis."

"He is a good man," echoed Ovid. "He was an excellent member of the squad of course, but only served a year before going to the legions. He had a way of thinking that was quite different to the others. Together we solved a lot of murders. Well, encountered a lot, solved a few murders."

"What is the procedure in Rome?" asked Menis. "If one finds a dead body I mean?"

"We would get the body to the family," said Ovid. "And if they found out who did it, they could bring a case. Of course, if the murderer was still standing over the body with a dripping knife in hand, we could usually take a guess and make an arrest."

"And if there wasn't an obvious killer? Did the family often succeed in prosecuting successfully?" said Menis.

Ovid shrugged. "Sometimes," he said. "Especially if they had a pretty good idea. But often, no. Rome is a big place, and people get murdered every day. What do you do here in Tomis?"

"Well, we don't have many murders and as you say they tend to be pretty obvious. But yes, it's up to me as Archon to find out who did it and punish the guilty party," said Menis. "Small town life you see — I get to do practically everything."

"I thought you would have a minion to do that sort of thing," said Ovid. "Should the Archon be investigating sordid crimes?"

Menis coughed. "Before the Romans came and made us a province, the Town Council ran everything including law and order. Now there is a Governor in residence and a small detachment of troops. We haven't yet reached a clear understanding of where responsibility lies. For all sorts of things. Of course, now I know, if I do get a murder, I shall call upon you and Avitius."

Ovid wondered if Menis was annoyed at this state of affairs — was he, a Roman, trampling on local sensibilities?

"Well," he said in a consolatory manner, "will you consider a joint venture? Rome and Tomis looking at the mystery of the sacrificial horse?"

***

Menis was indeed gracious and even seemed quite excited at the prospect. Moreover, Apolauste invited herself and her maid along with them, and Ovid found himself amused rather than irritated by this.

"Maybe," he suggested as they left the house, "we should bring provisions for the journey and have a picnic?"

Apolauste smiled at him and said, "If we had a ship we could plan a voyage around the Black Sea and take with us a band of heroes so that we could fight any dragons we met."

"Ovid and I solemnly promise to rescue you from any monsters," said her father. And to Ovid, "I am the talk of the town already for over-educating her and thus spoiling her for marriage. The Greek community here can be a little conservative with their daughters."

"I made sure my daughter was as educated as she wanted to be," said Ovid. "And she turned out to be a gentle and domestic creature who uses that education to help in teaching her own children."

Apolauste determinedly turned this conversation back to the present by enquiring about Ovid's new job as animal killing investigator and how he had got it. To Menis' surprise, and smug pride, she not only listened carefully but had some ideas to offer, admittedly based on town gossip. Her maid Cotela was of great help here as well, being connected to one of the local tribes. Ovid was intrigued.

"What was the local reaction to a horse's ritualistic killing?" he asked. Cotela, directly appealed to, did not seem to enjoy being the centre of attention but obediently gave his question some thought.

"They thought that whoever did it was crazy or very rich," she said. "Nobody from a local tribe would kill a horse. It is more difficult to replace a horse than a child. And the Getans love their children."

Slightly taken aback by this prosaic view, Ovid gave her a look of enquiry.

"It is important to be logical," said Cotela. "Nobody can put a price on a child, that would be silly. But a horse, a good horse, is the biggest purchase a man can make. If a child dies, the man mourns and then he and his wife look to have another child. But if the horse dies, he either makes a terrible sacrifice to replace it or is unable. And that is not to be thought."

"I have a lot to learn from you, Cotela," said Ovid humbly.

"I cannot read or write very well, sir," said Cotela.

Apolauste hugged her and said, "You are my first and best teacher, Cotela."

"Our household cannot imagine life without Cotela," said Menis serenely. "And here we are, at the gate. What is your strategy, Ovid?"

Ovid was tempted to say, "Go through the gate and not stop until I reach Rome, of course." But that would be childish and he was, to his surprise, enjoying his strange outing, being bossed around by a lordly Greek, an intelligent teenager and her Getan nanny. In Apolauste and Cotela there was an echo of his wife and her mother, organising his life and unprepared to show any respect until they felt he had earned it. Menis was right — Apolauste was going to find it hard to meet a mate in Tomis. Back to the moment, he told himself severely.

"We find the groom and ask him for his story," he said. "Then we find out who was in the inn."

"We can't go around in a gang like this, can we?" said Apolauste. "We'll terrify everyone. Why don't Cotela and I go and ask at the kitchen and you and Papa do the stables?"

Ovid humbly agreed that this was an excellent idea, and he led the way under the wooden arch that opened into the courtyard of The River View Inn. They stood and looked around. Apolauste pointed off to the corner ahead and to the right, where a small passageway opened onto the courtyard.

"The kitchen will be down there, I'd guess. Come on Cotela. Papa, we'll come back here when we are done."

POETIC JUSTICE

"Certainly, my daughter," said Menis to her swiftly departing back.

***

The wooden stables were built into the wall of the courtyard on two sides, and Ovid saw a dark entrance out of which breezed the smell familiar the empire over. Straw, manure and sweat built up a tang that almost overpowered, but somehow was bearable, because one knew it was created by horses. Menis held his cloak carefully wrapped around him as he went in, and Ovid reflected how fortunate he was that Menis had agreed to come along. He could hear Menis calling out in Greek, then in Dacian, and an answering call came from the depths of the building. Ovid kept in the doorway. He was going to have this conversation outside. A slight young man in a very dirty tunic came forward, pitchfork in hand, and put it down hurriedly when he saw his two visitors. He grabbed a cloth hanging on the wall and wiped his hands with it, while looking politely at them.

"Could we have a word about the horse that was killed last month?" said Ovid in his best Greek, speaking a little more slowly than usual.

"It wasn't me," said the young man at once.

"I know," said Ovid. "You aren't in trouble, we just need to hear what happened."

"Why? Anyway, the groom who was there has gone." His Greek was as good as that of anyone in Tomis.

"You weren't the one who found the horse? That's a nuisance," said Menis.

"He left," said the young groom. "He said it was witchcraft, and he was going to go back to his tribe. And the boss hasn't replaced him yet, so I've got double the work."

"That must be very inconvenient for you," said Menis, dipping his fingers into the purse on his belt. "Here — a little compensation for your trouble." He stood still, holding out the money so that the man had to come forward to take it. In the light from the courtyard, he could be seen to be even younger and dirtier than Ovid had thought. He also looked wary.

"What do you need to know?" He asked.

"I know the story being told in the taverns," said Ovid, deciding that now he must take over the questioning. "But I think it's been exaggerated, so I need to know what actually happened and no more. Do you understand?"

"Yes," said the groom. "I'm Getan, not stupid."

"Well then," said Ovid. "Over to you."

"This is just what I was told, all right?"

"Understood," said Ovid.

"He was asleep," said the groom. "One of us always sleeps in the loft in case of emergency. It was just before dawn, when he woke and he said that was because the horses were nervous. You get so even when you're asleep you notice." He paused to check they were following. Ovid nodded solemnly.

"And when he got down, he found Aster in the stall nearest the door. Blood everywhere. The smell was upsetting the others. He ran to get me and bumped into the boss on the way and then we tried to get the others out past Aster and into the next lot of stalls. It took forever. So did cleaning up the blood. Poor old Aster."

There was a silence. Ovid looked at the groom — the young man was already bored of trotting out the story once more, his thoughts on how soon he could get rid of them and get on with his work. Even his sympathy for the horse had not been accompanied by a change in expression. Aster was over and done with, but there were living horses to look after and not enough people to look after them. All Ovid's prepared, boring questions fell by the wayside and he went straight for the kill.

"Who do you think did it?"

The groom looked surprised then wary. "Couldn't say," he muttered.

"Rubbish," said Ovid. "You've got your suspicions. And you will have talked about it, listened to other people's ideas. You know the people round here, how things go. I think you have a theory all worked out." As he spoke, he watched the groom's face and sure enough there it was, the relaxation of the jaw as a slight smile brought smugness to his face. "Come on, you do — so who do the people round here blame?"

POETIC JUSTICE

He saw that he had used the wrong word. He was a Roman, a member of the ruling, judging class. He should have been more subtle. The groom looked worried.

Menis decided to step in. "You're worried about getting someone into trouble," he said gently. "You aren't sure that you should report mere gossip. But that horse — Aster — was stunned then had his throat cut. Supposing that person thinks he's got away with it and does it again? You'll be the one discovering some poor animal lying in a pool of blood."

The groom flinched and made up his mind. "It's just what people are muttering," he said.

Ovid and Menis nodded.

"There's a man, got something wrong, can't speak properly, and won't ever look you in the face," said the groom. "People say he's cursed. They say he must have done it."

"Has he ever done anything like this before?" asked Ovid.

The groom shrugged. "I don't know. It's just what people say. He is cursed by a witch, has been since he was born. He limps as well."

"Ah, yes," said Menis. "You mean the lad whose parents run the laundry."

"Right," said the groom. "But I don't know. It's just what people say."

"Yes," said Menis. "I know. Have you ever noticed him hanging around here?"

"No," said the groom. "People don't hang around a stable unless they really like horses. Sometimes boys ask if they can see the animals, maybe even help with the grooming. But they like horses, see? You aren't after someone who likes horses. You're looking for a madman. Well, the only madman doesn't hang around, and the people who hang around aren't mad."

"Your logic is impeccable," said Ovid. He handed the young man a coin, thanking him politely for his help. Menis said something incomprehensible and they left.

"Do you know much of the local language?" asked Ovid as they went back into the courtyard and looked around for Apolauste.

"I picked up a bit of Dacian from Cotela," said Menis. "Apolauste knows it well of course. Cotela has been her nurse form the moment she was born."

"And do all the tribes speak it? Or are there variants?"

"As far as I can tell they all speak something like it, but Cotela says Sarmatian is completely different to Dacian, and Thracian is different again," said Menis. "Not sure I quite go with that — the words of greeting in each language are almost identical, for example. But they do have distinct accents. Fortunately for me, they all speak a form of Greek as well and have done for hundreds of years. All down to Alexander the Great, of course. He made sure that Greek became the language of everywhere he conquered."

Apolauste swept into the courtyard with Cotela in tow, their faces satisfied and their strides confident.

"They've had more luck than us," said Menis.

"The kitchen is the heart of every home," said Ovid. "And the heart knows all." He cringed inside a little at this, but Menis merely said, "Let us see."

***

"The kitchen is a hive of gossip," said Cotela. Neither her face nor her tone of voice showed what she thought of this. "They are all bees buzzing around their Queen and seek to please her by saying terrible things about their neighbours and friends."

Ovid appreciated her imagery and thought that she must have enjoyed sharing Apolauste's education. He nodded at her approvingly.

"A good cook is a powerful person, even if she is a woman," said Menis.

"I agree," said Ovid. "What else did you discover?"

"Sulla the owner of the inn is a gruesome creep," said Apolauste. Menis nodded. "And I agree with that."

"Everyone thinks you need to do something about the drains out here," said Apolauste, "the cook thinks the price of grain is being fixed by the Black Sea grain merchants, and there is a rumour that the wife of the barber in the marketplace is having an affair."

POETIC JUSTICE

"Anything to help with the dead horse?" asked Ovid. He might enjoy this little family conversation but needed to keep them on point.

"The groom that found the horse has disappeared, which I think is suspicious. Otherwise, most of them think it's the son of the couple who run the laundry," said Apolauste, "but Cotela and I think that is just ignorant superstition, because he limps and doesn't talk very well."

"Has nobody noticed anyone hanging around the stables? Or the inn as a whole? A stranger?"

"Strangers at a place like this is normal," said Menis. But his daughter was shaking her head.

"Everyone who stayed on the night of the horse was a regular, and the inn was dark from an early hour. The cook says they haven't had any rowdiness in an age."

"Would you stay in the inn if you were planning to do something like that?" wondered Ovid aloud, and immediately answered himself. "No, unless you were mad or so confident it doesn't bear thinking about."

"Our problem," said Menis, "is that we cannot imagine the sort of person who did this. We think along our own lines, trying to capture the essence of a person whose thinking goes along completely different lines. We need to imagine ourselves as that person, and that is unpleasant."

Ovid looked at him with respect. "I have severely underestimated you, Archon," he said, intending it as a lighthearted compliment.

Menis replied, "Well, you are a Roman. You underestimate everyone."

Apolauste laughed, and Ovid pulled a face of excessive sorrow.

"In which case, all I can do is offer you a drink, Archon, and hope to learn humility," he said.

***

They ended up in Hermes' Place on Main Street, while Apolauste and Cotela returned to home, "to do some weaving," according to Apolauste, though her expression did not inspire any confidence.

"She is being sarcastic at me again," said Menis.

"She is a very intelligent young woman,' said Ovid and thought he had better leave it at that. You never knew how a father would react to a compliment of his daughter. He thought of his own Ovidia, probably still with her two children in Africa while her husband did something unutterably boring to do with taxes. He wondered if she had ever regretted having him as a father: he regretted not knowing her better. While she was growing up, he had been at the height of his poetic fame, busy either writing or reciting, always off visiting people higher up the social scale than him. How old was she now? Twenty-five? She might even have had another child since he last heard from her. And he hadn't actually seen either of his grandchildren so far.

"You are very lucky to be so close to one another," he said. "I hardly know my daughter."

Both men drank in silence, while Menis waited for the moment of loss to pass.

"Has our visit to The River View produced any thoughts?" he asked after a suitable time. "I wasn't sure it helps you at all, I must say. No suspicious strangers were seen, nobody has any ideas apart from blaming a poor lad whose wits are not all there."

"It would be interesting to know why people are mentioning this boy," said Ovid. "Unless, of course, they just blame him every time anything goes wrong. I don't think anyone mentioned this lad to Avitius."

"Avitius is a Roman, I'm afraid," said Menis. "And not everyone automatically blames the laundryman's son. The Dacians for example love nothing more than muttering darkly about witches. They all know stories of an old woman who lives in a house of reeds by the great river. They thoroughly approve of our worship of Cybele or the Great Mother, who, they say, will guard us against witches. Which reminds me — we have a festival of spring in honour of the Great Goddess coming up in a few days. The whole town will turn out for it.'

"Noted," said Ovid. "Your latest inhabitant will be there.'

He stared off into the distance and added, "As for today, I don't know. It says to me that someone knows that to enter The River

View Inn at the dead of night is easy. There is no lock — if you climb the gate to the courtyard you can get into the stables and kill a horse, then be back over the gate in no time. But it would take someone sure of their own ability. Stunning and slitting the throat of a horse is not done so quickly and quietly by a complete beginner."

Menis grimaced and raised his cup quickly to hide his distaste.

"Someone who carries out sacrifices," said Ovid, "or a butcher. Or a hunter."

"I can round up a list of temple assistants, along with their special tasks," said Menis. "The ones who carry out the sacrifices will be easy to weed out."

"Thank you. It's a strange request, I suppose."

"I shall think of a reason," said Menis. "Something to do with levies of men capable of fighting that we can call up in times of emergency, I think. Actually, that would be useful to know, and we can add them to the reserves we call on to do wall duty in the winter."

He drained his cup and got up. "And a list of butchers will be easy. But my guess is that you'll find this man in another corner of the town. He won't be anything obvious."

With which unhelpful observation, he thanked Ovid for an interesting expedition and left.

It was now the middle of a colourless afternoon, and Ovid felt restless. He caught the eye of one of the serving-girls and she smiled. He smiled back, thought of Fabia and smothered any feelings of guilt. He was perfectly entitled, far away as he was. He ran his fingers through his hair, went over to the girl and received a firm rejection.

Chapter 12

March 22
FESTIVAL OF CYBELE

Cybele is the great mother who came from the East and even found a place in Rome. This has always amused me for any society less likely to approve of Cybele does not exist. She is the consort of kings, and though nobody likes to say it, is always the more powerful partner. Kings come and go but the goddess stays.

The Greeks brought her out of Phrygia many hundreds of years ago, and she is worshipped in their cities through the world. It was when Rome needed help against Carthage that they consulted the Sibylline books and were told to invite Cybele to their city for its protection. The oracle at Delphi confirmed this and so the Romans asked the King of Pergamum to send the goddess to Rome. Her temple still sits on top of the Palatine Hill, and the Romans call her the Great Mother. But it would be a mistake to think of her as motherly. She controls the fertility of the world.

And what do Roman men worry about? Why, that her chief priests are eunuchs. Fools! They should worry that the crops fail, that rivers run back into their sources and the lands are parched, they should worry that the sun will fail to rise. But a priest of Cybele offering his own fertility to the goddess? That is between him and her.

***

On the morning of the spring equinox, Tomis put on its finest — the Great Mother, Cybele, was bringing spring back to the world and she did it through the streets of Tomis.

Avitius met the Governor at Headquarters for a quick meeting before Caecina set off in full toga to be seen at the procession. The Governor let Avitius brief him on the latest reports from the Danube forts and the coastal defences, as a valet fussed over folds.

"Well, everything seems as peaceful as we may cautiously hope," remarked Caecina. "Later on this summer, I am going to need a more personal inspection though. I shall have a think about how I want us to do that." He nodded to himself and said, "But for today, we concentrate on the festival and we put on our best togas and sandals. If you don't mind my saying, you could do with a bit of a rearrange…"

Toga folds spruced up, Avitius was allowed to leave and he went straight to Ovid's house. He found Ovid up and at his desk already, annotating what looked like an already very messy sheet of papyrus. He was pale and had dark circles under his eyes but was very cheerful and enquired if Avitius wanted a drink. Avitius wasted no time.

"Put on your best toga and comb your hair," he ordered.

The poet looked interested.

"Festival of Cybele, the Great Mother," said Avitius. "Big stuff in Tomis."

"Oh yes, actually I would like to see that," said Ovid immediately, somewhat to Avitius' surprise. "And I did more or less promise Menis that I would be there. I'll get Baucis and Philemon too."

He bustled out of the study, shouting for them and said over his shoulder back at Avitius, "We all became initiates at the Sanctuary of the Great Gods on Samothrace on the way here, you know, and if Cybele isn't one of the Great Gods, then I'm a Gaul in checked trousers and a ginger moustache. Ask Baucis about it, she is adamant that all female deities wherever they may originate are aspects of Juno, Artemis or Venus. At least, I think that is what she thinks. She may have something. Ah, Baucis, Avitius has come to take me to the Cybele thing in town today."

Avitius stayed in the study while a small war raged in the atrium between Ovid and his housekeeper. Baucis was protesting at Ovid going out "looking like that," Ovid was trying to get out of combing his hair. The man was a complete child at times, thought Avitius, sitting down in the chair — the only chair — behind the desk.

Ovid's desk was quite neat, he thought, his eye falling on one pile on the left — notes, on papyrus and a wax tablet — and a row of rolled up volumes on the right. In the centre was the sheet Ovid had been working on, five or six lines of poetry, well-spaced and heavily annotated. It was a draft being edited then. After crossings out were taken into account, he read:

First day of May. Here I must sing of the Good Goddess. On an outcrop on the holy side of the hill, Remus once stood to scan the skies for birds — in vain! Here a temple which modestly shuns the eyes of men stands, restored by Livia, as always following her husband in all things.

In the margins were notes — "emphasise Livia somehow???", "mention Romulus?", "do I actually need to say it's the Aventine?". Problems, problems, thought Avitius and into his mind came a picture of the memos he was currently working on "Pros and cons of a possible move to Callatis," "check road gangs," "send firm negative."

Ovid came back into the study wearing a clean tunic and holding a comb.

"Do I really need to wear a toga?" he asked, then, "Are you reading that?" He carefully leaned over the desk and turned over the sheet of papyrus. "No peeking. I don't even know if it will go into the finished thing yet. Is my hair all right?"

Avitius came round the desk holding up a hand in apology.

"I'm sorry — I shan't peek now that I know," he said. "Although, if you can't trust the Security Advisor, who can you trust? And a toga would be appreciated but you will find that people won't mind if the folds aren't perfect." He hitched up his own cumbersome toga as he spoke and Ovid laughed.

"Yours looks pretty good," he said. "Who does it for you?"

"There's a slave at Headquarters who valets the Governor and is happy to help us lesser mortals on special occasions, for a tip," said Avitius. "Also, the Governor insisted. I hate the damn thing."

Ovid showed his hair to the comb, then they went into the atrium, where Baucis waited with a grim look on her face and a toga in her arms. She stepped forward and said very firmly,

"This has just come back from the laundry, and you are going to wear it."

Ovid said, "Don't worry, Baucis, I promise to put it on and keep it on. Avitius has shown me the error of my ways."

POETIC JUSTICE

He stood patiently while Baucis draped him with swift expertise. Philemon appeared in his own perfectly-draped toga and Ovid whistled at his freedman's elegant appearance. "You definitely outclass me and Avitius," he said cheerfully, and they all left, walking out into the pale sun of spring, with the ever-present salty breeze blowing over the headland of Tomis straight from the sea. Avitius led the way, taking them down the hill.

"Isn't the temple of Cybele in the marketplace?" asked Ovid as they marched past the turning into Main Street.

"Yes," said Avitius. "But the procession starts at the harbour. A boat brings the sacred tree to Tomis by sea, and it is carried through the streets of the city to the temple where the Goddess waits for it."

"The Goddess' consort Attis is back from the death of winter, and rejoins his mistress," said Philemon unexpectedly. "Me and Baucis have paid our respects at the temple."

"What, today?" asked Ovid

"No, sir, a few days ago," said Philemon. "We've been exploring the town and seen all the temples I think now. And Baucis helped with the baking yesterday."

"Baking?"

"Everyone gets honey cakes today," said Baucis, and she smiled. "It's a lovely tradition. The children have spent all morning delivering them."

"I'm impressed," said Avitius, wondering why no honey cakes had ever come the way of Headquarters.

"There are a lot of very nice little shrines, here," said Philemon. "Not like Rome of course, but mainly well-kept."

"And lovely statues," said Baucis approvingly. "I like a nice statue."

"Do you know, I don't think I've ever considered how many temples there are in Tomis until this moment?" said Avitius. "I've tended to focus on the ones involved in the official life of the town — meaning the ones the Governor has had to visit. So, Baucis, what's your favourite statue so far?" He grinned at Baucis and her face lit up in a smile back.

"Oh, the Cybele is lovely, sir," she said. "Her dress is so beautifully carved, with all the folds falling down to the ground just like she was there in front of you. And one of those beautiful expressions on her face, like nothing can disturb her. And a lion at her feet, although I've never seen a lion in the flesh."

"You've seen lions at the games, surely," asked Ovid but Baucis shook her head.

"I don't like the games, sir," she said. "I never go."

Ovid was learning a lot about his servants in Tomis. He looked at Philemon.

"What about you?" he asked.

"Oh, I go to the games," said Philemon. "I like the gladiators. But the animal hunts are boring, so I go and get food while they're on."

"Cybele would approve I'm sure," said Avitius. "She is a protector of wild animals."

"She is a goddess who disturbs people," said Ovid and Avitius looked at him to make sure that he wasn't being flippant. He wasn't.

They were already too late to find a good place at the harbour itself and Avitius said that a viewpoint from farther up the hill was better anyway. So, they stood on the steps of the Temple of Neptune and were in time to see the ship enter the harbour between the two embracing headlands.

"Why does the tree arrive by ship?" asked Ovid. "In other cities, the procession just goes through the city."

"The goddess doesn't just bring the spring here," said Avitius who had asked this question last year and been instructed by a local. "She is opening the seas again for us, so the ritual pine tree enters town by the sea. And we know that the shipping season is officially open again."

"Did it ever close here?" asked Ovid.

Avitius shook his head. "As long as we don't get iced up, there are always merchants willing to take a risk. It's easy enough to hug the coast around the Black Sea, and even beyond — after all, you got here safely all the way from Rome, didn't you? It means trade can operate all year. There's a reason this town was founded here, and a reason it's so nicely well off, thank you very much."

Ovid said nothing but Avitius detected that superior look on his friend's face. Of course, Ovid didn't do trade. Avitius decided to ignore it.

The ship reached the quay and a procession lined up to escort the pine tree to the Temple of Cybele. Ranks of men in togas and Greek robes led the way, then some shaven headed priests carried the tree in its own special transport, a box with carrying poles attached. Behind were dancers, and the rhythmic clashing of tambourines was soon heard as the procession came near.

It was quite a small tree, thought Ovid, as the procession marched past. They really should have fixed it more firmly in the box, it was lurching from side to side quite violently, the green branches occasionally dipping as though to brush the hands of the crowd as arms stretched out to it. He hoped the goddess would be pleased, though this seemed an inadequate offering for a goddess as demanding as Cybele. The prayer from the end of Catullus' great Attis poem ran through his mind,

Great goddess Cybele, lady of Dindymus,
Let all your raging be far from my home, mistress,
Make others run wild, drive others to madness.

"I really don't need that sort of madness in my life," thought Ovid soberly. "The madness of ecstasy, of a complete surrender to the gods. The Great Mother of Samothrace would not be satisfied with anything less than a couple of bulls and some ecstatic self-mutilation from her priests."

Memories from the disturbing ceremony were still fresh in his mind, and Ovid couldn't help a shudder. One day he must ask Baucis and Philemon how they had reacted. Maybe.

As the procession went in up the hill, the crowds fell in behind it and shuffled along in time to the tambourines with varying degrees of enthusiasm. Baucis was thoroughly enjoying herself, swaying and clapping as she thumped her feet down, and Philemon maintained a dignified march while looking strangely distant from the whole thing. Ovid let the noise wash over him, but there was a rhythm under the crowd's constant noise that began to intrigue him. He identified the lighter metallic clashes coming from the tambourines ahead of him, with a gritty trampling of many feet just a moment later. As he focused on these sounds, he lost awareness of his surroundings: the noise enveloped him, and he let it carry him. He was surprised when the crowd came to a halt. The small market square of Tomis was full and everyone faced north. It took him some time to see that the modest building in front of them was the temple of Cybele.

"The tree is being presented to the Goddess," whispered Baucis. "We have to wait and see if she accepts the offering."

Cybele did not keep them waiting. Scarcely had Baucis stopped speaking when one of the priests came out on to the top step of the temple — and Ovid had to crane his neck to see the man even so — and cried out in Greek, "The goddess is gracious!"

And with that, the crowd went wild. Hugs and tears and cries of thanks poured from Ovid's neighbours and many people actually jumped up and down. Even Avitius might have wiped his eyes and Ovid was unsurprised to find that his cheeks were wet with tears that he could not remember shedding. The crowd started to disperse, splitting in two at the entrance to the marketplace and dancing down the road towards the line of bars that lined the road on either side. Their own small party was carried away, and they went where they were taken, until the numbers thinned to the point where they could choose their own way.

"Only one place to go now," said Avitius. "Let me stand you all a drink."

***

Baucis and Philemon stayed for one modest drink, then left. Avitius looked at Ovid and cocked an eyebrow.

"Well trained," he said. "They are freed, aren't they?'

"Yes, and have been for years, in my father's will" said Ovid defensively. "I don't know why they volunteered to come with me. I didn't force them."

"I'm sure you didn't," said Avitius. "Their loyalty is commendable."

"And undeserved, I know," said Ovid. "I really have no idea what made them come with me. I was in a bit of a state when the whole leaving thing was going on. I can barely remember anything about it."

Avitius said, "Maybe they are just good people."

There was a silence neither of them knew how to fill.

Eventually, Avitius asked how the animal killings investigation was going. Ovid gave the most theatrical sigh and admitted to no actual success as such, but "I have ruled out a lot of things," he said, "and I'm sort of building a picture of our culprit."

"Oh yes?" said Avitius and hoped he had sounded inviting rather than cynical. Ovid gave him a look but carried on.

"If we assume for the moment that the same person did the cat and the horse, then we are looking at a native of Tomis, who has observed timings and routines and is confident that nobody will notice him as he goes about his business. He is free to move around the town so I'm thinking he must live on his own or is his own master. He managed to kill the horse without any problem, so he must be used to it or lucky to get it right first time. Menis has sent me a list of the town's butchers and temple assistants as the most obvious people who could kill an animal easily."

He paused and looked at Avitius for praise. Avitius was running through each point in his head, mostly with approval.

"That's all good," he said cautiously, "though I think if this man is his own master, then we should rule out the temple acolytes. Their absence would be noticed. I notice you didn't immediately go for the son of the laundryman, the one everyone suspects."

"I went to visit the laundry," said Ovid. "I needed to have my toga freshened up and they got it done for today very nicely. But the lad — well, he is a grown man but nobody will ever think of him as anything but a lad — he is hard to see as a sneaking cat murderer. His mother for one keeps a close eye on him, and the thought of him climbing silently over the gate at The River View Inn just didn't feel right to me. He treads the laundry in the treading pools and that I think is the limit of his capabilities. Poor boy."

"He is probably happy enough and has parents who feed and clothe him and he has a job," said Avitius.

"I wish that were enough," said Ovid.

"Your pity will change nothing. Move on."

"That's all I have," said Ovid. "And given that this is a task you gave me to stop me feeling sorry for myself and drinking too much, I think I've done pretty well."

He stood up and stalked off.

Avitius watched him go and wondered why he felt any need to help him. Macer came over to clear away cups.

"Can't help liking him, can you?" He remarked. "Poor old sod,"

"He could have had it worse," said Avitius. "The Emperor is harsher to his own family. He sent the Lady Julia, her brother and her mother off to uninhabited islands."

"Well by all accounts the Lady Julia did a bit more than write dirty poems," said Macer. "I mean she was pregnant, wasn't she and not by her husband. And the word was she and her brother had been plotting against the Emperor, sending letters off to the Rhine legions and all sorts."

"Nobody knows what they are supposed to have done," said Avitius and wondered why he felt so disgruntled.

POETIC JUSTICE

Chapter 13

March 30
FESTIVAL OF CONCORDIA

Ovid was reading a letter from Rome, written by his mother-in-law, Sulpicia. He did some working out – this must have been sent after his first letter reached home, the letter he wrote on Samothrace. He sighed. He had been miserable, full of resentment. Not that much different to the man he was now, he supposed.

"Written in Rome on the second day of February.

My dear son-in-law,

We received your letter dated the beginning of January and written on Samothrace. I am most impressed, my dear Ovid, that you persuaded someone there to carry a letter, and he must have had some lovely weather or the luck of the gods for it to arrive so quickly here. I'm afraid this letter will not reach you until mid-March, though we have made a particularly good arrangement with a courier service. We shall spend much of our correspondence a month behind each other, won't we?

We also received the sweet poem you sent and as requested have had it copied and sent to all our friends. Fabia insisted on following your instructions despite my misgivings. Ovid, I have to say that I am not sure about this strategy — a stream of poems entitled, "My Sorrows" is not going to persuade Augustus to change his mind and pardon you. However, I did think the beginning of this poem worked well:

Off you go to the city, little book.

I would have ended it there, Ovid. Whining is a limited art-form.

I shan't send you any of my poems. I don't suppose you are in any mood for them."

His mother-in-law was a wonderful woman. He had known Sulpicia since they were both in their twenties. Like him, she was a poet, and she was also a clever, extremely well-connected woman. She was that crucial class above him and betrothed to a beak-nosed wonder from the top shelf, a real catch called Fabius Maximus. The marriage had of course, not worked. Just after the birth of their daughter, a more advantageous marriage had been offered to Fabius, and he had taken it. But he had had the good sense to remain on civil terms with Sulpicia, and the two of them had brought up their daughter together in a most amicable manner. Sulpicia had refused to marry again, but she was made of a different material to Ovid, and she had played her life to a different tune. He carried on reading.

"Let me tell you our new living arrangements instead. As you know we planned on a move to somewhere less obvious, more in keeping with the family of a man in exile. Fabia closed up the house and moved to a much smaller place on the Viminal which has the advantage of being in an undistinguished neighbourhood, respectable but nothing special. Next door is a wine merchant: on the other side is Rome's smallest and least famous temple to Minerva. I have moved in with her, as that will look decent to everyone, and as long as I have a study of my own, I am happy. From here we can go everywhere a Roman needs to go, but of course nobody will make the journey up the Viminal to see us. Fabia organised everything beautifully and would barely let me help, but you know how she is. Being efficient is how she deals with all this."

Fabia was indeed efficient. Beautiful, twenty years younger than her husband and not a poetical bone in her body, her father's daughter. And now she was forced to move so that she could live in the appropriate silence of a woman brought down by her husband's disgrace, exiled in Rome as he was exiled from Rome. Ovid's eyes filled with tears. He dabbed them away, irritated with himself and continued reading.

"I found your description of Samothrace and the Sanctuary of the Great Gods there absolutely fascinating. You say you've become an initiate in the Mysteries of the Great Sanctuary, and surely that experience will do you good. It will be interesting to compare it with our own Roman festivals and can only inform your writing of the Calendar of Festivals poem. By the way, please find another name for this — "Calendar of Festivals poem" sounds tedious."

"You are so right," Ovid said to the letter. "It's a terrible title, and as soon as I have actually finished the damn thing, the matter will get my full attention."

He could almost hear Sulpicia laughing at this.

"Now onto something more serious. We have, as you asked, done some digging around for information on Moesia. Fabia went around to see her stepmother this morning and dear Marcia came up with the goods as usual. How she keeps track of the whole of Roman society I don't know especially as she hasn't a shred of intellect. It's a good thing she is so likeable, or I might have got very cross with Fabius for marrying her.

Caecina Severus, your Governor in Moesia, is a new man, one of those from the middle classes Augustus loves to promote because they will be devoted to him. Caecina was consul ten years ago, has a blameless wife from his own background, a parcel of children, lots of money because the family has been in shipping for years. He's a career soldier, was involved with putting down the revolt in Illyricum, and got a lot of cautious praise for his work there. So, a sound man but what nobody knows is who he supports to succeed Augustus — Tiberius or Germanicus? Though the money is on Tiberius — Caecina is more of an age with Tiberius and has similar military experience. Young Germanicus of course is everyone's darling but doesn't really move in the same circles as Caecina. Fabius thinks that Caecina is a genuine, old-fashioned loyalist, who will support only Augustus to the bitter end, and then be loyal to whoever succeeds Augustus. Not really an innovator, says Fabius, but a terribly useful man when you have a new province to establish."

Ovid nodded as his lips moved along with Sulpicia's words. It was good to have Rome confirm what Tomis said. Caecina Severus was not going to be a problem.

"As for Moesia itself, well, nobody knows much about it. Near Illyricum, probably a bit wild, full of strange people called Dacians and Getans. The librarian at Pollio's Library says he doesn't even have a book about it, but he says if I read up on

Thrace I should get an idea of the place. I told him I had no intention of ever reading up on Thrace. Interestingly, nearly everyone I speak to knows about the Greek cities on the Black Sea and says they are civilized so I hope that you will find life bearable in Tomis.

Moesia has not yet reached the point of being organised enough for sending in the tax-collectors – Fabius says there is some way still to go with infrastructure and formalizing the army settlement. I don't think a province really is part of the Empire until we can tax it.

Don't worry about us, Ovid. Fabia is managing everything; I won't say she is happy but she is coping. And may I make a request? I do realize how terrible this is for you, believe me, but could you think of Fabia when you write please? When you indulge in self-pity, what is she supposed to do? You should know better."

Yes, he should. Fabia did not do self-pity. He had known that from the moment Sulpicia had suggested he marry her daughter. "She is in need of someone who won't pity her and will welcome her little girl. She has wit and a sharpness that you will like. Though, I warn you, she won't give an inch and she won't let you get away with your histrionic streak."

Sulpicia had been right in every point, but Ovid also gained a wife who was as efficient as her father, as intelligent as her mother and loyal to a fault.

"I really don't deserve her," Ovid said to the letter, and in his mind he could hear Sulpicia's immediate reply, "No man deserves his wife, dear Ovid."

He should reply immediately, but he was too upset, he told himself, and so he called Baucis for his cloak and went out to wander the streets of Tomis and find a bar.

Once he had left, Baucis went into his study and tidied a little. When she was certain he wasn't going to be back early for some reason, she read the letter from Sulpicia. She liked to know what was going on.

Chapter 14

March 31
ANNIVERSARY OF THE TEMPLE OF LUNA

Avitius looked down at the little body and cursed under his breath. The violence of Rome, the violence he had known all his life, had travelled all the way out here to this small, slightly self-important town that would not know how to deal with it. Common sense told him that violence and depravity were not limited to any one place, no matter how large and important, and the gods had shown him that man mistreated man wherever one looked. He had been in the army long enough to know that. But there was something about this scene that made him feel so sad, not just for the young woman whose life had been robbed, but for her family, her friends, her town. Something had been taken from them all.

"Welcome to the Empire," he whispered.

It was well past midnight and the moon lit up the street beautifully, but Avitius still took a lamp as he prepared to look at the body. He moved his lamp carefully from side to side, then bent and held it as near the surface of the body as he dared, so as to make sure that his first inspection was as thorough as possible. The first look was, he believed the most important. He had developed a theory back in Rome — one of many theories — that this was his best chance to get an idea of the dead person, as if something of them lingered but faded to nothing within hours. He was sure that doctors and priests, soldiers and philosophers alike would disagree with him, so he never mentioned it. When the soldiers with him showed signs of impatience he said that it was a mark of respect to the dead person that one paid attention. The grumbling quietened.

It was as he moved the lamp he had borrowed to the face that he saw the glint of a chain wrapped around her neck. Gently moving the long stands of her hair, he saw a tiny crescent moon lying against the roll of flesh created by the garrotte. The chain was threaded into a thin leash of dull red ribbon, which almost disappeared into the skin of her neck. This then, was the tool of the strangulation, and a strange one. The twisted ribbon would have done the job on its own, so why add a chain, surely an expensive choice?

"I want the doctor to examine her," he said to the group of soldiers. "Take her to the infirmary at Headquarters and wake up Doctor Rascanius. Tell him I will be along shortly. And lads...." He made sure they all looked at him. "You treat this body with the utmost respect. As if she were your mother or sister." One mouth opened to object but thought better of it and closed. He looked back at them all and nodded.

He had been unable to find a stretcher quickly, so his men had brought a large piece of sacking with them. They laid out the sacking on the ground and gingerly transferred the body onto it. The girl was covered up with a blanket and carried off, each man carrying a torch and a corner of blanket.

Avitius listened as the footsteps — accompanied by a grumbling that did not escape him — died away and then took in a deep breath. He stood where the girl had fallen, on the temple steps, and slowly noted all he saw. Before him was the temple itself, a small building dedicated to the Lares, the Guardians of every Roman house, and now guarding Tomis on behalf of Rome. To his left, a row of bars and shops lit up then faded into the darkness as the bearer party made its way towards headquarters. He turned to the south and a line of small houses stared back at him from across the street, while just off to the east was the marketplace. It was a street that would never be quiet during the day, but at night only the bars would spill light onto the stones. And even they were closed now, waiting out the hours until dawn, when the homeowners and shopkeepers would send out their slaves to sluice down the road.

Another lamp made its way towards him. One bar was still open. Hermes of Sinope had discovered the body when one of his barmaids had disappeared, and he had gone up and down the street looking for her. Antiope. A slave, about seventeen, Hermes thought, a nice girl. "Everyone called her Ani." No enemies, a good worker, and definitely not a common whore. "I don't run that sort of place, and I look after my girls." Once Avitius had reached the scene of the death, Hermes had slipped off to his bar, and waited for the body to be removed — "Don't want to hang around, it's bad luck to be near a — you know...."

Avitius nodded in greeting as the bar-owner approached him cautiously. People reacted very differently to death, and he tried to be patient with them all. Hermes wasn't being callous in not wanting to hang around his deceased barmaid, just fearful.

"Thanks for the loan of the lamp. I'll make sure Antiope gets back to you quickly," he said. "I'm assuming you want to do the funeral?"

Hermes nodded. "She didn't have anyone else, poor little thing. I just don't know who would do that to anyone, let alone her. Nice kid, doing her best in the world, already saving up her tips to buy herself free — what's wrong with that?"

Avitius shook his head. "Nothing," he said quietly. "Nothing at all." He looked up and down the street once more, and patted Hermes on the shoulder.

"Get some sleep," he advised. "I'll be round in the morning to ask you more about her, just try and find out a bit about her."

Hermes looked at him with a startled expression and Avitius knew that the bar-owner had only just realised that he himself must be a suspect in this murder. Of course, if Hermes had really strangled his own slave just outside the bar, he was an idiot but it would be hard to do anything about it, legally.

Avitius walked through the silent dark city back to Headquarters, determinedly blanking out the picture of Antiope's swollen face and the silver chain sunk in her thin neck.

***

Ovid decided that The Lyre of Apollo needed his patronage for the last day of March in this gods-forsaken backwater. In some weird trick of the post, another letter from Rome had arrived, this time from his wife, and he was not in a good temper. His first few poems describing his journey to Tomis had made it back to the city and were being circulated, but, said Fabia bluntly, they were not gaining him sympathy. Fabia was a very level-headed and unfanciful person — he sometimes wondered why she stayed with him — but she was also an expert in the delivery of uncomfortable truths, and Ovid preferred avoidance of uncomfortable truths wherever possible. Truth is relative, he would tell himself, knowing perfectly well that Fabia would tell him not to spout rubbish and to face up to the real world. He resolutely put away thoughts of Fabia, as he knew from experience that reflecting on what she was going through because of him had the capacity to upset him for days – and was very costly in terms of the wine he needed to get through such times. He therefore entered The Lyre of Apollo with a determined smile and a prepared compliment for Vitia. Naturally Vitia was not there.

"Macer, how can I praise your wife's beauty when she isn't around?" he demanded, making his way towards his favourite table. He did not know why this table was his favourite but he always used it if possible. It was round, and one of its four legs was slightly shorter than the other. Bits of tile were used to try and even it up, but it still needed careful treatment. "It's like me," he thought mournfully. "I'm wobbly and people can't safely lean on me."

"She'll be back in a minute, just gone to get more bread," said Macer, who rather enjoyed Ovid's unconventional visits. Unlike nearly everyone else, he thought Ovid was handling his unhappiness rather well. Macer himself missed Rome hugely, and only the opportunity offered by running the inn kept him in Tomis. Even if it did mean that he was forever in his brother-in-law's debt. Macer could handle that, after all Avitius was a nice chap, a bit humourless, though he'd noticeably loosened since Ovid had arrived. And who would have thought the two of them had known each other all those years ago? The story of the murderous widow and the parrot had been a cracker. Macer smiled as he decanted a jug, the Bybline of course, and took it over. He made a big deal of mixing it with a generous cut of water and hoped that Ovid would take the hint. The poet was not a happy drunk or, come to that, a tidy one.

"Heard the news? We've had a murder," he said cheerfully.

"A murder? Gosh!" said Ovid, mimicking his host's bright tone. "Have we ever had one before?"

POETIC JUSTICE

Macer ignored the teasing and told Ovid what he knew. Barmaid, strangled, left on the road near the bar where she worked.

"Not one of the girls from The Amphora?" asked Ovid, mentally forming a list of his favourite bars and sending up a quick prayer.

"The Amphora? How long have you been here that you've found a dive like The Amphora already?"

Ovid remembered that The Lyre of Apollo was officially his favourite bar and said hurriedly, "Well, some days I like to slum it a bit, you know?"

"Funnily enough," said Macer, "I know exactly what you mean. But don't tell the wife."

"Don't tell me what?" said Vitia appearing at the table with a plate of bread and cheese. "Here, get that down you — you haven't eaten yet today, I'm thinking."

"I haven't," said Ovid, and broke off some cheese happily. "You are wonderful woman, Vitia. Your husband was just telling me about the murder."

Vitia pulled a face.

"It's a bar at the side of the Temple of the Lares," said Macer. "Called after the owner, Hermes' Place."

"No!" said Ovid. "I like that place." And he remembered a night not too long ago when a sweet barmaid had refused to negotiate with him for some of her affection. What was her name? Antigone?

"Who was she?" he asked, afraid.

Vitia said, "We don't know yet, just that it's one of Hermes' girls. He'll be devastated. He's a good man, treats the staff well."

"Pity he serves mouse pee and calls it wine," said Macer. Vitia slapped his arm lightly, and said, "I want you to call in and give our condolences, make sure he knows the bar owners will help him out. He might need some extra hands. You can bet that people will want to have a drink there now there's been a murder."

Ovid stood up, chewing bread and cheese and said with a miniature explosion of crumbs, "I'll come too."

***

They arrived at Hermes' bar at the same time as Avitius, who was fresh from talking to the army medic about the corpse and looked grim. Macer felt for his brother-in-law and patted his shoulder.

"I'm just here to make sure old Hermes knows we all feel for him," he said. "Can I have a quick word before you start? Then I'll be off." He ducked into the bar, and Ovid said awkwardly, "Bad business."

"Yes," said Avitius. "Poor little Antiope, no harm in the world, and gets strangled."

"Antiope! That was the name," said Ovid. "Not Antigone."

Avitius looked at him. "You knew her?"

"Not really," said Ovid sadly. "But I liked what I knew."

Avitius did not ask further. Instead, he took the red and silver twisted cord from his pouch and held it out.

"This is strange though — it's what she was strangled with."

The silver chain glinted in the sun, and the red of the ribbon seemed more cheerful in daylight. Altogether a strange choice of garrotte.

Ovid's brow wrinkled as he said, "That's book ribbon. It's identical to the stuff I use to tie up scrolls and book tubes. It's always that red for some reason."

Avitius looked again at the length of the garrotte and said, "But by the time it's around a scroll or tube, the length is much shorter."

"So, the murderer must have a roll of this ribbon and he has cut off the length he needed to make this," said Ovid. "That's a very refined way of killing someone, especially when you decided to add in a chain like this. Why hasn't the chain broken?"

"The ribbon took the strain. The chain is just for decoration if that's the correct way of putting it."

"Or the chain is the important component and the ribbon was added for support," said Ovid.

Avitius looked at him, and said, "That's a point. Maybe the chain means something."

Ovid bent over the chain again and pointed at the little moon pendant, saying, "Maybe this is the important bit."

"I must ask around, see if it's one of the chains sold by our Getan friends," said Avitius. "The inland tribes are good at anything metal, and their jewellery has a market here. I know one merchant who specialises in silver and shifts the local jewellery down the coast and into Asia."

"Book ribbon though," said Ovid. "We don't have a wide choice of stationery shops here in Tomis. Who would have a stock of the ribbon?"

"I'll ask the clerks at Headquarters about rolls of red ribbon, and where to get them," said Avitius. He looked at Ovid and was struck by his face, frowning as he stood holding the ribbon with its silver adornment.

"What is it?" asked Avitius quietly, loath to interrupt the moment of concentration.

Ovid looked up and asked, "Why did he leave this though? It's as if he left it deliberately, like he wants us to see this and wonder about it."

Avitius had no answer and they interrupted by Macer coming back out, and saying, "I'm off back to The Lyre now. Go easy on Hermes, brother. He didn't have anything to do with this."

Avitius nodded and waited for his brother-in-law to go before muttering, "Amateurs," and going into the bar. Ovid wondered if he was being included as an amateur, but curiosity got the better of him and he followed.

They all sat in the gloomy interior of the bar — Hermes was in no mood to open the shutters — and Avitius started.

"If you want to send the undertakers to Headquarters, I can release Antiope's body to you," he said. "But she was murdered and I need to investigate. You know that, right?"

"I want someone to investigate," said Hermes. "I don't care who does it. Do I pay you?"

"No, I'm doing it at the request of the Governor," said Avitius, in the hope that when he saw Caecina, the Governor would approve. The Town Council weren't going to be any good at this.

Avitius began by establishing the bar's routine and took a list of the customers who had been in the night before. Tactfully, he asked who Antiope's particular friends were. Ovid blushed and bent his head over the table, but his name did not get a mention, thank all the gods. As he listened, he traced the familiar pattern established all those years before when he and Avitius had approached investigations together. Establish the circumstances, find out the people involved, worry about a motive last.

It had been an ordinary sort of day in Hermes' place. Antiope and the girls had cleaned the bar thoroughly as they did at the end of every month, then they'd opened at dusk. Several of the usual customers were in, eating the usual food, drinking the cheap Rhodian wine that Hermes sold with no pretence to connoisseurship.

"Why did she go outside?" asked Avitius, and Ovid approved the way his friend's tone was calm, giving no indication of the importance of the question.

"The girls have a break if it's not too busy," said Hermes. "They sit in the kitchen and chat to my cook, Gorgo, or they get a breath of fresh air in the back yard. But Ani liked to go out into the street and sit on the temple steps and watch the stars. She said she got a better view there. Gorgo said Ani came into the kitchen and got some bread and cheese, saying she'd eat it out front, with her stars."

A murderer who approached his victim and killed her in the street, when anyone could have left the bar and seen something — he must be mad, thought Ovid. Avitius questioned Hermes more closely — had any customers arrived or left during the time Ani had been away? Had any of the staff? Not even to use the latrines down the road?

But the old Greek had little to tell them that raised any suspicions.

"Our customers are — well, they're so normal," said Hermes. "If I'm honest, they're a bit boring. They run small businesses, they come from respectable families, mainly Greek, they don't go drinking for drinking's sake. I'm like their club, their time away from the family, where they can moan about trade and prices and stuff like that. A couple of them have Roman citizenship. They don't make trouble, do you see? They don't like trouble, so they don't make it."

POETIC JUSTICE

Avitius and Ovid nodded, understanding exactly what he was saying. Hermes' place was not the place where rebels or murderers hung out.

Hermes also introduced them to Antiope's two fellow barmaids, who along with Gorgo the cook kept the place going. Nice girls, who knew they were in a good place, they all had well-muscled upper arms, and red hands. The former came from decanting amphoras into jugs, the second from cleaning. Hermes might sell cheap wine, but you wouldn't see much dirt around. Sophia and Zia were slightly older than Antiope, and their eyes filled with tears throughout their interview: those hard-working hands wiped their faces over and over. The story they told marched with Hermes' account. Antiope had a life plan, as did they all. They worked hard, they saved their tips, they all had arrangements to buy out their freedom from Hermes. His customers knew that his girls made good managers: a Hermes girl went on to run a laundry, or cook for a family, or even, like Gorgo, stay working for Hermes. Though Gorgo, as everyone knew, was hoping for marriage to her ex-master. At this the two girls brightened a little, giggling at the thought that two people as old as Gorgo and Hermes could contemplate marriage.

"Did any of the customers show a particular fondness for Antiope?" Avitius asked, but they shook their heads. They all obliged a customer every now and then if asked, but the regulars hardly ever asked. That was not why they came to Hermes' Place. Antiope, it transpired, had had a crush on the man who delivered the Rhodian wine, but he had no eyes for her. Hermes came over at Avitius' query about the Rhodian wine man.

"He has a ship and I think he might be in the harbour at the moment," said Hermes. "He has a boy in every port, as we kept telling Antiope."

"How long since he was last in?" asked Avitius. Hermes thought about it.

"Last I saw him was around the time of the Cybele festival, and he was planning the first long voyage of his season, like they all do. In winter, he hops along the coast, gets as far as the southern shore cities in Bithynia. Summer he goes down to Asia Minor,

Lycia, Cilicia, Rhodes and Cyprus. The harbour master will know if he is still around."

Avitius thanked him and gave the girls a few coins towards the freedom fund. They were pleased and as they stood up to go, one nodded at Ovid and said, "Is he your clerk? Only he hasn't written down a thing, you know."

By the time Avitius had stopped laughing, he and Ovid were out and walking down the street once more.

***

The girl from trusted us of course. Three respectable women, what threat were we to her? But at the end, she knew the blessing of the Goddess, and so the charm builds up. Hecate of the Underworld, in blood we bind your enemies!

POETIC JUSTICE

Chapter 15

Athens, April 1
FESTIVAL OF VENUS

Never in his five years working for the Praetorians, had Clemens of Athens been summoned to a meeting. Normally he was given a brief, he collected information, and he reported back via the imperial post, or to a designated official on the Governor's staff. This time, he was to meet Sejanus himself and what his boss was doing in Athens instead of Rome was anybody's guess. It must be the Ovid situation.

In his mind, Clemens ran over what he knew. He had an excellent memory and never wrote anything down, instead making mental notes which he then filed in categories. He was the central office for every agent east of Greece and their reports came first to him. He had received updates concerning the poet's journey from Samothrace and regular reports had already started arriving from Tomis, speeded up by the Praetorians' own messenger network. He had passed these on as required, and as far as he could tell there was nothing of any great interest in them, so what did Sejanus want? Come to that, why was Sejanus, son of the Praetorian Commander, actually here in Athens?

Why in the name of all the gods was Ovid so important? The official story was that the Emperor was exiling him for his poem *The Art of Loving* – not in tune with current thinking regarding social attitudes. But if this was the reason, the Emperor had taken a long time to get around to condemning the poet, and a lot of interest was being shown in the top circles.

Clemens had no illusions about his own value in the network of intelligence run by the Praetorians. He was good at what he did, very good, but there were many just like him, and until now he had imagined that his work was of relatively little importance. Sejanus' visit changed all that, and he did not like this change to his routine. He passed a small shrine to — which god? It didn't matter. Clemens went up to the worn statue, and rubbed the protruding stone toe for luck, as he said fiercely, "You owe me." The god stared past him, disdainful.

***

Sejanus waved as soon as Clemens entered the bar. He looked as fit and relaxed as ever. Dressed in a light-coloured tunic, as ordinary a garment as you could think of, he could have been anyone, though he was young and good-looking enough to get decent service from barmaids, Clemens noticed. The girl at the bar floated over as soon as he had sat down but she wasn't looking at him.

"Good to see you," said Sejanus, as soon as he had despatched the girl with precise instructions ("make sure the water is decent well-water, freshly drawn, mind"). Clemens nodded and said, "You too, sir," careful to make no eye contact.

He was under no illusions. However much Sejanus treated him as a sort of friend, Clemens was in fact his freedman, born a slave in the household, and freed because he was reliable and could be of use. The bargain was on both sides of course — Clemens appreciated his freedom, enjoyed so early on in life, and he liked his job, reliant as it was on paperwork, organisation of information, a lack of human interaction. And he made good money. The family weren't mean. But he never made the mistake of liking any of them, nor was he fooled by courteous treatment into thinking they liked him.

Sejanus gave no explanation of his appearance in Athens, and went straight to the Ovid matter, as Clemens had expected. Clemens found himself questioned closely on Ovid's routine, interrupted only when the barmaid brought the drinks. She was dismissed with a smile and a tip, and they got down to business once more.

"The man is lost and drinks to excess," said Clemens. "It was noted on the journey that he was up and down, but that he seemed quite cheerful when he got to Samothrace. Being in Tomis seems to have had a deleterious effect once more."

"What are your thoughts about him possibly committing suicide?" said Sejanus. "I'd prefer it if he didn't. Suicide is not in the Emperor's plan for Ovid."

POETIC JUSTICE

Clemens shrugged. "He isn't the suicidal type," he said. "Thinks the world owes him and is convinced he can't deprive the rest of us of his genius. And he is too law-abiding to try and escape. Too intelligent as well. He has nowhere to go, and if he behaves himself in Tomis he will at least get good treatment from the locals. Of course, they're Greeks."

Once Sejanus was satisfied that he knew everything about Ovid in Tomis, he moved onto a rare compliment.

"You've done well. That is an excellent summary of the man and his reaction to what has happened," he said.

Clemens nodded. He had done well, he knew, but he always did.

"But for now, move Ovid down to second in your list of priorities," said Sejanus. "I'm interested in what people think of Germanicus."

Clemens accessed the neat little bookcase of information in his head. He unearthed the file he needed in a second: "Imperial family — potential heirs — Germanicus (currently in Illyricum, tail-end of revolt, junior commander to Tiberius)."

Sejanus said in a smooth tone Clemens recognised, "And in particular I want to know what people say when they compare him to Tiberius."

"Ah!" thought Clemens. "Trouble on Palatine Hill."

It was now several years since Augustus had adopted Tiberius — and made Tiberius adopt Germanicus. The gossip that whispered that the aging Emperor was going to overlook Tiberius and make the young puppy the next ruler of Rome had started immediately, but Clemens had his money firmly on the old dog. Tiberius was tough, had his mother's backbone and was the best general Rome had. Not that this had put a dent in the popularity of Germanicus but what could you expect from the uninformed mob? Young Germanicus was handsome, had a lovely wife who was the Emperor's own granddaughter and the golden pair had got right down to the business of producing impeccably born little Romans for the Emperor to dote on. Two children now, and both sons of course. All that and a shiny smile… Germanicus had everything. Clemens couldn't help a sudden grin and Sejanus raised an enquiring eyebrow.

"I was thinking about what makes people like a leader,' Clemens said, not quite comfortable with expressing a view. He didn't want this particular conversation to develop either, far too close to discussing the death of the Emperor himself. Nobody mentioned that if they were wise. Even if the old man was now in his early seventies and everyone knew he was failing.

Sejanus merely nodded. "And our job is to keep our leaders safe and informed,' he said. "Rome needs stability more than anything else."

And Clemens made sure that he looked solemn, well able to notice a heap of pious nonsense when someone carefully placed it on the table in front of him. He decided to just push at the Ovid question once more.

"I expect Ovid is finding Tomis hard," he said. "From my agent's reports, it is small and unexciting."

"Well, I can certainly handle that, for a few days anyway," said Sejanus.

Clemens struggled but knew he had let his surprise slip.

Sejanus grinned. "I'm looking forward to visiting Tomis. I should get there in June, and I'm interested in how young Sabina has handled things."

"Oh, by the time Sabina has finished, it should be clear to everyone, especially Ovid, that his poem is being used by some madman to create trouble for him." Privately, Clemens thought that the plan that he had relayed from Rome was fanciful, but Sabina had reported a good start already.

"What are your impressions of Sabina?" asked Sejanus.

Clemens had never met Sabina, but approved of her reports which were very well organised. She made it easy for him to file the information. But she was a woman and though there were several women working in this network of information, Clemens found he could not regard them as he did the male operatives. He did not know many women in the flesh and had not been close to any female in his life. He found women troubling.

"She is a very good choice for the place," he said cautiously.

"Ah," said Sejanus. "What don't you like about her?"

"She's too independent," said Clemens. "Clever though, organised, not fussed about using violence. Where did you find her?"

"Oh, she lived on the family estate, or rather the nearby village," he said. "She was recommended so Father had her trained up. Just like you really, except not a slave. Citizen mother and father."

"Not at all like me then," thought Clemens.

Sejanus took a sip of his wine, looking quite thrilled with the idea of meeting a violent and independent woman. But Clemens had had enough of this conversation: he kept quiet, and sure enough he was dismissed, politely of course.

He walked back along the street, noticing that it was warm and spring was rampaging, with tiny yellow flowers peeking out of every dusty crack in the walls. Relief filled him as he looked forward to getting back to his office and going through the package that had arrived from Asia Minor. He loved sorting the reports from so many places without ever feeling any desire to visit himself. Let men like Sejanus board ships and ride roads, talking to a different man – or woman — in every town. This thought brought him back to the question that had troubled him since he first learned that Sejanus wanted to meet in person. Why was Ovid so important that Sejanus was prepared to go to Tomis?

Chapter 16

Tomis, April 2

Avitius had been to Antiope's funeral, the procession ending up at the town's communal burial pit to the south-west. A slave could not justify the expense of a funeral pyre, no matter how valued she had been. Hermes had split Antiope's savings between the other two girls, and when he said, "It's what she would have wanted," Avitius believed him and respected him for it.

When the funeral party came back to Hermes' place, Avitius was surprised to see Ovid sitting in the corner, being served by Gorgo who had missed the funeral itself to keep an eye on the bar. The poet was jittering with energy, to Avitius' surprise — he'd always seen Ovid as too laid-back. He went over.

"Doesn't take a philosopher to see something's up," he said quietly. "But not here, eh."

"Sit and have a drink then," said Ovid. "Then I can tell you."

"One cup," said Avitius. "I'm not too popular here."

"Ah," said Ovid. "No wonder Hermes is looking so crossly at you. You went around all his customers, questioning them about Antiope. You scared them."

"Yes," said Avitius, with the certainty of an ex-centurion. "But it was the place to start. Unfortunately, I got nothing yesterday but the garrotte that killed her."

"About that," said Ovid. "The chain — it wasn't hers, was it?"

"No," said Avitius. "I asked the other girls and they said that she could not have owned a piece of jewellery like that without them knowing. It also struck me that it is just that bit too expensive for a slave – someone like Antiope doesn't get given jewellery, at least not often. Sophia said that even if anyone had given Antiope something like that, she'd have sold it for her freedom savings."

"Poor girl," said Ovid.

"I searched her quarters," continued Avitius, "and found nothing. Her friends couldn't think of anything. The Rhodian wine guy is out of the picture. The customers all stayed in here and could back each other up. And I shouldn't be talking about the investigation here."

"Drink up," said Ovid.

"Just tell me. What do you have?" Avitius asked.

"The Rhodian wine-man," said Ovid, "is in the harbour now and has been for three nights."

"Ah," said Avitius. "Interesting."

"Is that all?" said Ovid. "I land your prime suspect slap in front of you and you say, "Interesting"? I mean, what is interesting is why everyone told you he was "out of the picture," to quote yourself. Isn't it?"

"Not really," said Avitius. "He told them he was going to Rhodes for the first long voyage of his season, and they just repeated it."

"And when would you have seen you were wrong?" Ovid demanded.

"When I went and asked around the harbour, like I did yesterday," said Avitius. "Or when some busybody told me. Like you did."

"Are we going to question him? Oh," said Ovid. "You've already seen him, haven't you?"

"I have," said Avitius. "Would you like to know what happened?"

"Are you supposed to discuss this with me?" said Ovid.

"If I want," said Avitius. "And given that you tried to help by going down to the harbour this morning and asking around, potentially screwing up my investigation, I think I had better."

Ovid kept quiet.

"The Rhodian wine guy is called Stephanos," said Avitius, "and he is in fact from Cyprus. He is happily single with a boyfriend in every major port along this western Black Sea coast, and he was sorry for Antiope's passion for him which he could not reciprocate. He thought she was a nice girl. He was on board his ship the night before last, a fact confirmed by the crew and the harbourmaster, who stopped off for a drink and fell asleep on the deck. The harbourmaster thinks that it is possible that Stephanos could have waited for everyone to fall asleep and crept on and off the ship, but when I look at timings, it is clear that Antiope was killed while everyone on board that ship was still conscious if not sober."

Ovid stretched and sighed. Looking around the bar, he thought that the wake had reached the point where guests needed to murmur condolences and go.

"Come on," he said to Avitius. "I'm disappointed of course, but we need to be leaving. Poor Zia looks as though she needs to sleep, and Gorgo is just sitting crying."

They slipped out and nobody missed them.

Chapter 17

April 3

Caecina Severus had been Governor of Moesia for two years and had not yet announced where his capital city would be, but it was felt that Tomis was in with a good chance. The previous governor had spent his two years just getting the new province to accept that it now enjoyed the blessing of being part of the greatness that was Rome: Caecina's mandate was to deliver the promised peace and benefits. Avitius thought he was doing a good job, especially as he had spent a lot of time in the last two years helping put down a revolt in Illyricum.

On the day after Antiope's funeral, Vitia was worried about the Governor.

"Supposing," she demanded of Avitius and Macer as they all sat having a swift breakfast in The Lyre of Apollo, "this horrible murder turns him off Tomis? Suppose he goes down the coast and settles all the main stuff in Callatis or somewhere?"

Callatis, a city just down the coast was a worrying rival, with a few more temples than Tomis, and a more distinguished heritage, being the hometown of a philosopher and historian called Satyrus. Privately, Avitius was convinced that Satyrus had never really existed. And as someone who had travelled all the towns of the coast, he maintained that once you'd seen one six-hundred-year-old Greek seaside town, you'd seen them all.

"Don't worry," he told his sister kindly. "I shall have a word with the Governor, tell him how you feel."

Vitia stuck out her tongue and rattled crockery unnecessarily as she cleared the table.

But as Avitius made his way to the Headquarters building, he couldn't help thinking that she had a point. The town of Callatis had had a treaty with Rome for over a hundred years, as it was very keen on pointing out. And if the Governor moved all the official buildings to another town, he, Avitius, would have to move with them. Avitius liked Tomis, he liked having property there and keeping an eye on it. And he liked having some family around, probably because he didn't have to stay in the same house as them.

He mused on this until he entered Caecina's study and was immediately invited to take a seat while he made his report on the murder.

Caecina said, "It is most likely to be a customer, isn't it? And this Rhodes wine supplier is a regular customer?"

Avitius said, "Experience says it's someone she knows. But every customer named by Hermes or his staff has been interviewed and has a reasonable alibi. Including the Rhodian wine man, Stephanos."

Caecina thought. Avitius liked this about his new boss. Caecina Severus was intelligent, a decent soldier, not averse to making his way up the ladder by virtue of hard work. He didn't speak without thinking, and best of all for Avitius, once Caecina had delegated a task, he trusted his men to get on with it.

"What's the feeling in the town?" the Governor asked.

Avitius had hoped he wouldn't be asked this.

"They aren't used to murders here and people aren't happy," he said.

"Oh, yes?" said Caecina, sounding interested. "They don't just dismiss it as one of those things prostitutes have to expect?"

"With respect, sir," said Avitius, "she was a barmaid rather than a prostitute. Hermes doesn't make his girls work like that."

"Oh," said Caecina. "And is that important? She was a slave after all."

"She might think it important," said Avitius. "And this is the sort of place where people know that sort of thing. If she is thought to be —" he struggled for the right words but could only come out with, "— a good girl, then people aren't going to let it go so easily. Sir."

Caecina nodded and gave him a smile. "Centurion, no need to look so stern. I'm glad that your years in the legions have not hardened you too much. To this poor child, no doubt it was important that she was not used as a prostitute."

"The other girls at Hermes' place talked about her as though she was their little sister," said Avitius. "As for the gossip in the town, a lot of people assume it's a rape gone wrong, but it isn't, there's no sign of it. And that garrotte bothers me. It was something the killer prepared and brought with him especially."

"And left at the scene deliberately," said Caecina. Avitius was impressed. Ovid was the only other person who had spotted that. Caecina continued, "So this Rhodian wine trader seems unlikely, and you are happy with his — er — alibi?"

"I am, sir," said Avitius. "I could, if you wanted, keep him under surveillance for a bit. He says he needs to go on a long voyage so I could send one of my men along."

"It isn't what I want but your judgement that matters here," said Caecina. "Let's leave the Rhodian wine man alone. Anything else?"

"I'm going to go around all the bars and spread the word that I'm interested in anyone who is acting suspiciously, or who was mysteriously absent the night before last. I'm also interviewing the jewellery traders to try and pin down where the chain came from," said Avitius.

"Good thought," said the Governor. "And are you going to take your old boss along? Keep our poor exile busy?"

"Maybe," said Avitius cautiously. "He was good at this sort of thing when we were younger. He hasn't made anything of the animals that were killed, but I didn't really expect him to. Yes, I could let him tag along with me, as long as it's all right with you, sir. I mean, him being in exile and all that."

"I don't think we need worry about that," said Caecina. "It isn't as if he were in exile for strangling barmaids."

"Does anyone know what he is in exile for?" asked Avitius.

"Upsetting Augustus," said Caecina. "Poor chap. He really is a very fine poet. One thing I can tell you is that he wasn't formally exiled. The Emperor himself told him to go then asked the Senate for confirmation. I can't recall anything like it before. He has not had his money or possessions confiscated and his family are as free as they were before, with nothing held against them. Of course, he has no male family, just a bunch of women. Wife, daughter, stepdaughter, mother-in-law."

"So, he is in disgrace in Rome, but not necessarily in disgrace here?" asked Avitius. Caecina shrugged.

"We can treat him well as long as he doesn't escape the town. Is he going to try, do you think?"

"No," said Avitius. "He will behave. Which reminds me…"

Avitius did not quite remember how Ovid had persuaded him, but it was as the poet's friend that he asked Caecina if Ovid might use official channels to convey letters to his wife. Caecina, knowing full well that Ovid would use this license to send more sad poems home, granted it straight away.

"He's a fully-paid-up member of the Ovid Sympathisers Club," thought Avitius.

Caecina saw his expression and chuckled.

"It's a small thing," he said. "Not everyone in Rome has hardened their hearts to him but we all know that his pleading poems aren't going to make a wool-tuft of difference where it matters. Your friend is *persona non grata* and will stay here until he dies. He does know that doesn't he?"

"No, he is an unreasonable optimist," said Avitius. "But he will be grateful to you, Sir."

Caecina looked at him.

"False hope is cruel," he said quietly. "Remind him of that, would you?"

Avitius wondered when he had become Ovid's nursemaid.

"Sir," he said and turned to leave, with a small scroll containing the license to use the Governor's couriers and official ships. Caecina had not quite finished though.

"This murder," he said. "Let's not make too much of it, eh?"

***

Avitius left the scroll at Ovid's house and set off for Hermes' Place once more, musing on his boss. Caecina had many good points, such as calling him "Centurion." It pleased Avitius who had been proud of his rank, and Caecina said it did no harm to remind civilians. This, thought Avitius, showed you the measure of the man, thinking of his people as well as himself. On the other hand, Caecina did not share the sense of unease that Avitius felt over the murder of Antiope.

Hermes was staring into a cup of his own gut rotting Rhodian wine, minding an empty bar. He looked up and nodded at Avitius, and Avitius was surprised to see that Hermes looked old. When had that happened? The Greek's skin had sagged into wrinkles under his eyes and round his chin, and his eyes were dull pools of woe.

"Maybe I'm not the person to say it but you look terrible," said Avitius, taking the stool opposite Hermes. "And where are the girls, and Gorgo?"

"Shopping," said Hermes gloomily. "I've just done something as dumb as dumb or very clever and I don't know which."

Avitius waited, trying to relax his shoulders and lean slightly back on his stool, so as to look less official. Eventually, he decided Hermes needed a prompt so he tried, "What are they shopping for? Anything in particular?"

"Wedding clothes," said Hermes and Avitius couldn't help it as his eyebrows shot up. "Wedding clothes? Who is getting married?"

Hermes gave a dramatic sigh, broke out into a smile, and said, "I am." Avitius thought that it was like seeing the two masks of drama at once, tragedy and comedy, sharing a single face.

"I asked Gorgo to marry me," said Hermes. "It seemed the right thing."

Avitius understood the impact of Antiope's death on her ready-made family in the bar. They all now needed to seize life and use it wisely. There was a cynical side of him that wondered how long this would last even as he applauded Hermes' generosity.

"My congratulations, friend," he said.

Hermes shrugged but his blush gave him away.

"It's an expensive business, but what is money for? Don't know why I didn't do it sooner," he said. "I'm never going to find a finer woman than Gorgo."

"Well, I say you are a lucky man," said Avitius. "Pour me a cup and let's drink to your future happiness."

They poured, saluted each other and drank. Avitius wished there were much more water in the mix. Hermes' wine really was terrible.

"I've been thinking about it — you know, Ani, what happened to her," said Hermes, gazing once more into his cup. "I don't get it, I really don't. I'm Tomis born and bred, you know. And I'm not saying we're perfect, of course, but this..." his voice broke, and he drank and coughed while Avitius diplomatically studied the menu scrawled on the wall next to Gorgo's serving counter. Someone had made an attempt to rub it off, but ghosts of dishes remained. Beans in a ginger sauce should clear your head of a hangover, and for the less adventurous, cheese, bread and olives.

Hermes wiped his eyes and Avitius felt for him. "You're right about Tomis. This is different," he said.

"Have you ever come across this sort of thing?" asked Hermes.

"Yes, when I was younger, in Rome," said Avitius. "I was in a sort of city guard, long before the Emperor set up the Watch we have now. We had brawls to sort out, murders, rapes, all sorts."

"Will you set up a Watch in Tomis?" asked Hermes.

"We shall have to think about it," said Avitius and thought of the cost. Nobody was going to be willing to fund that. Not to save a slave-girl who worked in a bar.

"Did you think of anything else about Antiope's murder?" he asked. "Anything that could help me find this bastard? Anyone spring to mind as an admirer, anyone she rejected?"

"You asked me that yesterday," said Hermes, "and all I could think of was the Rhodian wine-man."

"Stephanos is in the clear," said Avitius. "Though as my friend Ovid found out, he is still in the harbour here."

"Is he?" Hermes sounded vague, and then he looked at Avitius sharply. "I've just remembered something. Your friend Ovid got turned down by Ani sometime last month — let me see... Sometime before the festival of Cybele."

Avitius tried not to look taken aback and shook his head. "Unlikely," he said. "As a murderer I mean. I can see him as an unsuccessful admirer."

He concentrated on keeping his voice calm while seething inside. "And I can also see him as a man with some explaining to do," he thought.

"He's written enough poems about being a rejected lover," said Hermes.

"You've read his poetry?"

Hermes shrugged. "Hasn't everyone? The funny ones anyway. I didn't bother with *The Metamorphoses*, a bit long-winded for me."

Avitius was once more surprised by Ovid's popularity as a poet but got back to the more important subject.

"I've asked all the owners of nearby bars if they can think of anyone who set them thinking, anyone who behaved strangely," he said, "but I think you will do better than me. They are a bit wary of me."

"I've asked everyone I know," said Hermes. "Didn't really know what to ask them, mind, but at least it's made them think a bit more about their own staff. We're going to miss Ani but I haven't the heart to start looking for a replacement."

"You hard-hearted businessman," said Avitius. He left the rest of his wine, hoping that Hermes wouldn't mind, pushed his stool back.

"Let me know if anything occurs to you," he said. "And keep asking your bar owner friends if they think of anything. Anything at all."

"And why," he thought, "did Ovid not tell me about this attempt to seduce Antiope? He really can be a prick – but he really isn't a killer. Though I never asked if anyone could vouch for him the night of Antiope's murder. Should I ask Baucis?"

Avitius stomped out of Hermes' Place, wondering why he had ever been pleased to see Ovid that morning in March when they had painted The Lyre of Apollo together.

***

Avitius' final visit of the day was to a silversmith who operated a small and extremely well-built shop on the outskirts of the market square. A guard stood outside the door and nodded politely as he went in, and Avitius nodded back, looking at the man and saying "Auxiliaries?"

"Thracian cavalry, attached to the Fifth Macedonica, Centurion," said the man with a grin.

"And this work suits you?" asked Avitius curiously. He remembered the Thracians well. Fierce cavalry, they babied their horses and drank to the despair of their officer.

"I miss the horses," confided the man. "But I did my service, and now I've a wife in this town and four sons. It is good to go home to them every night."

Avitius smiled and took a coin out of his pouch. "Peace has its advantages. Buy them a honey cake each from me," he said. "Tell your boys that their father was a noble warrior for Rome."

The coin vanished, and the Thracian cavalryman opened the door for him.

"Good day, sir," said a quiet voice in perfect Greek. The man behind the counter could also have been in the Thracian cavalry, tall and wide shouldered and with an air of being able to take care of himself in a fight. His beard and hair were combed and trimmed, and his fingers flashed with rings, but nobody would have seen him as anything but a fighter. Avitius introduced himself and the man nodded.

"And I am Seuthis. I am of the Getae, as you have probably guessed. And I would guess that you have not come here for a necklace for your sister's birthday."

Avitius noted that Seuthis of the Getae knew all about him. This was not entirely surprising, but it still made him a little uneasy.

"I need your knowledge, Seuthis," he said. "I have a piece of silver recently used in a crime, and I would like your opinion on it."

Seuthis raised his eyebrows.

"And in return, Avitius of the Romans?"

"He's having fun," thought Avitius, trying not to be annoyed. Aloud he said, "I would indeed like something for my sister's birthday, but not a necklace and not until October. What I can buy now to compensate you for your time and expertise is a small ornament, suitable as an offering to the gods."

"Jupiter, no doubt?" Seuthis quickly produced a box and opened it. "This is I think perfect. You can nail it to the temple wall."

POETIC JUSTICE

Inside the box were hundreds of little silver zigzags, Jupiter's thunderbolts, ranging from tiny to as long as his palm and fingers. Avitius smiled. These were indeed perfect. And maybe he could warm up the chilly Seuthis with some bargaining. Maybe he would even let Seuthis get the better of the bargain.

It was some time and a very expensive little thunderbolt later that Avitius was able to show Seuthis the silver chain with its moon pendant. Seuthis wrinkled his nose at sight of the piece, but examined it very carefully, talking as he did so.

"This is not particularly well-made but even so, it has been misused, the links stretched and here, look, almost broken," he complained. Avitius thought of the use to which this chain had been put and kept his peace. Seuthis continued, "And the moon is not the best work either. This is a necklace made by an apprentice or maybe by a man who does nothing else but make them, as quickly and as cheaply as he can. I would not sell something like this. It is not the work of the Getae or of any other tribe along the river. We pride ourselves on our metalwork."

"Where would one find this sort of thing?" asked Avitius, feeling increasingly nettled by the man's tone.

Seuthis shrugged. "A large town, a place with many visitors, a place where many people look for cheap goods. Alexandria or Rome, maybe. The towns of Asia Minor."

Avitius had been afraid of this. He nodded to Seuthis and said, "Thank you — for the amulet and for the information."

"And you will be back in October for your sister's present," said Seuthis. "Or even before, who knows?"

And that was it. Avitius left the shop and wondered what Seuthis of the Getae had against Romans. Aside from all the usual things people here had against Romans.

***

As evening drew near, Ovid came around to Avitius' office and was interested to hear about the silversmith's verdict on the moon pendant chain.

"Does he really think that the chain came from Rome, I wonder?" he said. "Or is he just being uncooperative?"

Avitius pondered this briefly then shook his head. "I don't think it's that. I saw him examine it carefully, and if he says it is cheap and mass produced then I shall go with that. He said Rome to annoy me because he has some sort of issue with us. But there are all sorts of places where someone could have picked up a chain like that. Any ship's captain or crew visiting a large town could have got it as a present."

They were silent. Ovid took a scrap of book ribbon lying on Avitius' desk, and started to fiddle with it, tying it into knots and undoing them. When he thought of it wrapping around Antiope's neck he shuddered.

"Would it have been quick?" he asked.

Avitius did not answer. Instead, he picked up the silver chain and ran it between his fingers for the thousandth time.

"Why use this?" he asked.

"The moon?" suggested Ovid. "Or it's a reminder of someone, the killer's mother, girlfriend, wife. Or it's the silver that matters, maybe?"

"How do you make that out?"

"No idea," said Ovid. "I don't go round killing barmaids with bizarre garrottes. Gods, that was tasteless. Sorry."

"Which leads onto a very interesting question," said Avitius. "Why did you not tell me that you tried to get Antiope to sleep with you?"

Ovid looked startled. "I did?"

"You did," said Avitius. "Just before the festival of Cybele."

Ovid wrinkled his brow, and Avitius watched as the realisation hit him. It was beautifully done. "Oh. Ah, yes, I remember. Yes, indeed, that must have been Antiope. Dear gods, I'm glad she said no." He took a quick look at Avitius. "You can't possibly think that I…"

"No, I don't," said Avitius. "It just would have been useful to hear it from you and not Hermes. No, this sort of bizarre stuff is too much for you. You aren't a killer, are you?"

"I've never even done any military service," said Ovid. He cheered up immediately, springing back like a puppy being trained unsuccessfully. "You are right, it is bizarre. So next question is —

why?" He shook his head, answering his own question. "I haven't heard anything that made me think of Antiope as a target, have you? The only thing I can think of is a rejected suitor, and surely someone at the bar would have noticed if she'd had an admirer. Someone a little more successful than me."

Avitius laughed at the delicate language. "Suitor! Admirer! And from you, Rome's premier poet of daring love elegy."

"Well, your doctor says she wasn't raped," said Ovid. "And she wasn't robbed, in fact the murderer left something valuable behind. It wasn't spur of the moment, because he was prepared, he brought a specific weapon with him. The motive has to be something else."

"I'm not sure that Antiope was necessarily the target," said Avitius slowly. "He wanted to kill someone, and maybe she was vulnerable at the right moment. She liked to sit on the steps of the temple and look at the stars, Hermes said. If she was there as he was on the prowl…"

"What a horrible thought," said Ovid. "But if she was the victim for no other reason than that she was handy, then what is our murderer hoping to get out of it?"

"Maybe he enjoys it," said Avitius. A thought struck him.

"I was going to ask you about the animal killings — did you have any thoughts?"

"Only the one that has just struck you," said Ovid. "Someone enjoys doing it."

"Maybe the same person," said Avitius.

Ovid looked out of the tiny window and saw that darkness had fallen. "You need to go home and eat," he said. "I'll walk with you — or you could come to my place and let Baucis complain that I didn't warn her you were coming."

They left Headquarters to a respectful, "Night sir," from the sentry and walked along the street, heading back towards Tomis' marketplace. The street was the soft dark grey of twilight and a bat fluttered bemusedly overhead as they reached the crossroads.

'This was all silver with moonlight two nights ago," said Avitius and Ovid laughed.

"You sound almost poetical" Then he stopped, grabbing at Avitius' sleeve. "Moonlight... Was the moon full when you discovered the body?"

"I didn't discover..." began Avitius and was surprised to find Ovid shaking his arm and saying, "Never mind that. Was it a full moon?"

Avitius thought. "Not exactly, I'd say," he said slowly, beginning to see where Ovid was going.

"And let me just check the dates again — Antiope on the last day of March, the horse just before the end of February, the cat a few days before the end of January. Right?"

Avitius stared at his friend. "You mean the moon was full or almost full every time? The moon was certainly shining when I was called to Antiope's body," he said. "The whole street was silver." He massaged the back of his neck, stretching his head back to look up at the sky.

"I don't think the dates quite match," he said. "As far as I can work out, Antiope was killed two days after full moon. I'd have to check the horse and the cat."

Ovid shrugged. "Does two days out matter if you are one of those full moon nutters?"

"Dear gods, I hope we don't have some sort of lunatic. When is the full moon this month?"

Ovid gazed off into the distance and his fingers fluttered like a flautist's as he counted.

"Four days before the end of April," he said.

POETIC JUSTICE

Chapter 18

April 4
THE MEGALESIAN FESTIVAL

"Letter to my dear wife Fabia, and my revered mother-in-law, Sulpicia, written on the fourth day of April in Tomis on the Black Sea.

And our big news is that we have a murder! Apparently this is a very rare event in Tomis, apart from the usual domestic instances, where the culprit is obvious from the start.

This murder unfortunately was not domestic or obvious. In fact, there is something quite disturbing about it and I hope you don't mind if I write it all down for you. It will help clear my thinking, and of course you may have insights on the whole affair. Though I hope that by the time I receive your undoubted wisdom, Avitius and I will know who the murderer is. This long-distance communication is such an irritation, though I trust that my letters are getting through quickly and regularly now that I have the Governor's permission to use his official courier. Apparently, he is a fan of my work.

So — to the murder. Now, when I was a young man, I ran the Commission for Prisons and Executions for a year and what I learned from it has come in useful here. Well, maybe not exactly useful, because I haven't made any progress, but let me explain. Have I told you about Avitius? Security Adviser to the Governor, excellent chap, and by strange chance, a member of my patrol when I ran that Commission thirty years ago? He asked me to help out with a small problem, a couple of strange animal killings and we had no luck, but several days ago unfortunately we got a real murder. The victim was a slave girl who as far as Avitius and I have been able to find out never did anything wrong in her life apart from being born a slave. She was strangled on the night of the full moon with a cord that had a silver moon charm on it. We have tentatively tied this to the two animal killings I mentioned earlier. The first was a cat on the day before the end of January, and the second a horse two days before the end of February. No doubt you, clever mother-in-law, will have made the full moon deduction already.

So, we might well have a moon madness here in Tomis, slightly chilling, eh? Stories of murder at the full moon were rife in Rome, and there never seemed to be an actual foundation to most of those stories, but a doctor I once met claimed that he had recorded patient numbers and diseases over several years, and noticed a distinct increase in disorders of the mind up to and including suicide around the time of the full moon. He recommended prayer to Hecate and abstention from alcohol. I wonder if there is a temple to Hecate here in Tomis? If there is, I intend to visit it before long, I can assure you.

Avitius and I spent yesterday trawling the bars of Tomis asking for full moon stories from the landlords and bar staff but haven't been able to track down anyone who shows abnormal behaviour associated with the full moon. What do you, the most intelligent ladies of my acquaintance, say to all this? I would ask for ideas, if I didn't know that it will be a month or two before I get a reply. Really, even using the official courier, communications are abysmal."

Ovid's mother-in-law Sulpicia found this letter extremely interesting, and it resulted in her spending an evening looking through many scrolls as well as consulting a calendar before she scribbled a reply that would not reach Ovid for many days.

POETIC JUSTICE

Chapter 19

April 15
FESTIVAL OF THE FORDICIDIA

Apolauste stood at the entrance to her father's study. She was holding a scroll and looked serious.

"Papa, I know you must be busy, but — this has arrived, and I thought you should see it."

"I'm only sort of busy," said Menis, looking at an unfathomable diagram of what he knew must be a drain. "I can't figure out how this will work, when we can't maintain the drains we already have, though..." and his voice trailed off as he saw his daughter's expression. "Never mind — what is "this"? And where did you get it?" And he stretched out a hand.

"You know the stall near the harbour that sometimes has books? The seller had several copies of this," said Apolauste. "It's a poem by our exile."

"And did you manage to understand the Latin?" asked Menis, smiling. His daughter's spoken Latin was nearly as good as his, but she found reading it harder.

"Someone had added a Greek translation," said Apolauste. "I wanted to make sure it was accurate, so I thought I'd better show you."

She stood patiently, while Menis read, his eyes darting from Latin to Greek as he checked. His face fell almost immediately and stayed there. Eventually he looked up.

"What are people saying?"

"They aren't happy," said his daughter. "He's been here all of two months, less actually. The translation is accurate then?"

"Oh yes," said Menis and his gaze fell once more on the poem supposedly written by Ovid. "I didn't know he had been so ill."

"He hasn't," said his daughter with the brutal scorn of the young. "He drinks too much and wallows in self-pity, everyone knows that."

Menis was about to object then thought of the comments he had just read about his town and shut his mouth.

"What he says about Tomis is most unfair," said Apolauste, unrelenting in her disapproval. "We have doctors, we have good food, and people have tried to befriend him. And as for saying that there isn't even a house fit for a sick man, that is just rubbish."

"It is indeed," said Menis, thinking of house given to the poet by a generous town.

"And here," Apolauste moved to look over the papyrus in his hand and read until she found the place she was looking for, "here, look at what he says."

Menis read, "… but my body shall lie in a barbarian land, unmourned and without the dignity of a tomb…."

"Well, he has ensured that none of us will come to his funeral," said his daughter. "Barbarian land indeed!"

She flounced off, skirts swirling, and he could not blame her. What a fool Ovid was!

He laid aside the problem of the drains and once more walked up the street to the poet's house. He did not care how much Ovid's head was aching, the poet had some explaining to do.

***

Ovid had suffered one of his chills in April and he spent several days in bed, feeling that he was breathing with a weight on the centre of his chest. Back in Rome, he would have gone to the hills at the first signs as the city air exacerbated the condition. In Tomis, Baucis thought, the sea air also had a beneficial effect, but Ovid decided that she was wrong. The illness plunged him into gloom and he stopped eating. Baucis and Philemon kept their own contact with him to a minimum and tried to put off all visitors, not always successfully. While Ovid's friends at Rome knew to keep away, Tomis tried to be kind and people brought little gifts and themselves to cheer him up. It was not a success.

On this day, Ovid made the effort and sat at his desk wrapped in a blanket and feeling miserable. Philemon had decided that now was not the time to keep his master short of wine and while Ovid could usually judge the amount needed to keep him mildly hazy, today he had been in a rage with his life and already drunk too much. He felt queasy and hated everything and everybody.

He gazed at the papers on his desk, and wondered why he had ever thought he could write poetry. What in the name of the Muses themselves was this rubbish?

"On this day, third after the Ides of April, the Fordicidia — a sacrifice to the teeming earth…"

He put his head in his hands. "You," he addressed himself out loud, "are a pretentious, talentless prick!"

"Possibly a prick, definitely pretentious," said a voice from the doorway. "Not altogether talentless, which is why I have come to see you."

The poet looked terrible, Menis had to admit. Wrinkles dug in deep, dragging his mouth and nose down and the little fan of lines at the outer edges of his eyes did not make him seem more cheerful. Those wrinkles clung to his eyes and clawed at his face.

Menis felt his usual compassion for this man, who was suffering his disgrace so physically and obviously, and he accepted Baucis' hissed information — this was not drink, this was a real illness. But he still had to explain to Ovid that he had no right to talk about Tomis and its inhabitants as he had done. He hardened his heart and got out the little pamphlet brought to him by his daughter, and said, pretending to peer at it, "I see we haven't been up to your standards."

Ovid did not seem to take in his words at first, huddled in his chair and scrutinising the depths of his cup with gloom. At last, he focused on the papyrus in Menis' hand, shrugged and said, "What are you talking about?"

"A poem, supposedly written by you about your time here, has arrived from Athens," said Menis. He watched Ovid. The poet's face went from misery to guilt in one moment.

"Ah. Which one?"

"It's addressed to your wife," said Menis. "How is she doing by the way?"

Ovid looked up and blinked at him. "How is she?" he repeated. "She's at Rome, so she's fine, of course."

Menis thought, "The selfish bastard hasn't a clue because he has never asked. Why hasn't she divorced him?"

Aloud he said, "I am glad to hear it. Please pass on my best wishes when next you write. However, I was disappointed with this, and I would like to know why you wrote it."

"I wrote it because I am bloody miserable and want to go back home," Ovid explained carefully.

"Yes, but it appears in this poem that you are — er — bloody miserable because you are, in particular, here in Tomis, a place where you have not yet lived for two whole months, and yet you can describe its winters from personal experience. In fact, according to you it is winter all year round, and fruit trees can't grow. The wine here — not that we make wine because according to you we can't grow vines — the wine still manages to freeze so that we have to consume it by licking it. Oh, and it is so barbaric that none of us speak Latin — shall I go on?"

Ovid shifted crossly on his seat and drew the blanket closer, emphasising his ill and sorry plight.

"How did you get hold of a copy anyway?" he asked.

"It's being sold by an enterprising stall holder near the harbour," said Menis. "He has a contact in Athens, who sends him cheap volumes of poetry and Alexandrian romances, as well as any pamphlets doing the rounds. My guess is that you used a rather unscrupulous courier who decided to sell your work, and the result has winged its way back here. My daughter informs me that these pamphlets have already sold out, after going on sale just yesterday and whoever produced them kindly provided a Greek translation for the benefit of us barbarians. That is a joke, by the way, though I don't suppose anyone in Tomis is clever enough to understand it."

Ovid said, "It's just poetic license." There was a mutinous tone to his voice, the sort of tone familiar to Menis because Apolauste used it when she was about to have one of her teenage strops.

"Well, be prepared for your poetic license to have some repercussions," he said. "On the way here, I was accosted by one of my fellow councillors who informs me that at our next meeting he intends to bring up the question of your freedom from town taxes here. You were going to be exempted from winter wall duty as well, and I think you can expect that to change. Do you see?"

Ovid said nothing.

Menis stood. "I've said what I came to say," he said mildly. "I'm having the Governor to dinner the day after tomorrow and would like to invite you to join us."

Ovid winced, and mumbled, "No. Not yet." And then, "I mean, thank you, but best not."

Menis gave up.

"I'm coming tomorrow, to check on you," he said. "Don't be ill."

"I can't help being ill," said Ovid.

Menis nodded at the wine jug and said, "I think that in your case, yes, you can." He knew he was being unfair, but there was a point to be made.

Outside, in the warmth of a perfect spring day, the sky an intense and a cloudless blue, he smiled to himself. Romans! Who would have thought that they could be so feeble?

Chapter 20

April 27

Avitius had increased patrols over the days leading up to the full moon, but the night itself passed with no incident. He did not intend to relax yet though. It was almost a month since the murder of the barmaid Antiope, and he had made no progress in finding out who had killed her. He hadn't been able to trace the origin of the silver moon chain beyond the Getan jeweller's opinion that it was mass-produced and probably from Rome.

"The one solid thing we have, it should be the key," he mourned to Ovid at The Lyre of Apollo, just as the evening was falling over Tomis. He took the chain out of the purse hanging at his belt, and once more the two men gazed at that little crescent moon, hanging from the middle of the chain. It should have hung around Antiope's neck, a present from a lover, something to express tender feelings.

Avitius and Ovid had decided that the connection with the full moon was their biggest clue, though Ovid suggested that given the physical locations of each incident, temples and bars should be warned. Avitius heard this out with admirable patience, and agreed, before telling Ovid that he had in fact already done this. The poet was unabashed. He had fully recovered from his illness and was back to peak confidence.

"He is settling into Tomis and quite enjoying himself," thought Avitius. "If he forgets how miserable he is, he is good company. I wonder how much he is drinking?"

Aloud he asked Ovid how the writing was going.

"I'm really making progress," said Ovid with unfeigned enthusiasm. "I've started doing a major overhaul of a poem I started years ago, all about the stars and the calendar and the great festivals." He went on for some time and Avitius knew better than to do anything other than nod.

"He is definitely drinking less," he thought.

"How are things otherwise?" he asked aloud.

POETIC JUSTICE

Ovid shrugged. "I've given up on the animal killings," he said far too casually.

Avitius shook his head. "I don't blame you."

After a pause, Ovid said, "Maybe a little tension has arisen with some of my neighbours."

"Oh? What did you do?"

"I have had no trouble that wasn't completely of my own making," Ovid admitted. "I'm writing poems and sending them back home, as you know. And the idea is to get some sympathy, persuade a few friends to lobby Augustus, get me pardoned or something. I may have exaggerated my life here for dramatic effect. Unfortunately, one poem got back here and some of my observations did not go down well. Can't blame people really, but I need to do some serious work to regain ground lost."

"You mean you need me to find you some more work?"

They both laughed at that.

"I've been a bit useless so far," said the poet. "Couldn't pinpoint your animal killer, couldn't help with poor little Antiope. I've lost my edge."

"You never had an edge," said Avitius.

Ovid shrugged and Avitius wondered if he'd been too brutal.

Chapter 21

April 28
THE FLORALIA

Ovid was indeed drinking less these days. Baucis and Philemon were pleased, Avitius was pleased, Fabia would have been pleased if she had known. Everyone loves me when I don't drink, thought Ovid gloomily.

He was at his desk, but he wasn't writing sad poems of exile to be sent home to Rome. Instead, he was editing passages of the great poem he planned that centred on the rolling course of the year, the stars, the religious festivals, things that never changed and would be playing out their course long after he was dead. It was going to be his legacy work, the work that everyone would think of first when his name was mentioned. Ovid knew that his name would be mentioned. The concept of modesty, let alone false modesty, was alien to him.

Today as he tried to review his work, the chain from Antiope's neck kept flashing across his mind, a silver thread that tried to wind itself into the lines of his poem. He looked at the words in front of him, already a mess of scratches, deletions and insertions. March, the month of Mars, warrior god. He'd written about Mars himself of course, covered the Ides with its festival of Anna Perenna, the trumpets' purification on the 23rd, the festival of Luna at the end of the month.... Ovid stopped. He read the last two lines of March again and there it was, both in his poem and hanging from the silver chain.

"Luna, the Moon, rules the course of the months: and this month ends with her worship on the Aventine Hill."

March ended with the festival of the moon goddess Luna — that was the key. Before the thought was lost, he took a clean piece of papyrus, and in the middle of the page wrote, "Last day of March — Luna." His pen hovered over it as he thought of what to write next. He hardly dared imagine what the finished shape of this thought would be. Once he started writing he wrote at a fast pace, scratching deep into the papyrus' weave, and spattering it with trails of ink.

Baucis and Philemon were having a quiet sit-down in the kitchen when they heard a clatter and then the slap of running feet as their master burst out of his study shouting, "The robbery" and ran through the front door. They exchanged glances.

"There's a thing," said Philemon.

***

Ovid found Avitius in his office at the Headquarters building. He looked tired and not particularly happy to see Ovid.

"I've been on patrol these last two nights," he said immediately.

"Never mind that," said Ovid dismissing all excuses.

Avitius groaned. "I have been patrolling bars for two days and managed to achieve an extraordinary combination of fear and apathy," he said. "The whole town is talking about my strange behaviour, and every woman is nagging her husband to do something because I've told people to be careful. The men are annoyed with me because they don't know what to say to their wives. And I have been told several times that my theory is wrong and I'm upsetting the town for nothing."

"You aren't wrong and I can show you why you are right to warn them all," said Ovid. "Come on, I'll take you for a walk. It will clear your head."

"Given that you never suggest a walk that doesn't end in a bar — no. I'm too tired."

"If I promise not to drag you into a bar, will you come for a walk — please?"

Avitius gave in and followed Ovid. They walked slowly down the street and turned left towards the corner of Tomis where Ovid lived. Passing houses and the occasional shop punctuating the blank walls, they barely noticed the familiar as Ovid tried to describe his moment of revelation earlier that morning.

"It was the moon pendant on the chain round Antiope's neck," he said. "It was annoying me."

"Annoying you, eh?" Avitius was sarcastic but Ovid ignored him.

"First, I have to tell you something that will sound irrelevant at first so just hear me out. When I was still in Italy on the journey here, someone went through my things and some of my work went missing."

"Oh, yes?" and Avitius wondered what this was leading to. "Strange thing to lose — are you saying it was stolen?"

"Yes, because I don't just 'lose' my poetry," said Ovid. "The important thing is that it was an old draft of my Calendar of Festivals poem, the one I told you about yesterday, and don't think I didn't notice you yawning. As it happens, I have already reconstructed most of what was lost, and of course I've improved most of it along the way. Now, earlier today, I was working on it as usual, but I couldn't concentrate because I kept going over and over the idea that the moon has something to do with these killings. Then I was looking at the March segment of the poem and it hit me. I realised that Antiope died on the day that the Temple of Luna on the Aventine Hill holds its foundation festival."

"And the Temple of Luna makes good poetry, does it?" Avitius was genuinely curious.

"Yes," said Ovid, "I use the stars, the constellations rising and falling, and that always leads onto myths, and then I mention lots of important and not so important religious festivals. And March ends with the foundation festival of Luna, the moon."

"Well, yes, on the Aventine, in Rome," said Avitius. "Surely it's of no relevance for most people here?"

They were now at Ovid's house and Ovid took them straight through to his study.

"I suppose Roman festivals aren't really relevant here, or most of them," he said, "but something else struck me." He picked up a scroll and unwound it to where he had marked a passage. "Sit down, sit down, while I get the right passage…ah, here. Remember the dead horse?"

Avitius remembered.

"It was killed on the day of the Equirria festival," said Ovid. "How was it killed by the way? Remind me."

Avitius remembered all too well, and so did Ovid, he knew. "It was stunned and then had its throat cut. Just like in a sacrifice of a bull or sheep. But — what about the dead cat in January? I thought that there was some sort of mad animal killer about, remember?"

"Yes," said Ovid. "The cat, which was killed on the Festival of the Altar of Peace. Then there was the horse and now this girl — both killed on festivals."

"Coincidence," said Avitius. "You yourself said that there are so many festivals — surely, the strange thing would be if anything happened on a day when there was no festival."

"The chain though," said Ovid. "The totally unnecessary chain. With a moon pendant hanging from it."

"So the moon is important to this person," said Avitius, "which we had already worked out."

"I'm onto something though," said Ovid. "And before you say anything, yes, it sounds ridiculous. But isn't it as believable as someone committing murder because it is the full moon? And back in our days patrolling Rome by night, didn't we see stranger things? You've served as a soldier for so many years — weren't you surprised by how people did absurd things, so often, against all sense?"

"Of course," said Avitius, marvelling at the Ovid he now saw.

"And there's this," said Ovid, quietening down after his enthusiastic theorising. "Look at the numbers – in my Fasti, for January I talk about – well, maybe twelve, festivals. February has ten, and March only eight. Surely it is very unlikely that anyone would coincidentally kill a cat, a horse and a woman on dates I mention?"

Avitius frowned. "Who would find those festivals of any significance though?"

"Ah that is a problem," said Ovid. "You'd have to be a fully-fledged, city-living Roman to know about all these festivals."

"Or someone so struck with you they were prepared to steal your poem while you were on the way here," said Avitius.

Ovid ignored him. "Romans from Rome," he mused. "There aren't many of them in Tomis." He sat and stared at the papers covering his desk.

Avitius said soberly, "And it would be a political mess if it were a Roman doing this. What, my friend, do you suggest we now do?"

"Patrol the bars and temples," said Ovid. "And when you catch the man who killed Antiope, ask about festivals. Jupiter, Juno and Mars, you never know. Maybe I'm right."

"Don't worry, it's an idea, and I welcome all ideas," said Avitius. "And thank you for your confidence in me." When Ovid looked blank Avitius added, "You said "when" I catch this bastard."

"Oh, you'll catch him," said Ovid. "Someone who is killing by the festival calendar or the phase of the moon is a complete madman. He won't last long."

"One thing," said Avitius. "There are just three days left in April, including today. Which festivals do I watch out for?" He was almost amused to see Ovid looking surprised. The poet's stroke of inspiration had not gone as far as to consider that, if he was right, there would be some sort of tragedy soon. He said patiently, "Which festivals for the end of April do you cover in your calendar poem?"

"Give me that scroll," said Ovid and almost tore the scroll in snatching it from Avitius' hand. He unrolled it to the end and stared at it.

"The Floralia," he said, in a whisper. "The festival of Flowers. It started today."

"Well," said Avitius, "no need to be so dramatic, you can't kill anyone with a flower. And there is only what — a day or two? — to the end of the month."

"And he might not kill every month. I mean, even if I'm right, we don't know why he is killing do we? So, we don't know that he has to kill every month."

"Let's hope so, but the moon was full last night," and Avitius turned to go, already giving the poet's theory some thought. Almost immediately he realised something and turned to Ovid.

"Can I have a copy of your poem?"

Ovid looked as though Avitius had asked him for a particularly grotesque sexual favour.

"Dear gods, no. It isn't finished."

Avitius waited but apparently this was the only objection. The poet was back to being an irritating, arrogant idiot, product of the privileged upper classes and far too pleased with his own importance.

"In that case, let me ask something different — could you make me a list of the festivals that you cover from today until the end of

May? That's all I wanted it for. I didn't intend to actually read it as poetry. Or offer you a critique." He laid on the sarcasm in the last sentence, hoping it would prod Ovid into complying and he was right.

The poet looked relieved and a little embarrassed, and said, "I can do that, it's just the poem itself, it's like…"

"Yes, I know," said Avitius.

"There isn't anything else this month but the Floralia," said Ovid.

"The prostitutes' festival," said Avitius, remembering the streets of Rome filling with exuberance as spring weather warmed the streets and the prostitutes led processions holding wicker arches woven with flowers.

"Do you think that is important?" asked Ovid, self-doubt once more creeping into his voice.

"Well, a horse was killed on the Equirria, which is interesting. And Antiope was linked to the moon with the chain," said Avitius and thought about it for a few seconds, before shrugging. "Oh, who knows?"

And with that, he left.

***

Avitius had spent the rest of the day going around the town's brothels, warning them to look out for strange men. This had amused everyone considerably and he hoped that they knew that he was serious. He was just about to retire for the night when a small boy delivered Ovid's list to the Headquarters building, insisting that he had been instructed to make sure the message got to Avitius himself. He got his way, a tip from Avitius and a faux clip on the ear from the duty sergeant as he ran out again.

Avitius unrolled the scroll, noting the short length of ribbon tying it. He supposed that he was always going to think of Antiope, every time he untied a scroll. Ovid had not sealed it, no need in Tomis. There was the list, and it was long.

"May festivals covered in my poem.

Note: May is a month to be avoided if you are thinking of getting married. Better mention that to old Hermes.

1st — an altar dedicated to the Guardian Lares, who also have a temple here, next door to Hermes' place. Where poor little Antiope sat to gaze at the stars. It's also the anniversary of the temple to Bona Dea, the good goddess. Two points of interest here — first, she came to Rome from the mysterious East, just like Cybele, and second, Livia has just restored Bona Dea's shrine, to much modest acclaim. Never underestimate the impact of our beloved leaderina.

2nd — the Games of Flora. I give them a lot of space in the poem, emphasising the colour and light-heartedness. Not an obvious candidate for a murder?

9th, 11th, 13th — the Lemuria. Maybe this will appeal to our murderer? It is the foremost festival of the dead. Suitably miserable and spooky?

14th — this is the day the Vestal Virgins throw straw dolls into the Tiber. It's usually supposed that this ritual goes back to an ancient human sacrifice to the river. I think our killer might find this attractive.

15th — festival of Mercury. He is the god who guides souls to the Underworld — possible?

21st — the Agonia, a damp squib of a non-festival if ever there was one. Nobody knows why it happens at all, let alone on this particular day. It is supposedly in honour of Janus. Blah.

23rd — the Tubilustrium. Ye gods, please don't tell me that anyone is going to be inspired to kill because it is the ritual washing of the sacred trumpets?

25th — dedication of the Temple of Fortuna. Is there a shrine to Fortuna in Tomis? If so, I'd say that was a possibility. He needs all the luck he can get.

I had a word with my friend, the attendant at the temple of Jupiter, and together we worked out that the full moon in May falls two days after the Fortuna festival. I can't think of any festivals that happen on that day or the next."

Avitius frowned at Ovid's levity especially the reference to the Emperor's wife. Would the idiot never learn? Why did he think he had been exiled if not for his habit of frivolous observation? And everyone knew that Livia, a scary and unforgiving woman, was instrumental in anything regarding morality. Her son Tiberius was looking set to take over when Augustus died, and Ovid needed to cultivate these people. Avitius wished that the poet would decide on one, nice level mood and stay with it. Up and down all the bloody time, thrusting his theory at him like it was a prophecy sent from Jupiter himself one moment, then backing off, asking needy little questions. Then he remembered what the Governor thought. Ovid was never going to be forgiven, never going to return to Rome. The exhaustion of keeping up an optimistic front was probably getting to him.

Avitius sat back and stared into the darkness beyond his desk, where a single lamp cast yellow flickering fingers over the scroll and its list of men's attempts to control their lives by means of offerings to the gods. If there were some madman compelled to go out and kill on one of these festivals, which would it be? There was plenty a lunatic could seize on if he needed an excuse for his killing. If — and he sternly told himself that it was still "if" — Ovid was correct of course.

"I must beware of setting this killer in stone," he told himself. "I don't know if this murderer even exists, this strange human who kills according to the moon or obscure religious rituals. Whoever he is, I must not pretend to know his motivation and future behaviour. That is dangerous."

It was time to leave off for the night. Tomorrow he would see the Governor again and Caecina Severus would not be interested in far-fetched theories.

***

It is in the spring that things die. You see the plants growing, nests bristling with tiny beaks, and you think "Ah, life has come back to the world!" But death surges forward too – think of the wasted eggs pushed out of the nest, the predators gathering to attack the young and the weak. Don't expect the goddesses of the spring to be all flowers and sunshine.

Hecate of the three faces, three-bodied goddess,
to you we burn incense, herbs of the night,
moon-cut and woven on your altar.
Your sacrifice awaits —
show us the future we desire.

Chapter 22

April 29

Avitius, as it turned out, was forced to cancel his meeting with the Governor.

"We knew!" he shouted at Ovid. "We knew that prostitutes in particular celebrate the Floralia, and dear gods, I went around all the brothels, every bar. The whole town has been on edge because I did all that and still…" His voice trailed away as he felt the exhaustion of failure dragging him down.

Ovid shuffled a little on his chair, watching the unaccustomed sight of Avitius in a temper, striding around the study. He waited for Avitius to sit down and asked in as measured a voice as he could manage, "Do the girls here celebrate the Floralia?"

"No, apparently the local girls don't, but they do in Rome, and in your poem, thus giving the idea to someone that a prostitute must be the target," said Avitius spitting the words at the poet as if to pierce him with them. He continued more calmly. "I am coming round to your idea — this is about your poem. You were right."

Ovid looked unhappy.

"I really don't want it to be, you know," he muttered.

Avitius sat down.

"I know. This man is not sane. But he has decided to kill based on your poem, and we cannot say that it has nothing to do with you."

Ovid groaned in frustration. "Why me?"

"Don't you mean why the prostitute Cynthia?" asked Avitius sharply. "Who was nineteen years old and has a baby of just under a year?"

Ovid tipped his head back and screamed to the ceiling of his study, and for once Avitius did not tell him he was a drama junkie. Baucis popped her head in at the doorway, looked enquiringly at Avitius and ducked out again.

POETIC JUSTICE

"Time to get logical about this," Avitius said when Ovid slumped onto his desk. "When we were back in Rome, patrolling the city — how would we approach this?"

"We would look at the scene and ask the people around it," said Ovid at once. "But we can't, I assume. You've already removed the body, haven't you?"

"Yes, but I can take you there and describe it to you," said Avitius. "Given that I can't think of anything else, let's do that. Come on."

"I take it that the Rhodian wine merchant is not in harbour?"

"No, and let's face it, we never expected him to be," said Avitius. "He isn't our Calendar murderer."

They left the house and turned south.

"I'm going to have to stop calling my poem the Calendar poem," said Ovid. "Especially if you are going to nickname this man the Calendar Murderer. I've been thinking of giving it the title *Fasti*, after the official record that gets carved in Rome. Does that sound all right as a name for a poem? You know, got a bit of authority?"

"Fasti. The *Fasti* murderer," said Avitius.

"No!" said Ovid sharply. "He is not that."

They walked on in silence for a while.

"I'm sorry about the girl, really I am," said Ovid. "What will happen to her baby?"

"She has a colleague, a girl calling herself Bella," said Avitius. "She'll have to deal with it. I don't do babies."

"Bella?" mused Ovid. "Catullus coined that word, you know. Good name though. Is she — she can't be — Roman?"

Avitius laughed. "No, you don't find Romans doing that sort of work in Tomis," he said. "We are too high up for that. Cynthia and Bella are both of local descent, I'd say, mostly Greek with a touch of the tribes from this area. There are plenty like that here."

"And how are they regarded?" asked Ovid. Avitius looked at him.

"How do you think?"

Ovid shrugged. "I honestly have no idea. Where are we going?"

They were now passing the Headquarters buildings and headed for the gate in the old Greek wall.

"You have lived here for nearly two months now," said Avitius. "And everyone has treated you like royalty, even though you aren't. That is because you are a Roman, and a top-drawer Roman at that."

"I certainly am," said Ovid.

"Also at the top here are the Greeks who can trace their families back through the six hundred years or so that this city has been here since foundation by some obscure Greek hero or other," said Avitius.

"You know," said Ovid, "I'm not sure I believe that."

"Says the man who thinks a she-wolf suckled the founders of his city," said Avitius. "Anyway, if you are not Roman or founding family Greek, then being Greek of some sort helps. The locals, who are usually from Getan tribes or Dacian or Sarmatian, are at the bottom of the heap, and beneath them are the mixed bloods. These people are the result of a local fathering a child on a prostitute, or a Greek merchant charming a Dacian girl on the banks of the River with tales of his glamourous life on the ocean wave. Add into the mix a few foreigners, from Syria or the east coast of the Black Sea, and there you have Tomis. Fortunately, as always, money helps if you want to be taken seriously here."

"And I'm the only prisoner," said Ovid mournfully. Avitius gritted his teeth.

"Yes, sir," he said. "You're the only rich, upper-class Roman poet we have serving his exile in this city and you still are treated as only slightly lower than the Governor. Do you like the house the Town Council voted to give you?"

Ovid stopped in the shadow of the town gate and said, "I don't know that I'm allowed to pass beyond here. Maybe I had better just stand here until you come back. Or go back to my lovely free house."

"Oh, don't talk rubbish, you're with me," said Avitius. "Besides where are you going to escape to? This road goes to nowhere but the river. And that's a day's ride."

They passed through the gate — unguarded in spring and summer — and carried on past a water fountain and a narrow track that followed the course of the wall on their right.

POETIC JUSTICE

Ovid gazed at the flatness stretching ahead. Last time he had been here, with Menis, he had been listening to Apolauste's chatter and had noticed very little. Now he looked around. To their left was a large field which showed signs that cattle and horses had been kept there recently though it was empty now. A few hundred paces ahead were a couple of substantial buildings, and Avitius pointed.

"The larger of the two is of course The River View Inn," he said.

"I know, I've been there, remember?" said Ovid, adding generously, "I do like someone who can use comparative adjectives."

"Don't be a grammar snob," said Avitius.

Ovid thought that Avitius would never have spoken to him like that in Rome, thirty years ago. Being a disgraced exile was a levelling experience.

"It's no bad thing," Ovid told himself. "He is a good man, and you, Publius Ovidius Naso, don't have the luxury of standing on your dignity anymore."

He found that he was standing still and staring off into the distance watching the road disappear as it merged with the horizon. It was time to return to the here and now, he told himself, and ran to catch up with Avitius who was disappearing into the gap between two small and rather ramshackle houses on the right-hand side of the road. Glancing down the alley, Ovid could see the signs of struggle and poverty — no fresh paint here, but tired woodwork, flaking walls and piles of rubbish heaped up in corners. He took a deep breath and followed Avitius down the narrow path.

***

Avitius had told him nothing more about the murder as they made their way through the residential area that had grown up outside the walls, an area filled with rows of one storey houses. The end of each little row bordered on the main road and the houses got more ramshackle as he and Avitius walked away from civilization.

"Who lives here?" asked Ovid.

"This is like the Subura of Tomis, where the poorest live" said Avitius. "And the sewers haven't reached here yet, so watch out."

Ovid hastily looked down and began the genteel tiptoeing of a man who did not think to put on his oldest boots that morning.

"I've never really thought about it before, but Tomis does have a water supply and waste disposal," he said conversationally. "Why hasn't it reached here yet?"

"This bit is new," said Avitius. "It's only grown up in the last five years or so since it was decided to form a new province. People thought that Tomis was likely to be the new capital, so the population grew. We have a lot more traders, and house prices inside the walls shot up. A sort of village began to grow up here, like the settlement outside the gates of a fort. The water supply follows the road, serves the inns and so on, but the further away from the road you go, the further it is to reach a public latrine or fountain. It's difficult to persuade people not to just throw their filth into the alleyways."

A squelch from under Ovid's feet confirmed this. The poet winced but put on a brave face, hoping Avitius would notice him not complaining. Avitius strode on, until the narrow path between houses had almost run out and knocked on the door of one of the saddest-looking houses Ovid had ever seen. Its wood and plaster walls bulged in places but looked as though someone had gouged holes in the plaster in others. To one side of the door, the wall was stained yellowish-brown in unlovely arches, a last farewell from leaving customers, he assumed. The brothel was so tiny it had no notice outside, though someone had helpfully scrawled "TARTS" on the wall, in Greek and Latin.

The knock on the door had gone unanswered and Avitius knocked again, shouting in Greek, "It's the Governor's representative. My name is Avitius. I was here earlier."

The door was opened. Ovid saw a face of hollows, large eyes set in sockets so deep he imagined for a moment he could see the empty holes of a skull. But he looked harder, and saw a face of grief, overwhelming sorrow that had shrunk the woman's face to the bone. The eyes were reddened, and the daylight, as she stepped out into the street, showed up the blotched skin of tears. She was a young woman, dressed in a brown tunic that covered her in a manner so modest even the Emperor's wife would have approved. It was stained from the knees down in water.

"I'm trying to get the blood off the floor and walls," said the young woman in Greek, though with an accent Ovid had never heard. "You probably don't want to come in."

Avitius used his gentle voice as he said apologetically, "I'm afraid we do. I need my colleague here to see the setting of this appalling act."

She looked at Ovid and said, "Well, it's a mess. Don't say you weren't warned."

She had turned and vanished inside so quickly that she must have missed their muttered thanks. Avitius ducked his head to follow her, and Ovid felt a sense of foreboding as he squared up to the gloom inside.

He took his time, pausing to look around to gain a sense of the dimensions of the room. It stretched to right and left of the door and opposite him was another wall, surprisingly fresh white and pierced by two curtained doorways. A small table with three stools around it lay to his left and to his right, was a bucket, several rags, and an exceptionally clean floor.

Ovid has barely taken this in when he was aware of a sudden confusion of movement as Avitius caught the girl's arm, and steadied her, then sat her unceremoniously on one of the stools.

"Head down now," he commanded, "Ovid, look for some wine, water — something."

Ovid went through the door ahead of him and looked around a tiny kitchen. The shelves held a few bits of crockery, no wine, and no food that he could see. He heard Avitius saying, "Here, you be sick in this, if you need." But he didn't think the girl had anything to throw up. He looked again. Such lack of anything — it was beyond him. He pushed back through the curtain and said to Avitius, "I won't be long."

Out in the fresh air, he breathed in to dispel the smells of the little shack. Despite her efforts, the girl had not managed to erase the faint odour of waste and blood. Ovid was overwhelmed by pity.

Back at the main road, he hurried to The River View Inn, where he haggled rapidly, then walked back up the alley leading to the house labelled "Tarts." With him he had a jug of water, a jug of wine, a loaf of bread, and some olive oil. He had to walk carefully to manage all this and not step in any of the alley's pungent offerings and was hugely relieved to reach the house. He walked straight to where the girl was now sitting slumped on the stool and began to lay out his finds on the table. She gazed up at him, a sheen of sweat on her forehead, and he heard Avitius clashing pots in the kitchen area. He took a quick look around and saw the bucket, still half full of dirty water but nothing else.

"Have you been sick?" he asked trying to sound like a doctor, kindly but professional, one who had seen all this before. She shook her head.

"Good. Avitius, we need cups and a small dish and a plate."

Avitius looked pleased to see him and placed a small pottery cup on the table. Ovid splashed neat wine into it, poured in a tiny amount of water and said, "Down that in one, please."

The girl drank. They all waited. Avitius nudged the bucket nearer her. She said in a small voice, "I'm all right, I think."

"Good," said Ovid. "When did you last eat?"

The girl shook her head. "I haven't eaten today."

"And that is why you aren't feeling so well now," said Ovid, wondering if he was over-doing the hearty doctor persona. "Now we are going to try just a little bread, small pieces only, and I'm going to pour some more wine, and I want you to eat and drink — slowly."

She nodded. Ovid tore up the bread, poured a dish of olive oil and mixed wine and water in her cup. Avitius said nothing but passed plates as needed, and they waited in silence while she ate. So intent were they on watching her, that all three of them jumped when a baby's wail erupted from behind the curtain to the right of the stairs. The girl froze in the act of eating, the guilt in her expression saying clearly that she had forgotten the baby's existence. She scurried behind the curtain and emerged holding a hiccupping and angry infant, and sat down once more, dipping her finger in the wine and giving it to the baby to suck, wincing as the little teeth chewed on her. Avitius took a small piece of bread, dipped it in the olive oil and held it out, saying "I take it this one is weaned?"

"He got his teeth early," said the girl, proudly watching as the child snatched the bread from Avitius and chewed on it with enthusiasm.

Ovid settled himself on another stool and said cheerfully, "And what's his name? Come to that, what's your name?"

"Cynthia named him Astyanax," said the girl. "She heard it meant "Lord of the city." It's a really old name. She always said there was no reason he couldn't grow up to be a big man in Tomis."

Ovid found this unbearably sad. The girl saw his face and said defensively, "She was right, that's what Astyanax means you know. I checked when I had a Greek customer."

"Yes," said Avitius. "It's a fine name for a strong young fellow like this one. Let me introduce you properly, Bella — this is Ovid, a friend I consult in serious cases like this one. Ovid, this is Bella."

"I like that you think this is a serious case, sir," said the girl. "Thank you." She broke more pieces of bread off for Astyanax.

Avitius nodded and said gently, "Now I need you to take yourself and Astyanax into the kitchen or the back room. My friend and I need to discuss details and I don't want you upset. You were very brave this morning, and I think I remember everything you told me. No need to upset you by making you go over it all again, eh?"

She nodded and took Astyanax back into his nursery, and Ovid gathered up the jugs and cup and bread to take through to her. He waited awkwardly as she laid Astyanax into a box lined with tiny blankets, took another from a neat pile by the doorway, and covered the baby carefully. She sat on a mat beside the box, and took the food and drink with a polite, "thank you," a little voice from the box echoing her with, "Ta!" She laughed and turned her attention completely to Astyanax, telling him what a clever boy he was, and Ovid backed out of the domestic scene and into a room where the baby's mother had been killed a few hours previously.

Avitius took him through the events quickly. When he had arrived, Cynthia's body was still warm.

"How did you get here so quickly?" asked Ovid.

"I was up early," said Avitius. "I couldn't sleep last night, kept thinking about your *Fasti*, wondering which festival would be chosen, so I got up and walked around, checked out the bars and so on. I was already at The River View when Bella discovered the body and came running down the alley."

"Did she see who did it?"

"No. The two girls take — took — it in turns to sit at the table in the front room, on duty as it were. They get custom from The River View. Bella said it was the end of the night and Astyanax was fast asleep, so she just lay down next to him. When she woke, it was dawn, and she went through to see if Cynthia had finished with the customer. Found her dead instead. She was lying by the table, face down, her throat cut."

"And she didn't hear anything?"

"Apparently not," said Avitius. "But Cynthia was hit on the head first, and then her throat cut."

"Ah, the sacrifice thing strikes again," said Ovid. "You have to admit it, whoever this is has nerve."

Ovid stood in the house's doorway, looking in. "So, he stood here to ask about price and whatnot, she said come in. He hits her straight away, and ... well. There must have been a lot of blood — where is it? It should be all over the walls."

"Bella's done a good job," said Avitius. "But look — there's still a spray of blood on the wall by the kitchen, and if you look closely at the table you'll see. I think he hit her, turned her round to cut her throat from behind and lowered her head onto the table to bleed out."

"He will have needed to wash," said Ovid. "Even round here people would have noticed a man covered in blood."

"Unless he's a butcher, or has brought a dark cloak with him," said Avitius. "And theoretically he could have had a quick wash at the public fountain near the gate. He would probably be early enough to be ahead of the women getting their first water of the day."

"Worth checking?"

"It's always worth checking," said Avitius, slightly pompously.

Ovid laughed and then said, "Are we just going to leave Bella and the baby?"

"For now," said Avitius. "You can give her a few coins if you're in a generous mood, she'll be grateful for anything, I'd imagine. She's a nice kid, kept her head this morning, would have been a great witness if she'd just taken a look at the man."

"And now her friend is dead, and she is left looking after the baby. She'll never feel safe again," said Ovid bleakly. There was a pause.

"Ask your friend Menis," said Avitius. "Someone might take pity on her and give her a job in town."

"What about your bar?" asked Ovid. "She could work there."

"Yes," said Avitius. "I could take her home now and tell Vitia that here's a prostitute, oh, and a baby that belongs to her dead friend, they both need somewhere to live, and a job for the girl. That will go down like the joke of your drunken uncle at Saturnalia."

"My uncle was brilliant at jokes," said Ovid.

"Give her the money and let's go."

***

Just before the gate, they stopped to look around the old street fountain. Ovid looked around.

"Are there springs and whatnot around here?" he asked, aware of his ignorance.

"The River View has a well in the back yard," said Avitius. "I had a scout around when I was looking for property in the town."

Ovid looked around: in front of him to each side the old Greek wall stretched over the hill and down to the sea. Behind him the road ran into the distance. He turned and looked over the road to the open space which surely was ripe for development. Avitius followed his gaze and said, "The Governor has forbidden any building there. He is going to use it for troop drills, and as a potential camp. We might need to build on it in the future, maybe a fort. For the moment, the local farmers use it when they bring their stock to market. The Getans are good farmers, breed decent cattle and better horses, when they're allowed to."

"Why wouldn't they be allowed to?"

"Other tribes," said Avitius. "To you and me the people out there are Dacians or Getans or Sarmatians, but really those are just words that cover a whole lot of tribes. Take the Getans. The Getans are made up of lots of small tribes and to a Getan his tribe means a lot more to him than being Getan. And within the Getans there will be tribes who hate other tribes because of something that happened two hundred years ago, and so every now and then they have a good bust-up."

"And let me guess," said Ovid. "They all hate the Dacians and the Sarmatians."

"Actually no," said Avitius. "Though a particular Getan tribe may well hate a particular Sarmatian tribe because of something that happened two hundred years ago."

"Marvellous," said Ovid.

"Some winters, say once every ten years," said Avitius, "the river ices over, and food is short for everyone. Then the Dacians on the other side of the river cross over and make for the nice rich cities on the coast, and all the farms near Tomis get ransacked. The farmers have to run back into town to escape, and we watch the farms being looted. Then the tribes retreat, spring comes, and we begin again."

"Would anyone actually attack Tomis?"

"If they are hungry enough. The winters can be tough here," said Avitius. "Sometimes the sea freezes and we are stuck in the town for a month or two. Really, we need a proper wall, built beyond The River View, stretching across the peninsula and permanently garrisoned."

He stopped as Ovid's eyes began to lose focus.

"However — this fountain. I can't see any blood, but I suppose we are too late for that."

Ovid gazed at the fountain. It was built into the town wall, and there was a paved area all around it. A few paces along the wall was a small altar built into a niche, a wilted wildflower lying on top. Ovid bent to read the inscription, but it had not survived those bitter winters Avitius had mentioned. He pointed at the flower and said, "I'm assuming nobody round here would celebrate a Roman festival like the Floralia?"

Avitius shook his head. "I reckon if you knocked on half a dozen random doors and asked which god that altar was to, you'd get six different answers, and you wouldn't have heard of half the deities anyway."

Ovid nodded absently but was already off pursuing another line of thought, walking along the track that ran beside the wall, and looking into the ditch that ran alongside. It wasn't a very deep channel but had obviously been in use as a general waste disposal area and it smelled. He pinched his nose as he went forward, focusing on a scrap of material in a light brown colour whose cleanliness marked it out for notice. Gingerly, he picked it up and held it at arm's length as he made his way back to Avitius. The faded red brown streaks on one side were obvious, layered upon one another, bleeding palely into patches of damp. Avitius used a handy twig to hold up the bottom of the material and looked closely, even sniffing cautiously, though Ovid saw that this was not a success. But then Avitius looked at the edges of the material and stiffened. He manoeuvred the twig to stretch out a different area of the cloth and pointed at the sharp corner. Ovid saw it immediately — tiny little stitches hemmed this rectangle all the way round, and the size was familiar.

"It's one of the baby's blankets," he said. He looked at Avitius. "He went into the back room and took a blanket to help clean himself. He must have seen Bella asleep, and Astyanax."

"And left them sleeping," said Avitius. "Cynthia was enough."

***

Avitius strode into Headquarters, Ovid at his shoulder. A tall man in his fifties, dressed unusually for Tomis in a toga, was striding towards them. He wore the toga easily, Ovid noticed, and his face was blessed with the curving nose of the true Roman. It could only be Caecina Severus, the Governor of Moesia.

"I've just been talking to Doctor Rascanius," he said, then noticed Ovid. "Good to meet you at last, Publius Ovidius Naso.

Unfortunate circumstances of course, so you'll have to forgive my lack of manners. Into my office both of you and tell me about this."

He raised his voice, "Timomarchos!" and the secretary, wax tablets clattering from his belt, came running.

"Timomarchos, fetch the doctor to my office, would you? I want him to tell Avitius what he's just told me."

Timomarchos dashed off and Caecina led Avitius and Ovid to a large room that was clearly an office, for use not ornament. It was extremely neat, Ovid noticed, as he looked at the shelves around two of the walls, one filled with wax tablets, one with scrolls, and the rest with boxes. A professional map of the western coast of the Black Sea was drawn on the wall opposite the door and Caecina saw Ovid looking.

"Once the surveyors have actually finished going over the whole of Moesia, I'll have a decent map of the province to put up as well," he said cheerfully. "I love a good map. Ah, Doctor, thank you. I thought you had better tell Avitius yourself about the girl. If I tell him, he'll only come and ask you to check."

The doctor managed a small smile before embarking on his report.

"The pertinent points are very straightforward. The girl was struck on the forehead, then had her throat cut. I gather that there was a lot of blood where she was found?"

Avitius nodded. The doctor nodded. Ovid had to stop himself nodding too as the doctor continued, "There were no signs of violence indicating that she had been forced. There were no indications that she was beaten before death. It was a quick and uncomplicated affair."

And so, Cynthia was reduced to a couple of wounds and a pool of blood. Ovid wondered whether anyone would be comforted by the news that she had not been raped.

Avitius told the Governor about their visit to the scene of the crime, and their thoughts about the full moon and Ovid's poem. It sounded thin even to Ovid as he listened to it rolling out as a military report. Nevertheless, he saw that Avitius was held in enough respect by the Governor to ensure a courteous hearing. Caecina listened carefully and even made notes.

POETIC JUSTICE

At the end, Caecina looked thoughtful and said, "And you're sure that it's the Floralia back in Rome?"

"Ovid's checked," said Avidius. "Technically, the festival of the Floralia started yesterday, and it will continue into May. It is especially celebrated by prostitutes."

"Yes, yes," and Caecina waved irritably. "Which reminds me — the girl who survived, Bella. Is she involved?"

"No," said Avitius and Ovid together. Caecina was amused but moved on.

"Very well. Is she in any danger, do you think?"

Avitius was a little taken aback. He had not met many men of substance who ever expressed concern for a prostitute.

"If this man is killing according to festivals, and once a month, then I don't think she is, sir. My guess is that he will move on to planning for his next murder."

"Dear gods, his next murder, and in a place this size. At some point, someone in this place is going to blame the Romans and the whole town will be queuing up to complain to me or the Archon." Caecina stood by the small unglazed window in his office and gazed into the courtyard around which the Headquarters buildings clustered in a rather haphazard fashion, roof dipping up and down. He came to a decision.

"Avitius, where can we put this girl? I'm thinking of somewhere she will be a little more protected than on her own in a slum. I accept that the killer is likely to leave her alone, but I don't want to risk it. Any ideas? What about your place, The Lyre of Apollo?"

Avitius struggled to find a reply and Ovid came to his rescue.

"Why not ask Hermes? He needs the extra help after Antiope's death, and there will be enough people to make sure the baby gets looked after."

"He might put two and two together though," pointed out Avitius. "We'd have to tell him about Cynthia's murder, and he would see the connection with Antiope's death immediately."

"He would also see the benefit of not scaring people," said Ovid. "And Governor, I know you have to be cautious, but I imagine that the murders of a barmaid and a prostitute are not going to be taken very seriously by many people. Professional risks. It's if a respectable woman gets killed that you'll have panic."

"Cynical, if probably correct," said the Governor. "Nevertheless, Avitius, place the girl with Hermes, tell him as much of the truth as you think wise, and urge discretion."

Ovid cleared his throat meaningfully.

"There is something I feel we must consider, Governor," he said. Caecina's eyebrows went up at the word "we", but he said nothing. Ovid went on.

"I think we are agreed that these killings seem to be on Roman festival days. These festivals are not usually celebrated in Tomis, am I correct?"

"A few official observations take place at the temple of Jupiter and the temple of Rome and Augustus," said the Governor. "Apart from that our Greek and Getan people worship their own gods as they see fit."

"Yes," said Avitius. "Which begs the question: why Roman festivals? Is it a protest at Roman rule?"

"And where is the murderer getting his information?" said Ovid rhetorically. "Where in Tomis can one find a calendar with all the festivals listed?"

"Nowhere," said Avitius. "Unless he has read your calendar poem."

"*The Fasti,*" said Ovid. "It's called *The Fasti* after the official engraved calendar in Rome."

"Could our murderer have read your poem?" asked Caecina. "You haven't been giving public readings, have you?"

"No," said Ovid. "It isn't finished yet anyway; I've only got as far as June. But a draft of it was stolen from me while I was travelling here."

If Ovid was hoping for a reaction, he was disappointed. Avitius and Caecina looked at him in silence. Eventually, Caecina said, "And — what? You're not suggesting the murderer stole it from you? Where on the journey did you lose it?"

"I'm not entirely sure, but I noticed it was missing in Brundisium, when I was about to sail for Athens and Samothrace," said Ovid, beginning to see how this was going.

POETIC JUSTICE

"Oh, Samothrace?" Caecina was distracted. "I was initiated myself there, several years ago now. Did you go through the ceremony? Remarkable experience, isn't it? Now look, Ovid, you must admit that this theory is a little far-fetched. Yes?"

"Well," Ovid began, but something made him stop. He looked at Avitius, who nodded in the direction of the door.

"Maybe I am just worrying about nothing," he managed. Avitius winked at him, then looked towards the door once more.

"I — er — I think it is time I went," Ovid said.

"Don't let us keep you," said Caecina, heartily.

***

Once the poet had left, Avitius relaxed and turned back to the Governor who was looking at him with amusement.

"Dear gods on Olympus, save me from the ego of a poet," said Caecina with a smile. He sat down behind his desk and stretched both hands over his head, as relaxed as Avitius had ever seen him.

"Time for a drink," said the Governor. "Would you do the honours, Avitius?"

Avitius, wondering what was up, poured and mixed. The two men sat and drank and Avitius waited for whatever it was that his boss wanted to discuss. On cue, Caecina gave a theatrical sigh.

"If we are right, Avitius," he said, "then something strikes me about this and I'm sure it has you as well. This person has killed on festivals which are, for want of a better description, very Roman. We must consider the possibility: is this killer a Roman? Even more — could he be your poet friend?"

Avitius thought this was unfair.

"You've seen him, sir," he said. "What would you say?"

Caecina said, "He's a poet and so I would say that the only thing that troubles him is getting blood on his tunic trim. Is that fair, Security Adviser?"

"Hades' teeth," thought Avitius. Aloud he said, "Not fair at all, sir."

"Interesting," said Caecina.

"Our man isn't Ovid, sir," said Avitius. "Apart from anything else, he wasn't here for the animal killings earlier in the year."

"Well, let's move on," said Caecina after a long swallow of the wine. "If we are right — which festival in May are we looking at?"

"My money is on the 25th day of the month, anniversary of the Temple of Fortuna in Rome. There's a shrine to Fortuna in the northeast corner of the city, kept up by the locals. It seems Fortuna appeals to all."

"Why not the Lemuria?" asked Caecina. "It is the festival of the dead after all."

"It takes place over three days," Avitius pointed out. "I'm just praying that it isn't the Lemuria because them we might be looking at three murders."

"We are looking at a difficult situation," said Caecina frowning. "Extra patrols on all festival nights?"

"Yes, sir," and Avitius braced himself for complaints about costs and manpower. Once more Caecina surprised him.

"I'm getting a couple of squads down from the river fort at Axiopolis," he said. "You'll have them at your disposal. I suggest you make the extra patrols high profile and say that it's because of the two murders. We'll reassure the good people of Tomis that we are taking this seriously and are prepared to act when their safety is threatened."

"Thank you, sir."

Caecina looked at him. "I'd still prefer it if you caught this lunatic first," he said. "And back to my main worry — do you think this man is a Roman? It could get very awkward if we had to go round questioning the Romans here. Not really enough of them in the town for it not to be very obvious. And Ovid, the most famous Roman ever to live in Tomis, has only just arrived…"

Avitius kept quiet as Caecina went around the whole question of Ovid's likelihood as murderer again, then sighed heavily.

"It's no good, I can't make him fit," said Caecina regretfully. "Well, I'm sure he will have gone straight to Hermes' Place, or your Lyre of Apollo, and he will be waiting for you there. I had better let you go."

"Sir," said Avitius thinking that the Governor really had got Ovid's measure.

"Talking of Hermes, is the old goat married to his cook yet?"

"Tomorrow, sir," said Avitius. "Gorgo decided that the last day of the month would be lucky."

"How very Roman of her," said Caecina. "My grandmother always said, "Marry in April, not unlucky May." I've never wondered until now — do the locals have lucky and unlucky days for weddings? Ah well. I assume the wedding feast is at the bar itself?"

"Yes, sir," said Avitius hoping that Caecina wasn't going to suggest a personal visit.

"I might pop in and wish the happy couple well," said Caecina. "A personal visit should go down well at the moment, don't you think?"

"Yes sir," said Avitius as enthusiastically as he could. "But if you went now, you could ask Hermes about taking in the girl and the baby. Make him feel important."

"And why can't you do it?" asked Caecina.

"I'm not important," said Avitius. They both laughed, but he added, more seriously, "I want to go and check on the girl, Bella, get her to Hermes' Place safely. And it will give me the opportunity to look around the place a bit more."

"Just in case our murderer left a signed letter?" said Caecina.

"Exactly, sir."

"Maybe it is time we went a little more officially public with these two murders," said Caecina. "I shall leave that to you to decide however, Centurion."

Avitius knew that this meant that if things went wrong, whichever way he had decided it would be his fault. But then, that was what the job was for — advising then taking the heat for the Governor. He nodded.

Caecina got up, shrugging his toga off.

"Well, then, I shall pop along to Hermes and tell him he is getting a new barmaid," he said lightly. "And I'm buggered if I'm going to wear a toga to do it."

***

Back at the shack outside the walls, Avitius helped Bella pack. There wasn't much, but the girl was taking everything.

"Or it'll all be nicked the moment people hear I've moved," she said.

"What about your landlord?" asked Avitius.

"Her next door takes our rent, but if she's our landlord, I don't know. Anyway, she's as bad as any of them," said Bella, but her expression was mild. "They aren't well-off round here. I don't blame them, sir."

Avitius looked at her and saw her acceptance of low-level crime. He'd seen it often enough in the Subura back in Rome. It was the peculiar, resigned empathy of those at the bottom of the heap — they resented the petty pilfering but understood the desperation.

"You'll be all right, you know," he said. "There are good people here in Tomis. Even the Governor wants you to be safe."

"Then he's the first Roman ever to think of me," said Bella. "Apart from you of course — and your friend was a nice old man. Who is he?"

"He is the most famous and important member of this town," said Avitius solemnly.

She laughed. "Yes, right!"

She had unfolded a large sheet over the now scrubbed and dry table, and was carefully piling her possessions in the middle, wrapping a couple of breakables in the spare baby blankets. Astyanax was asleep, swaddled tightly, and settled carefully in his box in the corner. Bella took a little glass bottle last, checking that the stopper was tight, and placing it in a cup, before nestling the cup in a small pan. Perfumed oil, Avitius guessed, and he wasn't going to ask where she got it. A sheet wound tightly around this group kept everything in place, and then she slung the sheet around her shoulder and across her chest. She pointed at the blanket bundle and said, "I'm ready."

"How will you hold the baby?" asked Avitius and she grinned at him.

"I reckon you won't mind doing that," she said. "You look like a man who can cope with babies." And the cheekiness in her look faded and she said sadly, "I think you'd do it for his mother."

"I think you might be right," said Avitius. He went over to the corner and gently picked up the sleeping baby. Astyanax made no noise but nestled his face into Avitius' shoulder. He was heavier than Avitius had expected.

As Bella picked up her bundle and adjusted the sling in which her precious glass bottle nestled, he took a last look around. The only signs of life now were the rough box in which Astyanax had slept and a straw-filled bag that served as mattress. Bella saw him looking and said, "I don't want the mattress and the box, he was growing out of that already. I don't want anything else."

Avitius saw nothing else. He nodded and took a last look round, focusing on the area where Cynthia had lain, tracing the ghosts of blood stains and spatters. He stood where he imagined the murderer had, wondered what had made him go and look for that little blanket to wipe the blood off himself. Ah well. No use speculating too much over that, though it gave him a nauseous feeling when he imagined the murderer watching Bella and the baby as they slept.

Avitius turned and ducked his head under the door lintel. He ran straight into Bella, and Astyanax shifted a little and creased his little forehead: Avitius held his breath until the baby settled again. He looked at Bella smiling, only to see her staring at him so seriously he wondered what was wrong.

"Bella?" he asked. "What is it?"

She said, "I've got something for you. I found it when I was washing the floor, cleaning up the blood. Hid it at first because I thought I would sell it. I was worried about money. But if you really have got me somewhere to live, if there really are people to look after me," her voice caught a little, "well, I think you should have it. Here."

In her free hand, she held out something small and silver. He peered at it, realising that this must have come from the night of Cynthia's death. Maybe...

"You think he dropped it?"

"Must be him," she said. "We'd have found it if it had been one of the others, trust me."

Avitius took it, noticing the regret with which she handed it over. He shifted the baby and peered at the little silver amulet, a sword hanging on a piece of silver wire than ran through a hole piercing the sword near its hilt.

"Thank you," he said to Bella. She nodded, turned and trudged down the alley, calling over her shoulder, "Good to see the back of this place. Come on."

He carefully and one handedly put the silver sword into his pouch, and hoisted Astyanax up his shoulder again, wondering how the baby managed to slide down so quickly, without apparently doing anything but sleep. That was why women holding babies were always moving, adjusting, pushing the little blighters back into place.

The next-door neighbour standing in the doorway of her own hovel sniffed at Bella's indiscreet comment, and as Avitius caught up said something in a language he didn't understand. It clearly meant something to Bella who jutted her chin forward and stalked on, with Avitius walking beside her.

"That's the landlord, I take it," he said quietly.

Bella said fiercely, "We don't owe her rent, no matter how loudly she says it. We don't owe her anything! She just can't bear that I've got away from her, and away from here."

"I've seen worse than this street in Rome," said Avitius.

"I've never met anyone from Rome," said Bella. "Not until you and your friend came yesterday," and she started to cry.

POETIC JUSTICE

Chapter 23

April 30

Ovid rose early on the last day of April, glad to shake off a night of uneasy and shapeless dreams.

"Dearest wife and mother-in-law too as I am sure you are reading this, Sulpicia, especially after my last letter, which I hope you have received. Dear gods, you are probably reading it as I write this, and it feels as though so much has happened. I'm sorry, I'm rambling, but something, or rather, a few things have happened, and I need to get it all down on paper, just to get it all clear in my mind because until then I'm not sure it makes sense. Bear with me, my dears, it really is all about me this time and I can't believe it. How unlike me, eh?

You know I told you that I was robbed? One of the trials of the road, and as it happened I lost very little, some money and a book bag with some work in it — a couple of descriptions of storms at sea and a draft of my calendar poem. I had another copy, so I didn't think too much of it. But now I am worried. Here is the thing: I know I've told you of the killings in Tomis, first a couple of animals, then a barmaid, but now a prostitute as well. Look at this list and tell me if I'm going mad in even suggesting it:

In January, on the anniversary of the Altar of Peace, a cat was found strangled and burned behind a temple.

In February, on the Equirria a horse had its throat cut.

In March, on the festival of the Temple of Luna a barmaid was strangled with a chain that had a pendant of the moon hanging from it.

In April, on the first day of the Floralia, a prostitute was killed.

All of these festivals appear in my Calendar poem. (Sulpicia, I'm calling it *The Fasti*. What do you think?) I am terrified that someone is using the stolen copy to plan these murders, and by the time you read this, another month will have passed and something else awful may have already happened. Fabia, you know I rely on your sense — tell me how tenuous and ridiculous this is. Because

155

if anyone makes the connection — my poetry and a run of lunatic killings — what will happen to me? I arrived in this horrible place at the beginning of March, but I am sure that the local officials are watching me now just in case I celebrated my arrival in Tomis by killing a barmaid. And no matter how ridiculous that is, no matter how easily my innocence is proved and believed, can you honestly see the Emperor ever pardoning me if there is a hint of a whisper of suspicion hanging over me? Just tell me I'm wrong, wrong about the whole stupid idea. Please.

In the meantime, Avitius is taking my idea seriously — as he must, but of course he has told the Governor. You can see why I'm worried, can't you? Suppose the Governor includes it in his reports back to the Emperor?

What should I do, Fabia? I wish you were here."

***

The wedding of Hermes and Gorgo was a joyous thing, and even Bella managed a smile or two amidst the bustling confusion into which she was thrust.

Ovid had helped Hermes and Gorgo with the planning and what had been decided upon was a simple affair that combined Greek and Roman elements and made sure that the union was publicly acclaimed and therefore legal. Gorgo was clear on that aspect, and so first Hermes made a formal declaration with Governor Caecina and Archon Menis as witnesses in the bar itself.

Gorgo, wearing her new dress, was overwhelmed by the Governor's offer to escort her on a solemn circuit of the marketplace and back to her new home: "It's a time-honoured Roman tradition, taking the bride to her married house," he explained. Once she had worked out that Hermes would never be able to backtrack after she had been seen on the Governor's arm by half the town, Gorgo thought it an excellent idea. The excited patrons of Hermes' Place made up the raucous wedding procession, and Hermes himself made a moving speech at the wedding feast on the subject of the great good fortune of men who find wives as beautiful and hard-working as his. And at the end of the feast, Ovid rose and declaimed the wedding hymn in Greek and then in Latin.

POETIC JUSTICE

*"The gods of love and marriage themselves
are whirling the wedding torches with joy.
The fires in each temple happily glow,
rich with incense, and garlands spill out
over the threshold, inviting in friends.
the doors are flung open, and in we all dance,
warmed by love and wine."*

Like everyone else by that point, Avitius had had a lot to drink, but he was nonetheless appreciative of his friend's contribution. Ovid's short poem was completely sincere and Avitius felt proud. He told him so as Ovid sat down.

"You must be drunk, but never mind," said Ovid with a grin. "Get me some decent wine. Hermes is serving his usual stuff, and I deserve better."

"Well, we've done our bit, and I need to extract the Governor before he gets to the point of no return," said Avitius. "Menis has already retired, so let's escort Caecina home, then go back to The Lyre and toast the newly-weds in peace."

Dragging the Governor away was a popular move — most of the wedding guests were waiting for the important person to leave so that they could get on with the party. And Caecina, to his credit, hardly stumbled on the way back to his house.

The Lyre of Apollo was quiet and Macer was happy to go in search of something "a bit special" for the two wedding guests. They toasted Gorgo and Hermes, and rather more soberly poured a little wine to the spirits of the two dead women.

"Funny to think Hermes would probably never have made this move if it weren't for what happened to little Antiope," mused Ovid. "And Bella now has taken her place. People have made the best they could from it all."

Avitius remembered the little silver amulet and scrabbled uncertainly in his pouch for it. As he got it disentangled from the miscellany of small objects a government official must carry around, he told Ovid the story of moving Bella out of the hut, and her reluctant decision to tell him of her discovery. Ovid took the sword and looked at it carefully, even polishing it on a corner of his tunic.

"Nothing special, I'd say," he observed. "It's Roman rather than from one of the local tribes here, isn't it? Has a look of those phallic charms they sometimes give boy babies. You know, the little winged willies."

"I think you'll find that the correct term is *phalloi*," said Vitia primly as she appeared at their table and set a dish of olives between them. "But what do I know, not being a poet? It'd be a good present for a lad joining the legions, wouldn't it? Keep him safe and remind him of home."

"You sentimental creature," said Ovid in feigned amazement. "You can't be the Vitia I've come to know and love."

"Juno, Queen of the gods, save me from ever becoming that Vitia," she said and went to refill their water jug.

"I'm right about provenance, though, aren't I?" said Ovid quietly. "That is not local."

"I'm sure you're right, though I shall check with my unfriendly silversmith," said Avitius. He put the silver sword away and picked up his wine-cup.

"And a lot of water in there first, if you please," said his sister sharply. "I don't want any mess here thank you."

***

A death and a wedding – the goddess is pleased.

It was an easy sacrifice, easier than the horse, and we were gone within a few heartbeats. The baby did not even stir.

POETIC JUSTICE

Chapter 24

May 1st
FOUNDING OF THE TEMPLE OF THE GOOD GODDESS

Avitius went back to the shop of Seuthis of the Getae next morning, unaffected by any trace of a hangover thanks to his sister's advice and his own good sense. Even Ovid had gone home merry rather than anything worse. And now the sun shone, and he was optimistic. He had a decent job, financial security, family and friends, and he would catch this killer sooner rather than later. He reckoned he was doing pretty well, and even paused at the Temple of Jupiter, Juno and Minerva, wondering if he should make another offering there. But no, not another one so soon, not when he hadn't discovered his murderer. The gods should be given time to fulfil their part of the bargain. He went on and greeted the Thracian ex-cavalryman guarding the shop.

Inside, he was addressed with the same icy almost-courtesy by Seuthis and Avitius knew he would have to work hard for his information once more. He was determined not to buy anything.

He began straight away, taking out the little silver sword and placing it in front of Seuthis.

"It is important," he said. "Someone dropped it and I need to find out who."

Seuthis looked up at him even as his fingers gently took the sword and turned it about. Out came the polishing cloth, and the sword was cleaned while Seuthis peered at it.

"This," he proclaimed, "came from Rome. The silver is of inferior quality and only you Romans would find it acceptable."

Avitius resisted the temptation to say anything. Or indeed to take the man by his beard and give him a centurion's kiss. He waited, keeping a look of polite interest on his face.

Seuthis clearly hoped for an indignant reply, and when he didn't get one, slid the silver sword back to Avitius, as if to say that he could tell him no more. "So — that's the game is it?" thought Avitius and mentally limbered up for the fight.

"A pity, but I suppose if it comes from Rome, then you will not know anything else," he said, taking the sword and putting it back into his pouch. "Thank you for your time and effort," he added as he turned away.

"Wait."

Avitius turned back, a polite eyebrow raised.

"Why do you want to know about silver amulets like these, the moon and this sword?"

"Because two young women have been killed brutally in this town by the man who owned them," he said.

"Little Antiope?"

"Yes," said Avitius. Not too surprising that the man knew her — she worked just along the street after all. Maybe Seuthis was not too Getan to drink at Hermes' Place.

"And the other young woman?"

"A prostitute called Cynthia, who lived beyond the gate on the river," said Avitius.

"I don't know her," said Seuthis. "But two young women and two silver charms? Maybe magic, maybe witchcraft is involved here, Advisor Avitius. You must take care."

"I don't think a witch would go to the trouble of buying charms from Rome," said Avitius. "Not that I have ever met a witch, you understand."

"I have," said Seuthis. "In my tribe — my little tribe, just one of many that called themselves Getae — there was a woman who could work charms and at first she used them to help, to banish a child's warts or help a woman having a difficult pregnancy. But when a man annoyed her, called her names, she cursed him and his family caught a terrible fever and died, leaving just him alive. He was torn apart by grief and stabbed her and his tribe ran him out of the village, for they were worried that the woman would haunt them."

"Why did the man insult her in the first place?" asked Avitius.

"Ah — that I do not know," said Seuthis.

There was a silence, and then Avitius said, "I'm curious. Why do you associate these little silver pendants with witchcraft?"

POETIC JUSTICE

Seuthis stared at him. "You Romans hang charms around the necks of your children, to protect them, don't you?" he asked. "Why should a witch not use a silver moon to call down the goddess? Or a sword to inflict a killing curse?"

He held out his hand, and said, "Let me see it again."

Avitius waited, slightly smug because his approach had worked.

Seuthis straightened up and said, "I stand by my first assessment, Advisor. This was not made here. It was made using a mould, as you can see here — do you notice that on this side the sword's pommel is rounded, but on the other flat? That is because the flat side has had a weight pressed on it, so that the silver filled the mould. But the mould itself was not perfect. Look at the sword from pommel to tip. Do you notice that the two sides are not quite the same? Here the curve towards the point is not level with the other side. This tells me that perfection was not needed. But there is a small thing that shows it was loved."

"Loved?" said a startled Avitius.

"Yes, Advisor, believe me," he said. "Look at the rounded side of the pommel. It is shiny. It has been worn. Whoever owned this wore it around his neck and when he needed luck or confidence, he held it with his thumb on the pommel and rubbed it. Maybe someone will remember that, Advisor."

Avitius could see it as the silversmith spoke, an unconscious gesture, variants of which could be seen everywhere, as people wished for luck or called on a god. He was on to a lead, he knew it.

"And one more thing," added Seuthis. "Look here, on the back."

Avitius bent to peer and saw it as Seuthis tilted the tiny charm to catch the light.

"A letter, scratched on the back," he said. "A Latin letter P."

"Or a Greek letter rho," said Seuthis.

Thanking Seuthis sincerely, he made his way from the shop and along the road back to The Lyre of Apollo, so absorbed he did not reply to the cavalryman's farewell.

***

Vitia washed down the tables at The Lyre of Apollo, singing a song she had learned many years before.

Avitius stopped in the doorway and watched, temporarily distracted from his thoughts about giveaway gestures and amulets.

"While you live, oh let your light shine,
don't you cry at all."

Avitius joined in softly as he made his way in.

"Life is short and there will come a time
to let the leaves fall."

"Ma used to sing that while she was spinning, didn't she?" he said. "Though how she found time for wool when she was trying to bring us up, I'll never know."

"She said it calmed her down at the end of a busy day," said Vitia. "You can spin and sing and rock a cradle with one foot, and the rhythm has to be maintained. You can't do anything else, so you stop thinking of all the things you haven't done. Anyway, it's a lovely tune."

"I haven't seen you spin in years," said Avitius. His sister laughed.

"I hated spinning, gave it up as soon as Ma let me," she said. "I took over the cooking and she forgave me. Talking of which, do you need feeding?"

Avitius sat and she ladled out a bowl of peppery bean soup for him.

"Pepper's so much easier to get here," she said. "When you asked us to come and run this place, and Macer was so keen for something new, I never really expected to like it. I thought we would be on the edge of civilization and worried about something new every day, but it isn't like that, is it?"

Avitius grinned and said, "Don't let the Town Council hear you say anything like "edge of civilization." You'll get the lecture about Tomis having been here for six hundred years and trading all round the Black Sea while Rome was still having to steal its wives from neighbouring tribes."

"Ouch," said Vitia.

"The soup's good, by the way. But why is it so quiet in here? Where is everyone?"

"Busy," said his sister. "Working. It's the first of the month, that's always a busy day. Bills due, rents paid, things starting or ending."

Avitius thought of his list of May festivals. It was going to be a busy month for him.

"Your face just fell a thousand miles," said his sister.

"I've got a lot on," said Avitius.

"And you can't tell me anything about it," said his sister. "Even though it's bloody obvious."

Avitius looked at her. "It would be useful to know what people are saying," he said.

Vitia stood over him and looked at him seriously.

"People are saying that we have a lunatic in the town, someone who kills women at the full moon," she said. "Not very useful I suppose?"

"Do these gossipers name anyone?" said Avitius. "I could do with some suspects."

"Every slow-wit in town has been mentioned," said Vitia. "But not seriously. They aren't what people expect of a vicious killer. But someone like that is a prime target when people get afraid. Even Macer makes the sign of the evil eye when he sees the laundryman's son."

Avitius thought about this. He was impressed that people were still using common sense, but another murder would change that, he was certain.

Vitia sat down and echoed this. "If there is another incident, someone will be accused, someone lame or poor, an unfortunate who gets tripped up in the street by boys. All sense will fly away and I'm not sure what will happen. I don't think Tomis knows what to do about it."

"Well, I will resign and go and live in the Syrian desert if this killer is the laundryman's son," said Avitius. "This killer is no idiot."

"That boy isn't an idiot, he just can't speak," said Vitia fiercely, and rose to clear away his soup bowl.

"The more he can convince people that he is an idiot, the safer he'll be," said Avitius to her back.

"Only for as long as sense prevails," she retorted. "You need to get this person."

"Would it help if people did not connect the murders to the full moon?"

"The full moon just makes them worry about madness and magic," said Vitia. "Soon, they will start gossiping about every old woman who has ever had an argument with her neighbour. People are basically not very nice, and they don't like feeling threatened."

***

"Letter from Sulpicia to Ovid, written in Rome three days before the end of April.

I'm sending this back to you as quickly as possible, my dear Ovid, because I noticed something in your last letter — the letter in which you told us about the barmaid's murder — which gave rise to thought. You may of course already have worked this out, but I think it is worth sending to you.

First of all, your point about the moon and Hecate is well-made and I hope that you did indeed appease the goddess, though I doubt that you found anything as grand as a temple to her in Tomis. She doesn't really go in for big gestures, though you will often find a small shrine to her within a larger one to Diana or Artemis. Anyway, she has a shrine on Samothrace of course, it's quite famous, you must have seen it when you were there being initiated. I shall go to our nearest Hecate shrine which is on a crossroads near the top of the hill and make an offering for you there.

It seems to me that killing these animals and a woman is not in keeping with Hecate at all. She is primarily a women's goddess, and while she is associated with witchcraft and the underworld, she also has aspects which are close to women's hearts and lives, such as love and childbirth. Her craft is concerned primarily with potions, and she is the patron of poisoners, but the idea that anyone would commit these violent killings to appease her is quite shocking. And no woman would, I am sure. The picture of witches that poets like you have written about is dramatic and unrealistic.

And secondly, you don't mention this but I am hoping you have noticed that every one of these killings was committed on a day of a festival which you discuss in your Calendar poem. I have a copy of your early draft from several years ago, and I have checked. Is this a coincidence? You of course will say that there is a festival on every day of the year, but I think that it is very unlikely that three killings committed by one man would fall by coincidence on days you mention in your poem. You made no secret of this poem, you have talked about it with everyone for several years. There are several drafts floating around in circulation amongst your friends.

You may of course dismiss all this, though I hope you won't. I am not showing this letter to Fabia."

Chapter 25

May 2

Ovid showed this letter to Avitius.

"My mother-in-law is a frighteningly clever woman," he said. "The fact that she has come up with the same ideas as us, and before she has heard about the murder of Cynthia on the Floralia — well..."

"Why is a clever woman frightening?" asked Avitius.

Ovid opened his mouth to answer, then shut it again. He thought.

"Women are frightening to men who don't like them," he said eventually.

"Or to men who have sisters," said Avitius.

"What would Vitia say if she could hear you?"

"Vitia doesn't bother listening to me," said Avitius. "She's practiced not listening to me all my life."

"Does she listen to Macer?"

"He thinks so, poor fool," said Avitius proudly.

"I wonder if I'm scared of women?" Ovid mused, with such artlessness that Avitius knew his friend was planning a poem rather than discussing his true feelings.

"Only if you can put your fear into iambic pentameter," he said. "I've never met anyone who liked women so much and with such pathetic results. Have you actually managed to get yourself laid since you arrived? Unpaid, I mean."

"It's unlike you to be so crude," complained Ovid. "Anyway, I'm a happily married man and you would tell Fabia if I strayed."

"Yes, of course," said Avitius, imagining himself writing a letter to a woman he had never met, to inform her that her husband had strayed.

"Moving from frightening women to a scary goddess, is there a shrine to Hecate in Tomis?" said Ovid. "My mother-in-law is right, it would be a good idea to make an offering."

"Ask your priest friend," said Avitius. "Or, your Baucis might know, mightn't she? Didn't she and Philemon do a tour of all the religious sites of Tomis?"

Ovid went over to the doorway and yelled.

"You are, of course, correct," he said cheerfully. "She'll know. Ah, Baucis, we need your expertise. If I wanted to make an offering to Hecate, where in Tomis would I find a shrine?"

"And why would you want to do that, may I ask?" said Baucis. "You haven't got someone pregnant, have you?"

Avitius was amused to see Ovid blush and intervened for his friend.

"Nothing like that, Baucis, I promise."

She looked at him suspiciously. "What have you got him into? Investigating these murders and the animals — it isn't nice, you know."

"We want to make an offering," said Avitius. "You're right, this isn't nice at all, and maybe Hecate will protect us. And maybe she will protect the women of Tomis."

"Oh," said Baucis and her frowning face relaxed. "Actually, that is a good idea."

"What would you recommend? Which temple or shrine would be appropriate?"

"Fortuna," said Baucis promptly. "It's a small temple in the north-east quarter. Turn right out of here, then left, and it's on one of those streets that goes off that road. It has a small altar to Hecate, like a household shrine, in one corner. The priestess is old, you might have to speak up. I'll get you some incense to burn and a little wine, just like you do at home."

"When you say "at home" do you mean here?" asked Ovid.

"Of course," Baucis replied, and turned to leave the room saying, "And make sure you tidy yourself up a bit…"

"She likes it here," said Ovid sadly.

"She is a sensible woman. As a matter of fact, my sister is happy here," said Avitius. "Happier than she was in Rome, I think."

"Macer is not so lucky, I'd guess," said Ovid. "Still, if our women are happy, so are we, right?"

Avitius patted his shoulder and said, "You have the intelligence of a block of wood sometimes."

After trudging up and down several streets in the northeast corner of the town ("Why can't we just ask someone for directions?" grumbled Ovid), they found Fortuna. The one-storey building built of brick and roofed with local tiles was not impressive but Fortuna, it turned out was a deity of long-standing at Tomis. Under her Greek name Tyche she had been worshipped for hundreds of years, or so claimed the ancient priestess who lived in the house next door and seemed uneasy at the sight of two men in her shrine.

"It's mainly women come here," she said. "Our Fortuna is a very female sort of deity, if you see what I mean, what with her sharing her shrine with Hecate."

"My housekeeper, Baucis, told us about the shrine," said Ovid hopefully.

"It's Hecate we'd like to make an offering to," Avitius and gestured to Ovid. "He's got some wine and incense."

"You're from Baucis, eh?" said the old lady. "Well, she's a good woman. Are you the one who had the vision on Samothrace?"

"Yes," said Ovid, a little startled. "Did Baucis tell you?"

"I am experienced in interpretation of signs from the goddess," said the old lady. "And Baucis had a vision of her own that she wanted to consult me on. A memorable visit for your whole party, I'd say."

"I didn't know Baucis..." and Ovid stopped as the old lady stared at him.

"Well, she wouldn't tell you, would she?"

She turned to Avitius. "And you're one of those Romans with the Governor, aren't you? We could do with a new roof."

"I'll have a word with the Governor," said Avitius, the lie coming easily. "What is your name?"

"They call me Tyche, after the goddess," said the old lady.

A generous financial contribution later they were allowed to stand in front of Hecate's shrine, with its small statue of the three-faced goddess and a tiny brazier, now smoking with incense.

"What is it that you want to ask the goddess?" asked Tyche.

POETIC JUSTICE

"We ask the goddess to protect us in our work and let us find the person we seek," said Avitius. "We ask her in her role as keeper of the night and guardian of women."

The old priestess chanted lengthily in a mixture of Greek and something else, and both men carefully kept still and respectful. The air became warm, and the smoke coiled into a fantastical spiral: for a moment, Ovid felt dizzy as he thought he saw animal shapes running through the grey wisps. He strained to hear the goddess' voice but though the old woman nodded and bowed her head, for him there was silence. He then remembered to breathe and couldn't help gasping as air seemed to enter and leave his body all at once. The priestess turned and looked at him carefully.

"She doesn't often speak, so you must be important," she said, sounding rather disapproving.

"Us? Important?" asked Avitius.

"He is the one she spoke to," said the old woman irritably, nodding towards Ovid. "Though only she knows why. I suppose you didn't actually hear her, did you?"

"No," said Ovid. "But I knew she was speaking. What language does she speak in?"

"Greek and Sarmatian of course," said the priestess. "Wouldn't be much use talking to me in anything else, would it? And now I suppose you'll want to know what she said?"

There was a note of expectancy, and Ovid took out his money pouch once more.

"She says you need to be careful what you write, and look out for the silver sword," said the priestess. "I hope you know what she means."

"Silver sword?" Avitius was astonished, but Ovid gripped his arm to silence him. His own question was much more important.

"How can I get back to Rome?" he asked quickly. "Did she say that?"

"No of course not," said the priestess. "That wasn't the question you were asking, was it?"

Ovid couldn't remember what question they were supposed to have asked. He remembered the smoke animals and the sense of wonder that the goddess was speaking to him, a man.

169

On the way back down the street Avitius kept quiet and waited for Ovid to say something. The atmosphere in the temple had left him feeling on edge, and the full moon was a few days away — why had Hecate not given them something more useful?

"The only silver sword I can think of," said Ovid, "is the one you found in Bella and Cynthia's house."

Avitius said, "And are you careful of what you write?"

There was a pause before Ovid said, "Sometimes."

Chapter 26

May 9
THE LEMURIA

The Lemuria dawned into a grey damp day and Avitius who had not been able to sleep rolled out of his cubicle in Headquarters to commence his daylong patrol of Tomis. It was an inauspicious start to the festival of the dead.

The people of Tomis were not used to wrapping up in May and the faces Avitius saw on the streets were grumpy until the sun burned off the mist, and the breeze from the sea cleared the air. The warmth and the light cheered him just a little, and he dropped into The Lyre of Apollo for a late breakfast. He was the only customer.

"They'll come in now the weather's broken," said Macer. "Everyone's running late on a day like this."

Vitia brought over bread and olive oil and sat to eat with them and impart the gossip.

"The baker says the laundry is in a flap this morning," she said. "Something about someone scrawling something nasty on the wall."

Such imprecision was unlike Vitia. Macer put his hand on hers and held it. She swallowed.

"I'm worried," she said to Avitius. "It's only graffiti, I know, but even graffiti doesn't happen here, not much."

"What does it say?" asked Avitius.

"It's a curse," she said. "I'm not saying it out loud."

"No," said Avitius. "I'll get over there. Remind me of the people."

"It's owned by a man called Geron and his wife is Artemisia. The boy is Cercion," said Vitia.

Avitius dropped in on Menis first to make sure he knew of the incident. He did.

"Old Geron is all right, though laundries tend not to be in the heart of the community because of the smell," said Menis. "I'd better visit, I suppose."

"Come with me," said Avitius. "He'll need reassurance."

The laundry was closed up as they approached, though one man was silently painting the wall next to the entrance. As Avitius drew near, the smell of urine and wet wool hung in the air, and the feeling of damp made his neck itch where his own tunic touched the skin.

He stood next to the man, who carried on working without any sign that he knew he had a visitor. The wall was clean, with no hint of the writing.

"Nasty business," said Avitius. "I take it you're Geron."

"He didn't murder them," said the man, his voice tight with anger. The brush went up and down over and over the same strip of wall.

"I know," said Avitius. "Do you have any idea who did it? The graffiti?"

"Any number of idiots in this town." The man turned to look at Avitius and there were tears in his eyes. "My poor boy is not safe in Tomis, and I never thought I'd say that."

"Did you or your family encounter any hostility before this?" Avitius noticed how official he sounded and knew he needed to develop a more relaxed style. He tried again. "Anyone spreading gossip, anyone dropping nasty little comments?"

"You get used to people being nosy, saying stupid things," said Geron. "Ever since Cercion was little and it became obvious he was – you know. Most people are okay, but some can't pass by without making the sign to ward off evil."

"Nothing like this though?"

"Nothing," said Geron, fiercely attacking another strip of already-covered wall. Menis, standing just behind Avitius coughed discreetly and Geron turned in surprise.

"Archon, I'm sorry, I didn't realise…"

Menis held up a gentle hand and said, "I was just wondering if I could help, Geron."

POETIC JUSTICE

Geron wiped his brush carefully before using it to gesture. Avitius turned and, sure enough, an audience had gathered some way down the road, not a crowd, but ones and twos stopped to watch. He glared at them and there was a shuffling dispersal.

"Just by coming to see me you've helped," said Geron turning back to the wall and scrutinising it. "Can you read anything now?"

"No," said Avitius truthfully, "but I would like to know what it said. If you don't mind."

"'May the Furies drive you from this place —'" Geron began and Avitius interrupted.

"It was Latin?"

"Yes," said Geron. "Which is strange. Everyone we know talks Greek normally. We only managed to read it with the help of that poet who lives here now. He was here collecting his tunics."

"Ovid?"

"That's the man. Shall I tell you the rest? It goes on 'murderer of women, may you fall before your time, and may you lie unburied in the sand.'" Geron tried to sound as though he did not care, but his voice cracked on the word "unburied."

Avitius had not expected to be listening to Latin and he had definitely not expected to recognise this curse, but it was familiar.

He raised his eyebrows at Menis who nodded in confirmation, and said, "I've heard that before."

He stared off into the distance then shook his head. "It will come to me."

He turned to Geron. "Let me know if your boy could use a refuge," he said. "I've a farm off to the north, not too far, and his mother could go with him."

Geron nodded briskly. "Kind of you Archon, but I need them both here."

"Bear it in mind," said Menis and they all knew what he was not saying – if things got worse, if the laundry was threatened again.

Menis and Avitius walked in silence for most of the way back to the centre of town.

Menis said, just as he prepared to walk on to his own house, "I wish I could remember where I've heard that before. It's the sort of thing that comes to one last thing at night, just as one is dropping off to sleep."

"Ovid will know," said Avitius.

"Strange that it was written in Latin," said Menis, careful not to weigh down the words too much.

Avitius did not find it strange at all.

***

He found Ovid later that day in Hermes' Place. The poet was chatting to Gorgo at the counter, and Avitius had time to notice how she was definitely enjoying her status as a married woman. Bella was serving the tables, and she gave him a wide smile as he lifted a hand in greeting.

"Hello," said Ovid genially. Two cups down and happy, in Avitius' judgement. Good. He nodded at Gorgo, and found a table for himself and Ovid, who tore himself away from the counter.

Bella swished past, calling, "I'll get you what he's having."

"Do I have a choice?" called Avitius and she laughed and shook her head.

"Did you hear about the laundry?" asked Ovid. Avitius nodded.

"I heard you were down there and helped with translation," he commented.

"It was a quotation from *The Aeneid* would you believe, almost word for word," said Ovid. "Now why was that?"

"Virgil's *Aeneid*?"

Ovid rolled his eyes dramatically. "Unless you know of another *Aeneid*?"

"I just didn't expect to find a modern classic inscribed on walls here," said Avitius.

"Oh, come on, Advisor," said Ovid, and took a hearty swig. "It's pointing at me again. The Roman, the poet."

"But that makes no sense – this can't be the *Fasti* killer again," said Avitius.

"Don't call him that!" said Ovid sharply. "And why can't it be him? He clearly reads Latin, now we know he writes it too."

Avitius shook his head. "So, you are saying that having killed a cat, a horse and two humans to annoy you, he has now turned to literary graffiti? Why in the name of the gods of the Capitol?"

POETIC JUSTICE

Bella had returned with a cup of wine, already mixed, and she placed it in front of him, saying, "With Astyanax's compliments."

"He's a cheeky baby," said Avitius smiling. "But thank him for me, will you?"

She laughed and pointed at Ovid's cup. "You need to start adding a lot more water if you're having any more."

"This is my last cup, I promise," said Ovid. She rolled her eyes and left them, and Ovid turned back to Avitius, saying, "We don't know why he is pointing at me, but he is. And he is using my *Fasti*, you know that. Now with the laundry, well, this is a poem, a Latin poem."

"You don't think maybe the people it is really directed at are the laundry family and their son?"

Ovid shook his head. "Whoever this is – he's attacking me and enjoying it. And he used the wall of the laundry to laugh at the superstitions of the ordinary people here, the people who think that the boy is cursed by the gods or some such nonsense. He is no threat to the laundryman's family."

"Of course he is a threat to them," said Avitius. "Geron – or rather his son – has been accused of murder. People will talk, and some will believe. Menis has offered to take the boy onto his farm outside the city for a bit. I hope they take him up on the offer."

"He'll be fine," said Ovid. "The whole family will be fine."

***

We aren't witches. Ovid himself has written a witch into one of his early love poems, portraying her with all the originality of a lazy man. His witch is old, drunk and a bawd, and while it is true that she knows how to use herbs – well, so do I and every woman who brewed a willow bark tea to soothe toothache or quietened down a restless spirit with camomile. No woman flies through the air or makes rivers run backwards, or makes the dead speak – these things are the territory of the gods. Witches, the sort of witches Ovid and Horace and Theocritus talk about, do not exist. Why then are men so scared? Are they scared of witches – or women?

To be clear then – I am not a witch. My companions and I worship Hecate and we carry out the goddess' commands, but we use normal human powers. And we turn people's fear against themselves.

The curse on the laundry wall is all the goddess demands this month, though no doubt the security man will increase his vigilance as the month proceeds. May is an unlucky month: no great endeavour for May. The goddess rests and waits for June.

POETIC JUSTICE

Chapter 27

May 23
THE TUBILUSTRIUM

Ovid scribbled furiously, completing yet another letter just in time to send a boy down to the docks where the Governor's messenger ship was about to sail. Once this was done, he allowed himself another look at the list of festivals for May that he had propped up against the wall of his study. The month had been peaceful so far, though Avitius had taken care to post patrols in the town during the middle days of the month. These were the days he thought might appeal to a would-be *Fasti* murderer, the Lemuria. But all had passed off peacefully.

Today, it happened to be the *tubilustrium*, the festival of the purification of the sacred trumpets. Ovid decided he could enjoy a well-deserved cup or two of wine. He set off for The Lyre of Apollo, as carefree as he had been since arriving in Tomis.

Unlike Avitius, Ovid had not been on tenterhooks about the likelihood of another murder; he was more worried about the effect of Tomis' troubles on his potential reprieve. If there were more murders, there was a greater chance of someone telling the Emperor about the use of Ovidian writings by a homicidal madman. Ovid had spent a month working on a new poem, a brilliant defence of his poetry aimed right at the Emperor and he had just sent it off to Rome. As long as Augustus were not distracted by anything else! But no – all Ovid had to do now was to wait for Fabia to make sure that it got to the right places.

He whistled as he strode down the road towards The Lyre of Apollo and wondered if he should drop into the Headquarters and drag Avitius along. That man had no fun in his life. It would be a kindness.

Decision made, Ovid turned back towards the Headquarters.

Tomis in May, even with a salty breeze coming off the Black Sea, was an attractive town, he had to admit. The buildings, he had noted before with approval, were well-maintained, and now every housewife had a tub of blue-flowering sage or lavender at her door, and the smell lined his walk. Shops had freshened up their painted frontages, and the streets were clean. Whenever Ovid was in a good mood, he allowed himself to be fascinated by the variety of people he passed in the streets, and today he was not only in a good mood, but the sun was also shining strongly enough to make one think of summer heat. The women had put on their pastel shades, the men were dressed in everything from workmen's tunics in useful dull colours, to trousers made of animal skins, and often a mixture. The men of the local tribes — Ovid was hazy on the details here, being unsure of the difference between a Scythian, a Getan and a Dacian — wore their hair long and often were bearded. Some plaited hair or beard, and Ovid wondered if they ever put ribbons in. This thought led him back to the death of poor little Antiope, and with that he arrived at the Headquarters, a large stone entrance reminding all who passed of the presence of Rome. He wasn't allowed in of course but gave his name to the soldier at the entrance, leaning on the wall to wait in the sunshine. He felt peaceful. He closed his eyes and imagined being in his courtyard garden in Rome, smelling the scent of the herbs and polishing his lines of poetry.

Avitius tapped him on the shoulder, and said, "Let me guess — you need a drink."

Ovid opened his eyes, blinked away a stray tear and agreed, but a shout made Avitius turn back.

"Avitius, could we meet tomorrow..." and he saw Ovid and smiled. "Good to meet you, Publius Ovidius Naso."

"Likewise, Caecina Severus," said Ovid carefully.

"I've been meaning to ask you if you would like dinner sometime," said Caecina cheerfully. "In fact, the Archon Menis and I are dining tonight at his house. Shall I twist his arm? I know he would be delighted if you came."

Ovid expressed thanks and hoped that nobody would ask him to recite his poetry. He was not sure that he was up to that yet.

"In the meantime, Avitius, tomorrow first thing, please. Unless there is a murder, of course."

POETIC JUSTICE

"Sir," said Avitius, ignoring the whimper from the poet at his side. The Governor nodded at them both and turned away.

They started off towards The Lyre of Apollo.

"Another murder? Did he have to say that?" said Ovid mournfully. "Does he not realise how the mere thought of it affects me?"

Avitius stopped, and put out a forceful arm, barring Ovid's way.

"Just in case this is going to turn into a "poor you" conversation," he said, "Don't."

He started to walk again. Ovid trailed after him. He wanted a drink more than he wanted to throw a tantrum at Avitius. The good mood of the morning dimmed and Tomis smelled of hairy barbarians and a sharp salt wind straight off the sea.

***

Ovid was behaving beautifully.

Dinner was pleasant, civilised, Roman. Menis watched his two star guests, the Governor and the poet, as they wrangled over the virtue of Virgil, the heroism of Homer, Cicero's coruscating rhetoric — anything but love poetry because that was too close to home. He had decided in a moment of caution that Apolauste should not be allowed to join this dinner just in case it turned sour, but he need not have worried, and she would no doubt be in one of her strops with him tomorrow.

He watched the two men with approval, noting the way Ovid's face had relaxed. Nothing to be done about grey hair and wrinkles, but animation lifted the man's face, and his smile flashed out more and more. Menis silently toasted his new Governor. He approved of Caecina Severus, for if Tomis had to be Roman, then he wanted it to be part of a safe and prosperous province that was properly under control. But now he had discovered that Caecina also loved literature. Menis found the high-born Romans he met almost universally well-educated and interesting, often philosophers in their own right — oh, what a thing for a good Greek to admit — before they had to go off and deal with an uprising here, a rebellion there. Such a curious people, the Romans, he thought, and allowed his mind to go down a well-worn track as he watched and listened and occasionally applauded a point well made by tapping the side of his wineglass gently. Glass, not pottery. Menis smiled to himself as he remembered the excitement of this recent delivery from Syria.

"And how are you finding life now, Ovid?" he asked as a lull in the conversation gave him an opportunity.

"I am a little happier than when you first met me," said the poet, with a smile. He turned to Caecina. "Menis first had me to dinner just after I had arrived here and I was none too thrilled with my situation. I'm afraid I was a bore. I gravely disappointed your daughter, didn't I Menis? She was expecting someone vibrant and exciting, and she saw a grumpy old man instead."

"We can't be vibrant all the time," said Caecina. "And that must have been a difficult time for you, my dear Ovid. Although my Security Advisor helped you settle in of course."

"And Menis," said Ovid generously. "Between them, and these unfortunate – ah – incidents, I have got to know my way around Tomis pretty well."

Menis had hoped the subject of the murders would not need to arise, but he supposed that he had been naive. He decided to move the conversation on.

"Well, it has been an interesting year, in my official capacity," he said. "I am grateful that I only serve one year, thank all the gods. Then I'm on the Town Council for life and the annual dinners are the stuff of legend."

"Dinners?" asked Caecina.

Menis smiled. "Surely, Governor, you have learned that every time a group of men are put together for whatever purpose, they automatically turn into a dinner club? Every monthly Town Council meeting in Tomis ends with a dinner. The councillors take it in turn to host. Any excuse for a celebration here."

"Then you must co-opt your poet," said Caecina, immediately realising his mistake. "Ah — maybe in a year or so, when you've got more used to the place, Ovid."

"And when people here have stopped being annoyed with me," said the poet with a small grin. "You were right, Menis, my behaviour did not make me popular. Even my wine-supplier told me to stop complaining."

"Which reminds me," said Menis. "There is an amphora on its way to your house as we speak. It's a wine from Palestine and rather good."

Ovid inclined his head in thanks and Caecina held out his glass for a refill before saying, "A toast to poetry and the poet. May you both flourish here in Tomis."

Flourishing in Tomis was not something Ovid ever anticipated, but he smiled and raised his glass.

Chapter 28

May 25
ANNIVERSARY OF THE TEMPLE OF FORTUNA

Avitius was still on full alert and being tired and fearful did not suit him. Vitia commented on it and got snapped at, Macer silently kept his brother-in-law supplied with the special Bybline wine and both of them made him eat.

Every day that passed without a strange death should have been a blessing, but as the month approached its end, he felt more worried. If he did not catch a killer this time, what use was he to the Governor, to the town, to Rome? The only blessing was that there had been no further attack on the laundry.

On the day of the founding of the Temple of Fortuna, Avitius made a solemn offering at dawn. He poured wine and crumbled incense at the little shrine of Mars that stood in the corner of the courtyard at the Headquarters building. How any god could allow this madman to operate was beyond his understanding, but Avitius accepted that the ways of the gods were beyond most people. All one could do was ask and make an offering and hope. And Mars was the soldiers' god and surely would understand his efforts.

He had spent the most likely days so far this month in a personal patrol of obvious sites, even spending some nights of the Lemuria in the cemetery beyond the town walls, a decidedly uncomfortable business, and one that had tested even his lack of superstition. Ovid had told him he was mad.

"Nobody visits a cemetery on the Lemuria," he pointed out. "Everybody conducts the black bean ritual indoors, at midnight."

Avitius had thought that a cemetery would be the ideal place to drop off a body on such a night but kept this horrible thought to himself.

On this day, he was to patrol the small street in the northeast of the town, where the shrine of Fortuna was situated.

Avitius offered the old priestess the protection of one of his men, citing an unfortunate rise in vandalism on temple premises. She tsked and told him how unsurprised she was.

POETIC JUSTICE

"Ever since we were told the Romans were coming, people have been very badly behaved," she told Avitius, her forefinger accusingly levelled at his breast. Avitius blinked. He wasn't used to Rome bringing an increased level of chaos: most people however much they complained about taxes or made jokes about straight roads, grudgingly admitted that it was nice to have a bit of order. And everyone liked the fish sauce.

"Badly behaved, Madam?" he asked.

"Nobody comes to the temple anymore," said the old lady. "Nobody makes offerings. Look at it! Needs a good coat of plaster, and someone to get up a ladder and scrub the moss off the roof. You think I can shin up ladders? And when you were here with your posh Roman friend, you said you'd tell the Governor about my roof, but did you?"

Avitius had in fact mentioned it to Caecina who had told him it was the responsibility of the Town Council.

"Have you had any trouble with vandals?" asked Avitius, to distract her as well as keep up the pretence.

"Nobody can be bothered to even vandalise my temple," she snorted. "We get a few people in on festivals, a pinch of incense and they're gone. I tell you, if this town ignores Fortuna, they are going to be sorry for it."

Avitius nodded. "Have you told the Town Council that you need help?"

She snorted again. "Fortuna doesn't need their help," she declared in contradiction of what she had just said. "Bunch of money-pinching merchants. You know the trouble with this town? It looks outwards, over the sea. It needs to look inside, and over its shoulders. Those Getae aren't going to be happy for long. First cold winter and the Dacians will attack. Then you'll discover how Roman the local tribes are. Or aren't."

Avitius knew this was true.

"Madame, you have the right of it," he said seriously. "Thank you for your time."

The old woman looked at him. "And will my time mean that the temple roof gets cleaned?"

"Yes," said Avitius, seeing how he could keep a presence without being too obvious.

He spent the rest of the day sitting on the roof of the temple of Fortuna, while two squaddies who were on punishment duty carefully cleaned moss off the old, cracked tiles. The roof looked worse when they had finished, the need for repairs laid bare. With no moss sealing the cracks and holes, the temple would leak next time it rained. He decided to have a word about it with Menis next time they met.

Meanwhile, he sat and watched the street and thought about life. The view took in the whole street — not that it was a very long street — and he noted that despite the old priestess' laments, the temple was visited by several people, all women over the course of the day. All women – he didn't like that, felt that by attracting them, the temple somehow made them a target. He began to feel uneasy and swept his eyes up and down the street constantly, looking for a flicker of movement, a loitering figure. He had no joy: nothing and nobody stood out.

When dusk came and his two miscreant squaddies packed up the ladder and scrapers and buckets, Avitius stayed. He was still uneasy, and his back muscles ached. His jaw was stiff from holding it clamped shut for too long. After one last walk up and down the street, growing increasingly convinced that he was being watched, he went inside to take up his post in a corner of the temple, next to the little shrine of Hecate. From there, he could see both the front entrance and the back door leading to the house where the priestess lived. He was taking no chances. The statue of Fortuna though ignored him and gazed towards the main door, refusing to get embroiled in these insignificant affairs of mortals.

In the morning, as he stretched stiff limbs and massaged life into his backside, he reflected that relief and a sense of being let down were similar feelings, a sort of celebration but of something that had not happened. The old priestess tottered in from the back door, muttered, "Are you still here?" and stood in front of the statue, communing with her goddess in silence, while Avitius slipped out of the front door. He needed some sleep then tomorrow he would talk things through with Ovid.

Chapter 29

May 26

"Sounds like the old lady needs a girl to train up," said Vitia as they all sat around a table in The Lyre of Apollo. "I could ask around, check to see if anyone is lined up to take over. We can't have the Temple of Fortuna without a priestess."

Ovid thought helping out at the Temple of Fortuna would be an ideal job for his Baucis and Philemon. He said so and was gratified by the approving smiles this suggestion received.

"If only you didn't need them," said Vitia.

"Maybe when I'm recalled to Rome," he said optimistically. "Baucis and Philemon might consider staying here. They've earned retirement, the gods know that. I could buy them a little house."

The expressions had changed.

"What's the matter?" he asked.

"Nothing," said Avitius. "Just can't imagine you leaving them here."

"Only if they wanted it," said Ovid. "I do know how to treat loyal family retainers, you know."

"Any more news about the graffiti at the laundry?" asked Vitia. "Though why it's you dealing with that and not the Town Council, I don't know."

"Menis did help," said Avitius.

Vitia knew the deaths of the barmaid and that prostitute were eating away at her brother, but he wouldn't talk about it. Ovid wasn't bothered of course, but then that man only bothered about himself. She stood up, saying, "You know if you are genuinely concerned about graffiti, then I am a Gorgon with a headful of snakes."

Macer laughed out loud and said, "Come on, love, let's run this bar." He steered her back to the counter with an arm protectively around her hip, and Avitius looked at the pair of them with a small frown.

Ovid who had spent some time staring at the table as if debating something, waited until both Macer and Vitia were occupied behind the bar, then hauled a small wax tablet out of his bag. "Here," he said, "I made you a list of June festivals, just in case."

Avitius took it and looked at it sadly. He couldn't open it then and there, not in the comfortable atmosphere of his bar.

***

Back at Headquarters, Avitius opened the promised note of festivals and noticed at once that Ovid's usual careless commentary was absent — this was a list, pure and simple.

"Festivals in June, as covered in my *Fasti*. I can't see anything obvious, but there is the Vestalia, which is a big women's festival.

Note: weddings are unlucky up to and including the fifth day

1 — Carna, goddess of door hinges
3 — shrine of Bellona, goddess of war
4 — festival of Hercules the Guardian
7 — fishermen's festival
8 — festival of the Goddess Mind
9 — the Vestalia begins
11 — the Matralia
13 — festival of Minerva
15 — Vesta's shrine is swept out and the sweepings tipped into the Tiber
22 — anniversary of the defeat at Lake Trasimene – not a festival?
24 — festival of Fors Fortuna
27 — foundation of Temple to the Lares and Temple of Jupiter Stator
29 — temple of Quirinus

That's it. Nothing really leaps out."

"And what do I make of this?" thought Avitius and knew a moment of inadequacy, a moment where the centurion did not know what to do. This month might have been trouble-free so far, but he knew in his heart that this killer was not done. He ticked off the days to the end of the month on his fingers – five days to go.

POETIC JUSTICE

Chapter 30

May 31st

"I think we can safely say that our misgivings were in fact unfounded as nobody died then," said Governor Caecina. Avitius shook his head.

"Nobody died, sir, and I'm very grateful to the gods, but I don't feel that this is the end of it," he said. "And I'd like to know who killed those two girls and whether it was the animal killer."

"Yes," said Caecina. "That sort of escalation in violence is unsettling in a small place like this, but it's time we took a province-wide view. I have other jobs for you. It is, I'm afraid, as simple as that."

Avitius did not feel surprised at this. Politics had taken over for his boss, and he knew better than to interrupt.

"The Town Council are in charge of matters in Tomis," continued Caecina, "and they can, for example, decide whether to fund a City Watch along the lines of the Watch in Rome. I may have hinted that their bid to be recognised as chief town of Moesia may be helped by something like that. When they have decided, no doubt they will want to consult you, and I want you to encourage them."

Avitius grunted a "Sir" and waited.

"Meantime, there's the road being built from here to the Danube forts," said Caecina. "I'd like you to go and do an inspection. Make sure they're working at a decent rate. Then I'd like you to visit the forts at Axiopolis and Carsium. Catch up with the intelligence coming over the River. I'm going to show my face at the coastal towns, and meet up with the Black Sea fleet."

Avitius noticed that this would mean that the Governor enjoyed the cool summer breezes of the coast, while he would bask in the sweaty dust of the inland. But a stretch away from Tomis and the exercise would be good. He would also enjoy his own company for a few days and use the dull miles of riding to get his thoughts in order. Since Ovid had arrived in Tomis, life had got complicated.

"I'd like a couple of days to review this year's intelligence reports, sir," he said.

Caecina nodded. "Of course."

"I'm also going to visit Menis, suggest some ideas for the Town Council," Avitius said. "Then I'll be on the road. Maybe four days from now?"

"Three would be better," said Caecina, with the assurance of years of commanding legions. And Avitius was dismissed, striding back to his office with a slightly put-upon feeling. As an ex-centurion he was used to it of course. Being the link between policy and operations in a legion had never been easy, and Caecina was just like every other commander Avitius had ever worked under. When an upper-class Roman saw a problem, he listened to opinions, he issued an order, he moved on. And Avitius could see no better way.

Back in his office, he summoned his clerk, Geminus, and together they went through the administrative list of preparing for a journey: getting a horse, money, supplies, a passport sealed by the Governor, notes on potentially useful people. Then, leaving Geminus to pull everything together, Avitius set out through streets pinpointed with unseasonal bursts of stinging rain. It did nothing to improve his mood and he arrived at the house of the Archon in need of warmth and wine. Menis was happy to provide both, and Apolauste and her maid brought towels, and a tray of food and drink to Menis' study.

"I'm being spoiled," said Avitius, knowing that the household ran to a comfortable number of staff. He smiled at Apolauste but had no intention of discussing anything with a young woman in the room. He waited patiently until she had no option but to retire gracefully.

"I should have found her a husband, I know," said Menis in what was clearly a well-used excuse for his indulgence. "But she isn't keen, and I really don't want to lose her."

"Maybe one solution would be to marry again yourself," said Avitius.

"Yes, maybe," said Menis. His words and tone were polite, his face blank. "Yes, I'm sure the proverbial unkind stepmother would drive her away successfully. I must think about that, Security Advisor Avitius."

Avitius was amused but thought he had better switch to official matters.

"I have to go away again on provincial matters," he began and relaxed as he watched Menis become Town Archon once more, blessedly intelligent and easy to work with.

Quickly, he laid out his problem — he and the Governor were both out of town for at least a month, but the *Fasti* killings were still unresolved.

"I don't think that a gap in May necessarily means the murderer is done," he finished and Menis nodded slowly as he thought this through.

"Your options are that the murderer has died, is ill or has left town," he said. "And the first option apart, he may be back at any time. What Roman festivals are occurring this month?"

Avitius handed over a copy of Ovid's list of festivals and Menis scanned it frowning.

"Are you thinking that the time of the full moon may be important too?" he asked.

Avitius shrugged. "It's a possible factor in the timings," he said. Menis tapped the wax tablet.

"You are asking me and the Town Council to consider extra security around Tomis? The festival of the Lares, I am assuming is your main concern. It is around the time of the full moon if I'm reckoning correctly, and we have an official celebration at the Temple of the Lares lined up. The temple next to Hermes' Place."

Menis had noticed everything and Avitius' respect for the man was reinforced.

"It will be four days before the end of the month and I might be back," he said. "I have left instructions that all incidents are reported to you."

"And what you leave so tactfully unsaid is that the town needs a Watch," said Menis looking completely unenthusiastic at the prospect. "I shall do my best, but the Council are not going to be keen on the expense. They rather think that it is Rome's responsibility now. I pointed out at the last meeting that Rome had not yet established taxes in this province, and we should be using the time to set up these things, but they do not agree. You know in winter we form a citizens' rota to man the walls?"

Avitius knew. Of course he knew. He was given the job of liaising and making sure that the citizens turned up and were armed with more than pruning shears.

"Well, at the last meeting, one of our councillors asked why we were still having to do this. And you can point out until the River runs with gold that the tribes are not yet fully pacified, that most of Rome's soldiers are still involved in putting down the Illyricum revolt and that given we pay no taxes yet, why should Rome man our walls — they just sit there wilfully not listening."

"Rome is not going to man your walls in winter anyway," said Avitius, thinking he might as well get that said straight away. "It isn't how we do things. We simply do not have the military resources to set up a guard in every town in the Empire. You've managed perfectly well so far for hundreds of years."

"Like I say, even in the face of experience and logic, the ability of a group of old men to grumble remains strong," said Menis drily. "I expect none of this to come back to me via gossip, of course, Security Advisor."

"Of course," said Avitius. "In the meantime, you will think about what measures can be taken as the end of June draws near?"

"Of course," said Menis. "And we must all ask the gods to make sure that nothing happens once again, that the culprit is dead or gone. Two murders in two months is quite enough for our town."

As Avitius left, he knew that nothing would be done while he was away.

POETIC JUSTICE

Chapter 31

Tomis June 1
FESTIVAL OF CARNA, GODDESS OF HINGES

Ovid was surprised to hear that his friend was leaving for a trip into the interior of the province, then remembered that Avitius had a job.

"I keep forgetting you have to do what the Governor says," he complained.

"I never forget," said Avitius.

"Oh, a life of service must be a wonderful thing," said Ovid, waspish with the thought of enduring his own company over the summer.

Avitius made no reply to this but drank his wine. If Ovid was going to whine at him, he wasn't going to wait around. But he did have something important to say.

"I'm not satisfied that we have no more to fear from our murderer," he said. "I know the most likely explanation is that he's left Tomis…"

"Or that we imagined the whole thing and all the killings were unrelated to each other and to me," said Ovid quickly.

Avitius paused and said, "Is that what you think?"

"I don't know what to think, we've been over it so many times," said Ovid untruthfully.

Avitius continued, "Just keep an eye on Hermes' Place, and check that Menis is doing something. If you want to contact me, it's best done through the military. Ask for a clerk called Geminus, he'll see to it."

He took a sip and watched Ovid miming writing everything down conscientiously.

"You know, when I woke up this morning and there was no report of anything I felt so relieved. But if we are right, this may not be over. He may not have left town, he might have a reason for leaving us guessing. Gods help us, he might think it is funny."

"You know, when you catch him, he won't be anything special," said Ovid. "Nobody you'd notice in the street, nobody you've already considered."

"Your faith in me to catch this nobody is heartening." Avitius rose. "Vitia and Macer will look after you when I'm away."

"I don't need looking after."

Ovid wished he'd kept quiet as soon as the words had left his lips. Stupid childish words. How old was he? He sipped on his wine, refusing to catch the eye of either Macer, or Vitia, who he knew were watching him.

What was he going to do in the next month, as the town heated up? He had sent off his great poem to the Emperor Augustus, and was beginning the next poem in his *Sorrows*, but that was not enough. Working on his calendar poem, the *Fasti*, no longer appealed, though really he should get on with the second half of the year. January to June was not going to make a full poem. He hunched his shoulders in exasperation at his own restlessness and said, "I wish you weren't going."

Avitius got up. "You'll be fine," he said, and left The Lyre of Apollo with a quiet farewell to his sister.

"Oh well done," Ovid silently told himself. "Drove him away in no time."

Still, he could do something about Avitius' instructions, and make sure that he dropped in at Hermes' Place regularly. He cheered up at that thought. And the Emperor would surely forgive him soon. The poem he had just sent to Rome would do the trick, give Augustus a reason to pardon his favourite poet. Ovid began to do some calculations. His letter with the poem included should arrive in the middle of June, so if he gave the Emperor a few days or so the official pardon would reach Ovid by the end of July at the latest. Why, he might even make it to the Bay of Naples in time to enjoy the end of the summer season there. And, of course, he hastily added to himself, it would be good to see his wife again.

Vitia watched him as she polished cups and set them out in even rows on the counter.

POETIC JUSTICE

"Look at him," she said softly to Macer. "Already forgotten about Avitius, already dreaming of Rome. Who is going to convince him?"

"Nobody," said Macer. "It's not our job."

"Avitius wants us to keep an eye on him," said Vitia.

"If you ask me, this whole bloody town keeps an eye on him, and he repays us all by whining," and Macer saw he had caught his wife's attention.

"I thought you liked him?" she asked.

"I do," said Macer. "I even sympathise with the poor old sod sometimes. But that doesn't mean he isn't an annoying bastard."

Vitia looked at Ovid. Most customers, she reckoned, were annoying bastards. Come to that, all men could be annoying bastards. Macer was one of the good ones, and he still set her teeth on edge at times. She thought of the babies she had lost back in Rome, and how Macer had seemed unable to say or do anything right until coming here to run this bar had transformed her marriage – and maybe given her a last chance at motherhood.

"Come on," she said to Macer. "I need this amphora replacing." And as he hurried to lift the heavy wine jar for her, she smiled.

***

The man who climbed the hill from the harbour was cheerful. He was young, well-off and healthy, he came from a good family, he had a future worked out. Back in Rome, a well-connected wife had been selected for him, and his father ran the Praetorian Guard with an efficiency and loyalty that was much appreciated by the Imperial family. As a result, Livia and Tiberius themselves had indicated their willingness to personally oversee Sejanus' own career. All Sejanus had to do was remain on the path his own aptitude had marked out for him, and he would go far.

Ignoring the Temple to Neptune visited by nearly every arrival in Tomis, he turned right and made his way to the centre of Tomis, finding the marketplace without needing to ask anyone. At the temple of Jupiter, he asked if any message awaited him — he gave the name "Argenteus" — and was handed a sealed wax tablet. He only opened this once he had found himself a corner seat in a nearby bar, where he was served the worst wine he had ever tasted.

Thank Jupiter they couldn't get bread and olives wrong, wherever one went in the Empire, he thought. He ate and drank then asked for directions to the Temple of Fortuna and found himself in a street in the northeast corner of the town. The Temple was so small he nearly missed it, and from there he counted off the houses until he reached the one he wanted, complete with a yellow plant pot filled with thyme at the front door.

"Sweet," he thought slightly contemptuously. In Rome, a plant pot just got pissed in until the plants died. When the door was opened by an elderly freedwoman, he asked if there was a room available, and casually let his hand go to the silver chain around his neck and the sword pendant. He was ushered in and given a seat in the main room, while the woman went to fetch Sabina.

Sejanus had never met Sabina, though he did of course know all about her. Her mother had lived for a while on his own family estates in Volsinii, and the child who lived with her was bright and pretty, and caught the eye of the family steward, always on the lookout for new material. He told his master, and the child was given the same education as the intelligent lads from the estate. Sejanus' family believed in investing in people.

When Sabina entered the room, she brought a tray with wine and water on it and the freedwoman set up a small table at Sejanus' elbow. The necessary minor fuss allowed him to scrutinise Sabina.

He approved, apart from her hair, which was short, and held back off her face with a scarf. She was lean and her eyes were wary, even though she was expecting him and presumably had had the sighting of the sword pendant relayed to her by the maid. She looked straight back at him and made no tiresome enquiries after his health or voyage. She did not fuss with her draperies, tuck her hair behind her ear, or smile. All was business. He nodded.

He began by asking her about her family and if she was surprised at the question, she showed no sign of it. She answered in a disappointingly unfeminine voice, with little change in tone, and no emotion to drive her sentences.

"My mother died ten years ago," she said. "My father died before I was born."

POETIC JUSTICE

"And you lived near my father's estate in Volsinii, is that correct?"

"I was educated and trained at your father's expense and I am grateful," said her cautious voice. He persevered and was pleased that he forced her life story from her. After her successful education, his father had arranged for her to be sent to Bithynia, where she ran a small intelligence gathering operation to general satisfaction. When it became clear that a new Roman province was going to be formed south of the River Danube, she was sent to Tomis and began similar work there.

As he drank a much better wine than he had endured in the bar, she gave him her report.

"When I received the message that Ovid was coming, I used my contacts to gather information from the Town Council on how they were going to handle him," Sabina began. "I also started to work on the stolen poem. The robbery, by the way, I considered foolish. He might have noticed or even discovered the thieves."

"I recruited people from Ovid's own circle and they did an excellent job. Your reservations are unnecessary," said Sejanus mildly. "Please carry on."

"We also received the idea of performing some sort of antisocial act on dates significant in the poem."

She paused and looked at him, wondering if the whole thing had been his idea. He nodded. "Yes, a little fanciful but quite in keeping with the subject himself. Go on."

"A cat, then a horse was killed," said Sabina. "We made the deaths look like a ritual, maybe sacrifices. Unfortunately, this was before Ovid actually arrived, so I don't know quite what Rome hoped to achieve."

Sejanus was almost amused by her impertinence. Not afraid to speak her mind.

"Did it result in gossip through the town?" he asked. Sabina nodded.

"And it was linked to the time of the full moon. People thought there was some sort of a madman or maybe a witch going around. We encouraged this."

"All good," said Sejanus.

"Once Ovid had arrived, we needed to do something a little more — extreme. We killed a barmaid from one of the bars he likes and left a moon pendant around her neck. Ovid had been seen propositioning the girl a few days earlier. The town was shaken, the moon madness theory was firmly established, but Ovid himself was friends with the man who is the Governor's Security Advisor. If anyone suspected him, the Advisor must have quashed it. We decided to carry on until someone realised the connection to his poem. And so, we killed a prostitute during the Floralia."

And with that Sabina was done. She sat and looked at him and waited for his reaction.

"It's slightly irritating that the full moon thing obscured the link," said Sejanus thoughtfully. "What did you do in May?"

"Some graffiti made to look like a curse. No more was needed because by then they had made the connection and the poet was anxious. That was the extent of the orders conveyed to me — we were to stir up the town and make the link between the poet and the killings."

"Yes," said Sejanus. "I see."

He rose. "I shan't be here long, so whatever I decide I shall let you know quickly. In the meantime, I need to sleep. Where are the nearest baths? You may provide a slave, a towel and some olive oil."

"Phoebe!" Sabina's freedwoman appeared swiftly and Sejanus assumed she had been listening nearby. He wasn't particularly bothered. Sabina looked a little disappointed, he thought, as Phoebe led him out of the room. Had she been ready for an argument? He had no reason to criticise her, and he didn't often encounter people who wanted to argue with him. He also had noted that despite her beauty — and she was beautiful — he felt no desire for her at all. She actually, if he was honest, repelled him. Ah well, there was no point to be made here and it would keep things on a business footing between them. He had many stops on this little jaunt around the East and there would be women if he chose. In the meantime, he would rest a few days here, get his clothes properly laundered and decide whether or not Sabina should be let loose again. He rather thought not.

POETIC JUSTICE

Chapter 32

June 7
FESTIVAL OF THE FISHERMEN

Late in the day of the fishing festival, the government courier had delivered the mail to Headquarters, and the clerk Geminus had kindly brought Ovid a single sealed roll of papyrus, a short letter Sulpicia had sent from Rome a mere sixteen days earlier.

"My dear Ovid, I am writing this in haste and without telling Fabia. We have just been to dinner with my ex-husband and his wife Marcia and have learned much that you might find interesting.

Firstly, Fabius holds out no hope that you will be pardoned. This will be a hard thing for you to read, but I see no point in withholding it from you. The upsets of late have had an impact on the Emperor. Fabius says he has suddenly become an old man, and it is all too easy for him to blame you, however unfair it might be. Fabius says Augustus is being very tight-lipped about it, but your poetry, especially the *Ars Amatoria*, certainly influenced him.

Now — Marcia was her usual delightfully indiscreet self and came out with a snippet that surprised Fabius. Apparently, the intelligence agents of the Praetorians all have a token so that they can recognise each other. It is an amulet in the shape of a silver sword, so small one can wear it as a pendant on a necklace. It occurs to me that if anyone in your Tomis is an agent, it will be your friend Avitius so I thought I had better warn you."

Ovid read and reread this, eyes wide from the beginning. There was too much to take in. Never being pardoned? How ridiculous! Augustus might be fixated with people's sex lives, but surely one poem written years before was of no importance? Why didn't the old bastard just die? Ovid took a sharp breath and looked around guiltily, hoping that he hadn't really just thought that. He read the end of the letter again and was struck once more, so hard that all thought of Augustus' wrath fled. A silver sword…

He remembered all too vividly the silver sword pendant found at Cynthia's murder. Did this mean that her murder been —

official? Sanctioned by the Praetorians? Ovid found that he was actually clutching his head, like some damned tragic actor about to die on stage. And what about this idea that Avitius might be a Praetorian agent? Everything in Ovid wanted to dismiss this, but he told himself it had to be considered. If Avitius was an agent of the Praetorians, how would he, Ovid, know? It wasn't as if spies routinely declared their presence. Had he ever seen a chain of any kind around Avitius' neck? He stood and strode around his study, thinking. In the end, he decided that he could only work on the assumption that Avitius was just what Ovid had always thought — an ex-centurion, an advisor to the Governor of Moesia. Very well – Avitius was merely Avitius.

What was Ovid's next move? Well, he needed to speak to Avitius urgently, because the pendant found at the scene of the murder had taken on a new and very frightening aspect. But Avitius was away inspecting roads or something. Ovid groaned. Should he tell the Governor? It was already heading towards evening and the Governor would almost certainly be either bathing or preparing for dinner. Ah, no — curse it all, the Governor was in Callatis. And Ovid could not go there to ask him. He must send a messenger, or maybe tell Menis? It was all too much to think of, now. Better to leave it until the next day, surely. He called for Baucis and told her to fetch him a jug of the wine that Sulla the businessman had sent him. He needed something special tonight.

She nodded and was about to go when Ovid thought to say, "And Baucis? Have you ever seen anyone here wearing a little charm in the shape of a silver sword? Probably around their neck on a chain?"

Baucis' stunned look made him realise how bizarre he sounded. He waved his hands at her, dismissing her.

"Never mind. Just get me the wine."

As he fell asleep that night, Ovid wondered who else in Tomis knew about the silver sword.

***

The dream made perfect sense until a scraping sound woke him up. The sense seeped away as his mind shifted from trembling images of sea and storm to a single point in the darkness of his room. The point moved and let out a desolate squeak, and Tiberius the kitten padded over and stretched up towards him. Tiberius could scramble onto the bed perfectly well but preferred to be scooped up.

"Idiot animal," Ovid grumbled. He grabbed the kitten and lay back as Tiberius constructed a nest on top of him, organising the bed covers to a feline liking. As Ovid settled back into sleep the small weight settled on his stomach, lightly riding on the swell as he breathed. He smiled to himself, imagining the kitten bobbing up and down. He wondered how Fabia would react to having Tiberius in bed with her — if he took Tiberius back to Rome of course, it might be kinder to leave the cat here in Tomis. Maybe Baucis and Philemon would take him on. This led to an Ovidian favourite daydream, the one in which he stood at the ship's rail and watched Tomis slip further and further into the distance. His breathing slowed, and he slipped back into sleep.

And then he heard the noise again and was instantly alert. Tiberius shifted as Ovid's breathing stopped, then restarted, very quietly, trying to imitate the pattern of oblivion. He analysed the noise. It was the slight scrape of a chair as someone sits or gets up, and now he realized that the first sound he had heard could not have been made by the kitten. Tiberius could just about push past the heavy leather curtain in the doorway, but he was too small to push a chair. There was someone in his study moving furniture – why, in the name of all the gods? Maybe someone wanted to steal some more poetry said an unhelpfully flippant part of him. He grumbled inwardly and wondered why he didn't have a daring part of himself, one that gave instructions on confronting burglars. He threw off his blanket with a petulant flourish and Tiberius squealed as he fell to the floor tangled in blanket.

"Bloody animal!" Ovid hissed as he felt around the heap of material. The kitten helpfully dug its claws into his hand but Ovid bravely clutched Tiberius to his chest and struggled to his feet. Well, the burglar should be running now, so Ovid cautiously stuck a nose around the curtain. "Anyone there?" he called, pitching the last syllable so high it sounded as though he was singing it. He was stunned when a well-educated voice sang back in Latin, "I'm in the study." Slowly but without any feeling that he had a choice, Ovid left the safety of his bedroom and entered the study.

"Adorable!" said the man sitting at the desk. At his desk? An unknown man was sitting at his desk? Ovid was outraged.

"That's my desk," he found himself saying as he clutched Tiberius to his bosom.

"And you have a kitten," said the man. "What is his name?"

"Why are you sitting in my house and at my desk in the middle of the night?" Ovid asked. He was fairly confident now that this was not a run-of-the-mill burglar.

"Don't you want to know who I am?" asked the man. "Look, I shall change seats — you can have your chair and I'll pull up this stool. There."

There seemed to be a quite unnecessary scraping of chairs and fussing over seats, and Ovid kept reminding himself that this was the middle of the night, and in front of him was someone he did not know — although the more he looked, the more he wondered about that. The face was familiar. Someone from Rome, no, someone related to someone at Rome — could that be it? Whichever it was, it could not be good.

Still holding Tiberius, he sat in his own chair, moving in an elaborate arc around the desk, so as to keep a distance from the man who now perched like an eager sparrow — no, make that a sparrowhawk, this was definitely a hunter — on the visitor's stool. As he settled, Tiberius dug painful claws through his sleeping tunic and Ovid gently pulled the kitten off himself, picking out each claw in turn. He deposited Tiberius on the floor and said, "Shoo now," noting that the animal made straight for their uninvited guest.

"Well, if Tiberius likes you," he said in as disdainful a voice as he could manage.

The visitor looked at him blankly and said, "Tiberius barely knows me from Romulus. Why does it matter that he likes me?"

"Not the Emperor's heir," said Ovid. "The kitten. The kitten is called Tiberius."

"Ah," said the visitor. "How sweet. I am sure he would be touched. Tiberius, the man who will be our next Emperor, I mean." He leaned down and made little kissing noises to the kitten who treacherously ran up and allowed himself to be scratched behind the ears.

POETIC JUSTICE

"This is getting silly," thought Ovid, "and I want my sleep."

"Come on," he said. "What is all this about? And how do I know you? I know I know who you are from somewhere."

"Well," said his visitor, "we have only met once and I was in my official capacity which meant that you didn't look at me. It was at the villa of the Lady Julia on the Bay of Naples. You had come to give a recital at a party, and I was on the staff of the Emperor who was also visiting. My name is Aelius Sejanus and I am a member of the Praetorian Guard. In fact, my father is the Praetorian Prefect."

Ovid gaped, and felt his insides begin to rebel. A wave of nausea swept over him, so intense that he had to lean forward and prop himself up on his elbows. It left him hot and sweating and he concentrated on breathing in the cool night air and telling himself, "I must stay calm." He watched as Sejanus picked up the kitten and held it gently in his lap, stroking the little head between the ears and apparently getting it just right. And then with the hand not caressing Tiberius, Sejanus pulled at the silver chain around his neck, until the pendant was lying against the dark material of his tunic. It was a silver sword.

"I have not come to do you any harm," said Sejanus amiably, watching Ovid notice the pendant. "No physical harm anyway. I'm leaving to go on with my tour of the eastern provinces, and wanted to let you know what has been happening before I went. That is all."

"Do you mean — you —" and Ovid gave up. He did not know what to ask, couldn't see what this man wanted to tell him, and just needed sleep. If he was quiet and listened, maybe this Sejanus would speak, leave and never bother him again.

"You had a letter today, from your mother-in-law," said Sejanus, his fingers absently stroking the silver pendant. "I knew that it would make you worry, so here I am. Yes, you have been under observation since you came here, but you can hardly have thought otherwise, can you?"

"I thought the Governor would keep you informed," said Ovid.

"We keep away from governors," said Sejanus. "They all have too much on their minds, and political allegiances among the governing class aren't always what we would wish. Your Caecina

Severus for example, seems a good loyal servant of Augustus, but he isn't a known quantity really. Respectable enough family from Volaterrae, competent general, but that's it. No track record in Rome, which is important."

"There are hundreds of us with that sort of background," protested Ovid. "My family is very respectable in Liguria. Gods above, your background is almost identical. Augustus likes families like ours."

"Talking of whom, I have a message from the Emperor," said Sejanus and his voice became smooth and diplomatically quiet. "Please listen carefully and do not look for double meanings or loopholes. You poets over-interpret. You must not hope that you are forgiven or ever will be forgiven. The poems you have been sending back to Rome will have no impact on any future decision to pardon you. They are irritating and doing nobody any good, least of all your wife, who is clearly embarrassed by them. However — the Emperor wishes to emphasise that your family are in no danger at all. He has no intention of taking out his annoyance with you on women. That is all."

He gently placed the now sleeping Tiberius on the floor and rose from the stool, saying, "I have probably given you a lot to consider so shall see myself out. Don't look for me, I am leaving Tomis immediately. And you need a bolt as well as that lock on your front door by the way."

As he left the poet managed to speak. "But — you haven't told me anything at all — nothing I didn't already know."

Sejanus did not stop, but called over his shoulder, "Are you sure?" and was gone.

Tiberius staggered to his sleepy feet and did a stretch that must have doubled his normal body length, yawning after the visitor. Ovid slowly rose and said, "Come on, Tiberius. Back to bed."

He lay down, clutching a squirming kitten to him until Tiberius sank ungrateful teeth into his finger and was deposited onto the floor. Ovid lay in the dark, listening to the kitten snuffling around under the bed. His rage, held back while Sejanus was in front of him, gradually took over his whole body until he sank into a bout of frustrated tears.

POETIC JUSTICE

Augustus. Cold, vindictive, ruthless bastard. No wonder even the Imperial family all seemed to go off track — Augustus surely must realise by now that there was a reason he kept having to punish his own kin, daughter, grandson, granddaughter... the list went on. And everyone knew about the old goat's youth, when there hadn't been a virgin in Rome safe from him. But it seemed running an entire Empire still gave him time to send a personal message of hostility to a helpless poet living in exile. Bastard!

Chapter 33

June 8

The next day, Ovid had indigestion, a burning in his chest that made him miserable. He attributed it to lack of sleep and the visit by that young upstart Sejanus, though the more he thought about it, the more unreal the whole incident seemed.

"There's something wrong with the front door," said Baucis as she brought in a plate of bread and olive oil. "Philemon will get someone in today."

"See if a bolt can be fixed," said Ovid.

He could not eat, but Baucis forced a disgusting mint and honey concoction down him before he stumbled out of the front door with no real idea of what he was doing.

He trailed past The Lyre of Apollo, wondered whether to go in and burped at the thought of the stale smells of yesterday's food. And he simply could not face wine. A sudden determination swept over him and pushed him to Headquarters.

After remembering the name of Avitius' clerk, Ovid hung around at the entrance, under the suspicious eye of a veteran soldier who clearly never read poetry. The sunshine was cheerful, and people walking past chattered and laughed. All was well in Tomis. He felt his mood sink lower.

A tall middle-aged man with a nose larger than Ovid's appeared and looked questioningly at him.

"Publius Ovidius Naso? How may I help?"

"I need to get a message to Avitius."

Geminus stepped back and ushered him through the entrance, muttering something to the guard as Ovid shuffled forward. And then they were walking briskly across the courtyard and down the corridor to Avitius' office.

"Take a seat," said Geminus, and handed Ovid a clean wax tablet and stylus. "If you write the message, I shall work out where the Advisor is likely to be and arrange for a courier."

POETIC JUSTICE

They set to work, Ovid scribbling in the wax and Geminus clattering tablets and muttering under his breath. When Ovid closed the wax tablet and looked for something to tie it up, he was unsurprised when Geminus handed him a length of red book ribbon. He tied up the tablet and handed it to the clerk who carefully dripped wax over the knot.

"Do you want to put your seal on it, sir?" Ovid shook his head. He had left his seal ring on his desk.

Geminus put his head out of the room and yelled, "Courier," There was an excited slapping of sandals and he came back to the desk, saying, "I shall send the courier across country up to Noviodunum. The Advisor might have just reached there, depending on what he finds at the forts on the Danube. With Fortune's smile, your message will get to Avitius in two to three days."

Ovid nodded. Not soon enough but then it never was. He thanked Geminus, and rose, wondering what to do with his day now. Write poetry maybe.

Chapter 34

June 9
THE VESTALIA

Today in Rome, the women will celebrate the Vestalia, visiting the temple in the Forum and honouring the eternal flame that keeps the city safe. Vesta is a safe goddess, guarding the family and the fireplace which is the heart of all that makes a home comfortable. She makes women good wives and mothers, respectable, chaste and obedient. Sejanus still thinks we are like that, and has left, certain that his instructions will be followed. He wants no more killing.

But women have another side, and as neither a wife nor a mother, but a true servant of the goddess I turn to Hecate. The last element of the charm is about to be woven.

And now it is time for the binding.
Lady of sky and land and under the land,
we bring water and incense,
we garland your altar with bay.
Draw him to us.
Lady of the moon, who draws down the sky,
Lady of the streams, who guides the rivers.
Listen to my songs and draw him,
draw him home to us.
Take the threads, white, red, black.
Twist the threads, black, red, white.
Knot the threads, red, black, white.
Bind the altar, bind the man.
Draw him here to us.

***

Ovid nursed a large cup of wine and watched the world of Tomis go by from a table just outside the front door of The Lyre of Apollo. He was sure that it was the best place to catch the breeze off the sea in the whole town, and ended up there most evenings as the summer warmed the air. Often he just sat, speaking to nobody, occasionally trying out lines of verse in his head. The third collection of his *Sorrows* poems was coming on nicely, and soon he would start sending them back to Rome.

Ovid dealt with the unpleasant parts of life by wearing them down on a daily basis: in the morning, things like visits from Sejanus worried him and his mind would nag away in a circle of questions. But as the evening approached, his concerns faded, and he was able to push them into a deep corner of his mind where they resided alongside his worries about his health and the growing mystery of why the women of Tomis were unresponsive to his charms. With a cup of wine in his hand and several more under his belt, he found the confidence to dismiss any thought that urged him to be careful not to pester his family and friends, and the encouragement to focus on his glorious homecoming which surely could not be far away now. He had barely given a thought to Avitius and the message he had despatched only the day before. He was moving on.

When a small hand tugged at his sleeve, he felt almost outraged at having to leave his daydream of cheering Roman crowds.

"Sir! Sir! Are you the poet?" said a high voice in bad Greek.

"What is it?" Ovid asked the small child peering at him. The boy's face was beautifully proportioned with sun-blushed cheeks and his teeth were white and straight — an enviable appearance of innocence and youth, thought Ovid, tucking the picture away for the next time he had to describe the young god Eros.

The boy checked that he had Ovid's attention and stood up straight to deliver his message.

"The priestess at the Temple of Fortuna need to see you urgently. She say you if the security man Avitius not here. Please come."

Message over, he waited expectantly.

"That is all?" said Ovid, musing on how he had moved up in the world — to be consulted if Avitius were not present.

"Yes, sir," said the boy. He waited a little longer, sighed and turned to go, before Ovid quickly said, "Wait," feeling for his money-pouch. He held out a coin and said, "I'll give you another of these if you take me to the Temple. I got lost last time."

The boy nodded and took a couple of paces back, looking at Ovid expectantly.

"Ah well," Ovid said to himself. He swallowed a mouthful of wine and left the cup on the table. Macer would chalk it up to his account. He was comfortably hazy, and never thought to wonder why the priestess wanted him.

The walk to the Temple of Fortuna took Ovid to a street he just about recognised from his trip to sacrifice to Hecate. Only last month, he thought, looking around. It was a street where people lived in rows of small respectable houses, walls kept fresh with a yearly coat of plaster wash, and a pot of herbs at every door. When they arrived at the Temple of Fortuna, Ovid remembered Avitius telling him how he had spent a day on the roof just in case the murderer struck there. Ovid looked around and concluded that he had never seen a less likely setting for a bloody killing. He paid off the boy, who scampered off into the sunset.

Entering the shrine, Ovid was only aware of gloom and the smell of old incense. He waited quietly, breathing in air laden with prayers, remembering the warning of the priestess when he was last here. She had said to beware of a silver sword. What was her name? Ah, yes.

"Tyche," he called softly.

There was a swirl behind him that momentarily chilled his neck, but he did not have time to turn before the blow landed and he crumpled.

POETIC JUSTICE

Chapter 35

The east bank of the River Danube, June 9

Avitius stood and watched as the road-gang went about its work methodically. He had been gone several days, though he was barely a day's travel from Tomis, and he was enjoying the break. The further into the country he got, the hotter the weather, and he had managed to develop a hint of a tan. He gazed over the green-brown river and saw no sign of human beings in the thickly wooded far bank though he knew that the villages of Dacian and Sarmatian tribes gazed back at him, coveting the fertile farmland surrounding the Greek cities of the coast.

He had made so little progress because of the delay at the first fort on his itinerary, Axiopolis. A scout who had gone over the river in April was expected back soon, so he had stayed for the man's arrival and debriefing. While waiting he had met a former comrade in arms and had spent a couple of idle days enjoying his memories of the best the army had done for him. Then the scout had arrived and briefed him on all the gossip from the settlements across the river. There was reassuringly little chatter, except that a band of Sarmatians was rumoured to be on its way south in search of some decent agricultural land. There was the potential for some conflict, but nothing too worrying, as far as Avitius was concerned. Sarmatians were always on the move, and there were clashes over land all the time. Now a breeze sprang up and he breathed in the scents of water and greenery.

A shout from the road gang brought his attention and he strolled over to the little knot of men surrounding a swearing squaddie. The man held one hand tightly in the other and blood squeezed out between his fingers. A bloody-handled pick lay at his feet.

"Let me see, soldier," said Avitius and his voice held all the authority the young soldier needed. He stretched out the wounded hand, unfolding it with a wince.

"It's not too bad, sir," he assured Avitius. "Bit of stone leapt up and sliced straight into my wrist here, see."

"It happens," said Avitius. "Go and clean it thoroughly in the river. I want you to hold it in the water and count to a hundred slowly, right?"

"Sir!" And the young soldier jogged down to the water, while Avitius set everyone else back to work. He sorted through the gang's pack and found the pack of bandages, remembering the scores of times he had patched up a scrape or cut for one of his century. Sometimes, he thought, a centurion was nothing more than a strict aunt to eighty nephews.

The squaddie now made his way back towards him, a familiar sheepish expression on his face. Being bandaged by your centurion in front of everyone else only failed to be embarrassing in the midst of battle.

"Stand still, put the uninjured arm under the injured one," instructed Avitius and scrutinised the wound. The flap of skin was now smoothed back in to place and only thin trails of pinkish water slowly made their way across the brown and hairy forearm. He nodded approvingly.

"A quick bandage and you'll be fine," he said. "If it starts bleeding again show it to the medic and get a stitch or two in it." And he began to bandage the arm.

"You've done this before sir!" said the soldier, cheerful now he was sure he wasn't maimed for life.

Avitius laughed. "This time three years ago I was centurion in the Fifth Macedonica, about to march into Illyricum. I wouldn't even have bothered looking at a scratch like this."

He watched as the soldier moved his arm around experimentally, and all at once it happened. A glint of silver and he focused on the soldier's neck, a chain escaping from underneath his tunic and the phallus amulet lying against the dull red of his tunic. He stared, scrabbling in his mind for the memory he knew was surfacing. The silver sword? Yes, but more than that, a necklace he had seen on someone... and then he had it. The soldier shifted awkwardly as Avitius stared. He covered the amulet with one hand, quickly flipping it back under his tunic.

"All right, sir? Can I — er — go?" He gestured towards the rest of his gang industriously digging at the trench. "I'll just get on with it, shall I?"

"Yes," said Avitius. "Carry on."

And he turned and looked back over the river, seeing not the waters or the woods but the silver sword as it moved with the breathing of a woman, a woman in the marketplace at Tomis. He watched as her hand moved to clutch the amulet while beside him Ovid babbled an apology.

Abruptly, Avitius turned and made his way towards the small fort of Axiopolis a mile or so upriver. His summer journeying must wait. He had to get back to Tomis.

Chapter 36

Tomis, June 10

When Ovid tried to open his eyes, he found that he couldn't. His eyes did not want to open. He could not remember ever being aware of the effort it took to open his eyes, but before he could think any further a pain shot through his skull from back to front and across his forehead. He could not care less about opening his eyes but moaned loudly in protest.

After an eternity, the pain seemed to recede and he realised two things — that he felt sick, and that he did not know where he was. Very carefully he opened both eyes a fraction and was relieved that he did indeed see something. He had not gone blind then, even though it was becoming clearer every moment that he needed a basin or bucket soon. Cautiously he lifted his head, waited for the inevitable wave of pain, then looked around. He was in a small room with no furnishings and there was — thank all the gods — a bucket in one corner. As he sat up very slowly, he also saw that there was a cup and a jug against the wall nearest to him. He would investigate them in a moment.

Once he had crawled to the bucket and been thoroughly and miserably sick, Ovid debated the options now ahead of him. He could crawl as far from the bucket as possible and lie down again or investigate the jug. The taste in his mouth decided him. There was the most wonderful drink in the jug, he discovered, clean, cool water. He sipped, gargled, then sipped again, relishing the clean taste as his mouth began to feel normal again. He leaned against the wall and let his mind drift.

Sometime later he thought, "I can see so it is daytime. I must do something," and fell asleep.

When he woke, he ached all over but especially in his neck, and began massaging it so that he could lift it off his chest. It was then that he found a twisted coil of threads around his neck, fitting so closely that he could just squint down to see the colours of the wool, red, black and cream.

POETIC JUSTICE

"I'm a sacrifice," he thought. "I've been bludgeoned, and this strange necklace is my garland. I wonder if I am still in the Temple? And who hit me? Surely not the priestess?"

The little room was darker than when he had first woken, he thought. He must have been in here for a night and a day already, and it was drawing close to night once more. Time to start thinking of escape.

"Here is where a knowledge of mythology is of no use," he told himself. "When did Achilles ever get himself knocked out and imprisoned? Although lots of women get locked in towers, I seem to remember. I wish I knew what was going on." He refused to admit that he was extremely frightened. And his bladder was full to bursting so he would have to confront the bucket again. Of course, no sooner had he become aware of this, than he was aware of the revolting smell filling the room and he felt something near despair at the thought of what he would have to do.

Once this distasteful episode was done, his stomach rumbled and he almost laughed. Aching, empty and presumably locked in – he must start exploring.

A single small window, shuttered on the outside, let in what light there was. A wooden door was in the corner, with no visible lock. He tried it, but something very heavy had been placed on the other side of the door, and it barely moved. He went to stand under the window and listened carefully but could hear nothing. He was probably at the back of the building then. He cleared his throat which stung, and a tiny little voice squeaked, "Help!" Ridiculous.

Someone though must have heard him, for there was a murmured conversation on the other side of the door. He put his head to the gap between frame and door, but the murmurs stopped and there was the scraping sound of people moving the heavy whatever-it-was blocking the door. He was about to meet his captors, and his only weapons were a bucket of filth and the empty jug. He picked up the jug and waited. The door remained closed.

"Stand facing the wall opposite the door," said a woman's voice. Ovid was astonished for she spoke Latin. He stayed still, determined not to do as she ordered. The door opened, and he saw three shapes in the gloom of the Temple of Fortuna. They clustered around the door, and he could not see faces try as he might. He had a surge of panic then realised that they were all three of them, masked. And he was sure that they were all women. Why was he not surprised? He took a deep breath and gazed at them.

"Holy Mother, he stinks," said a voice. He recognised her – the priestess, Tyche.

"At least he found the bucket," said another voice. And this one was familiar. His memory itched.

"What in the name of all gods is going on?" he demanded.

"It's a pity you see fit not to do we asked. We'll try again," said a third voice, the one that had spoken to him before the door opened. "We shall take several steps back, and you will come out."

The three shapes withdrew. Ovid moved to the doorway and looked out. The interior of the Temple of Fortuna was lit by a couple of lamps and he saw immediately that the front door was closed. Probably barred as well. He looked again at the three women, now separated out but cloaked and hooded and distinguishable only by height. The one on his left, nearest the temple entrance, was the priestess Tyche, so who were the others?

"Who are you?" he asked.

"Come out and we shall tell you," said Tyche.

"No."

The woman in the middle gave an exclamation of disgust and strode forward. Before he could move, she had grabbed his arm and jerked him forward. He stumbled, head swimming, and automatically reached for her, but she just stepped to one side and whipped her staff round swiftly. The wood bit into his knees, and he fell, jarring his head and for a few long moments, everything was pain and noise.

It was as he strove to get back to reality that he heard a banging that was not in his head. The door? Someone at the door of the temple? He cried out but made no sound and the women closed around him. His arms were dragged behind his back, his hands tied, and a rag was stuffed into his mouth. For a moment he was convinced he could not breathe and panicked, jerking his limbs and rolling around in his desperation to get air. He was lifted up by the elbows and somewhere on the way up discovered that his nose was clear and he could breathe.

"Ye gods, I'm completely at their mercy," he thought, incredulous to be so weak, so lacking in any resource.

As he stood there shaking, the women remained still and alert — had the banging noise he had heard been real? Was there someone at the temple door? He strained his ears for footsteps but heard nothing. It must have been all in his mind, the result of hitting his head. The grip on him relaxed.

"There is no point to any sort of argument or resistance," said the third voice, the one he did not recognise. "You are about to die, but it will be quick, and there is nothing you can do to stop it. I won't ask if you understand because you're a man and therefore stupid enough to try and talk your way out. And maybe you genuinely believe that we are not going to be able to carry out our threat."

The second woman, the one behind him spoke. "You are the third person we have killed, just in case you are wondering," she said. A native Latin speaker, familiar, Ovid thought. He had definitely met her before. He began to go through all the women in Tomis he knew, standing still and trying to appear completely docile while working to get the rag out of his mouth.

"Tyche, make the shrine ready," said the first voice. "We shall kick his feet from under him if he moves."

As Tyche moved over into the corner, the second woman moved closer and he could feel her breath on his neck. Could it be Vitia? Ovid thought that Vitia might be nearly as tall as him. But why would Vitia now want to do this to him? He risked a quick look to the side. Whoever she was, she was the tallest of the three and the one who had taken on the physical tasks of restraining him. Not Apolauste, then. Apart from the sheer absurdity of even as indulgent a father as Menis allowing his only child to go unchaperoned around Tomis, this was no young girl, but a woman of middle age to judge by the worn hands. So, one middle-aged woman. And by the corner shrine was Tyche, he was sure. The third woman was the leader, directing the others, and by his guess the youngest of the three.

Ovid stood helpless as the women moved around the temple, arranging an incense burner, fetching vessels. What were they going to do to him? He quietly worked his tongue around the rag in his mouth until he had loosened it and spat the rag from his mouth with satisfaction. At least he wasn't going to go quietly. He drew in his breath and prepared to scream.

***

Avitius arrived as night fell in Tomis. He rode his horse through the streets at a trot ignoring the complaints of the people he passed. There weren't enough people to pose a danger of accidents, he reasoned, not in Tomis.

His first call was at Ovid's house where he met Menis and Apolauste coming out, two slaves and Cotela behind them.

"What's happened to him?" demanded Avitius. Menis understood his concern immediately.

"We can't find him," he said.

Avitius sucked in air and wished he had a century of men at his disposal, men who would do as he asked with no question. He must get back to Headquarters and see how many men he could round up.

"How long has he been missing?"

"We came round to check on him earlier this afternoon," Apolauste said, her voice high with tension. "The house was empty then, but not closed up. We tried the military where you work. And Papa went into all his favourite bars. Ovid's favourites, I mean, not Papa's. The last place he was seen was The Lyre of Apollo, yesterday, near sundown."

"Your brother-in-law saw him leaving with a boy. He thought the lad had brought a message," said Menis. "So we asked everyone he knows — that businessman Sulla, Hermes, the people at the laundry. Nobody had sent him a message. We've had a quick look round the house just now, though I'm not entirely certain what we were looking for. The place is definitely empty."

Avitius took a deep breath. "Think!" he told himself. Where would Ovid go, what sort of a message would tempt him? And where were Baucis and Philemon? Apolauste looked at him with wide eyes — he must be looking grim. Poor girl. He tried to smile and said, "It will be all right, I'm sure. Let me take over the search now. I'll let you know as soon as I find anything. Let Cotela look after you."

Menis gave him a hard look but nodded and said, "I can lend you some men for the search. I'll send them up to Headquarters. You don't think he's just trying to go back to Rome, do you?"

"He isn't that stupid," said Avitius, hoping to every god in the Pantheon that he was right.

Back at Headquarters, he gathered all the bodies he could find. He had a plan.

***

Ovid had almost been interested in the ritual the women were preparing until he had been stripped of his clothes. For good measure, one of them had slapped him across the face. Now he sat, head ringing and utterly humiliated, in the corner behind the shrine of Hecate and no longer able to see most of what was happening.

As far as he could tell it was now completely dark, and though he strained for the sound of footsteps, he could hear nothing outside the temple. The rag had been spotted immediately when he spat it out, and an elbow to his midriff had kept him quiet while a new gag was made from his own tunic. Now he was incapable of doing more than groan. He sat and pondered the awfulness of his situation and did not care that tears slipped down his cheeks and into the gag. They had left his hands untied though and he felt the twisted wool around his neck and started pulling on it. He was not going to be a docile victim.

"Can we start?" said the leader, sounding for all the world as if she were holding a poetry reading. Ovid almost expected her to ask if everyone could hear her.

"I have the drink ready," said Tyche and Ovid hear footsteps and a pause as the women drank. The second woman appeared at his side and hauled him up — gods, she was strong — maybe she was a barmaid, thought Ovid, all those amphoras to carry. He was pushed around to the front of the shrine and unexpectedly, his gag was untied. A cup was held to his lips. He smelled wine and nearly drank until a bitter odour made him cautious and he clamped his lips shut, twisting his head away.

"Wine, a smidgeon of poppy juice, and strengthening herbs." Tyche sounded scornful.

"Don't worry it isn't poison," said the second woman, and in the amusement of her tone Ovid knew her. He was so surprised he opened his mouth to ask why she was doing this, and the cup was returned to his lips. Head whirling, he supposed he had nothing to lose, and he sipped, feeling warmed by the wine and its hint of poppy sweetness. He tasted sage and rose water, cut with a bitterness he did not recognise, but which somehow suited the drink.

"My last drink is a good one," he thought and gulped it down. It hit his empty stomach, and for a moment he fought not to retch. They pushed him to his knees then left him to contemplate Hecate's three faced statue as behind him the women started humming, a one note sound, that every now and then pulsed. And tell-tale rustles of fabric and snicks of brooches being undone alerted him to what was going on, and he almost had to laugh.

"Alone with three terrifying naked women" he told himself. "I wonder if they are going to start dancing around me. Oh, I hope they start dancing around me!" It was no good. He was giggling.

The humming stopped and from behind him, the leader started to intone a prayer. It was completely serious, and yet he was still overwhelmed with laughter. His shoulders shook as he bowed before the shrine of Hecate and thought, "Hecate is the patron of witches. I'm being sacrificed by three witches. Witches, witches, witches." He began to sway as the prayer was intoned.

"Hecate, daughter of Asteria, honoured by Zeus,
nurse of the young, bringer of wealth,
you grant success to men in battle
and make our farms flourish.
You sit with kings in judgement,
and your favour is bestowed as easily as you take it away.
Lady of Samothrace, accept our sacrifice,
Lady of Miletus, hear our prayer.
Goddess of earth and sky and sea,
here in Tomis, you find your perfect home."

POETIC JUSTICE

By the time the prayer was being intoned by all three women for the third time, Ovid no longer cared about anything. He was drunk in a way he had never been before, sleepy and with mist filling his head, but also seeing shapes in the air around him.

"I saw animals in the incense when I came here last," he thought, and tried to remember who he had come with. He shook his head in irritation, and a memory came to him, of animals dancing in the smoke of the incense. He looked up. Someone had lit a lamp and, yes, there was smoke again, and in it a cat twirled before him – Tiberius? He stretched out his hands to stroke the cat, but it twisted away and was replaced with a galloping horse. Who had he been with last time? The horse reared in alarm as its throat pumped out blood. Ovid retreated inside his head and watched as the cat and the horse swirled around him. When they stood on their hind legs and clashed cymbals he was not in the least surprised, and then at last it was all gone and he became a twist of soft warm smoke, curling up into the sky.

Chapter 37

June 11
THE MATRALIA

The sun was shining which was strange because he was dead. Ovid was fairly certain that the sun didn't reach down into the Underworld. And he hadn't crossed the River Styx yet, either.

"It's very confusing," he tried to say, and found himself whispering because his mouth was dry and tasted terrible and he had a headache like the worst hangover he had ever endured.

"What's that?" bellowed a voice in his ear and he winced.

"Sorry," the voice whispered. "I got a bit excited. Say it again."

"I'm confused," Ovid managed to mutter, and wondered if he should open his eyes.

"At least you're alive," said the voice with a cheerfulness he did not associate with the owner. Who was it? He peeked out of one eye.

"Avitius?"

"Hello," and there was his friend smiling down at him in a most un-Avitian manner.

"I can see up your nostrils," said Ovid, his voice stronger.

Avitius looked taken aback and pinched his nose shut as he shifted back on the chair.

"That's better," said Ovid. "Gods, my head aches. Any chance of some water? Where is Baucis?"

Avitius looked at his friend and wondered what to say.

"What do you remember about the women at the temple?" he asked.

"Good gods, nothing!" Ovid retorted trying to sit up. "I was busy being drugged and murdered, remember?"

"Ah, so you do remember. How many of them were there?" Avitius persisted.

"Three. One was definitely the old priestess of the temple," said Ovid, falling back against the pillows. "Or I thought she was. My head!"

"We found three women with you," said Avitius carefully falling back on facts. "One was the Priestess of Fortuna, you're right. The others..."

Ovid stared up at Avitius, wondering why he looked so worried.

"The others were a woman called Sabina – and Baucis," said Avitius.

"A woman called Sabina and Baucis?" Ovid asked drowsily. "Strange name."

Avitius looked at the ceiling and counted three cobwebs.

"One woman was Baucis, your Baucis," he said patiently.

Ovid was silent for a while. Then, "I remember," he said. He sounded almost uninterested. Then, finally agitated, he tried to sit up saying, "Where is Philemon?"

"He has disappeared," said Avitius, trying to hide his irritation with this development. His men had been just too late at the harbour, and Philemon was now a passenger on a ship to Asia Minor.

Ovid looked around the room as if Baucis and Philemon would emerge from the corner and Avitius would laugh and admit he was wrong.

"We must be wrong," he said "because this is Baucus and Philemon we are talking about, and they don't kill people." But he remembered the amusement of the woman who had poured poison down him.

"Baucis hit you, imprisoned you, fed you drugged wine and nearly killed you," said Avitius.

Ovid did not reply and Avitius let the silence go on, unable to think of anything else to say. He saw Ovid's hands go to his neck, and said quickly, "I cut it off."

"Good, said Ovid. "It was my wreath, a sign that I was the victim. I'll never be able to look at a sacrificial animal again."

Tapping at the door caught their attention. Apolauste and Cotela were in the doorway.

"Hello there. Do you need anything?" asked Apolauste, blushing. "Cotela has made you some soup." She held out a bowl with a hopeful look.

"Can I have some?" asked Avitius, smiling.

"It's for the invalid," said Apolauste primly.

Cotela was already at the bed, and Avitius helped her to get Ovid sitting up. She fussed with pillows, but Ovid realised that she was careful and gentle, and it was nice to be pampered. He discovered that he was very properly dressed in a tunic, and soon he was sitting up and looking doubtfully at the bowl of soup. Cotela took no notice and fed him determinedly. He had no strength to deny her and swallowed obediently, while Apolauste and Avitius watched him in silence.

"That's better. What do you now remember of yesterday?" asked Avitius, as Cotela took back the cup and set it carefully on the table next to her.

"Everything, I think," said Ovid immediately. "My head aches but it's as clear as Syrian glass. And I have so many questions I don't know where to start." He looked at Apolauste and Cotela understood. She cleared dishes and cups and gathered Apolauste with her as she left the room. Apolauste did not even complain until she thought she was out of earshot.

Ovid smiled at Avitius. "Thank you for saving me by the way — I gather the noise I heard right at the end was not cymbals clashing but you breaking into the temple?"

"I don't know about any cymbals," said Avitius. "I just ran in, pushed three naked women out of the way and caught you as you fell."

"There was a clashing," said Ovid.

Avitius shrugged. "You'd obviously been hit several times, and…"

Ovid frowned with thought, shook his head, then winced and said, "Very well. Tell me about my rescue instead. Weren't you supposed to be inspecting forts and so on?"

"I was," said Avitius, nodding. "And I was conscientiously gathering material for a report on progress with road repairs when I had a revelation. I remembered where I had seen the silver sword charm – before we found it in Cynthia's hovel."

"We – how nice, that you say "we"," murmured Ovid. "So don't keep me in suspense – what about the silver sword?"

"Do you remember bumping into someone in the marketplace, a couple of months ago it must be?" asked Avitius. "You said she reminded you of someone." He checked to make sure the invalid was following him, and not looking too tired. "Well, I had a sudden memory of the necklace she was wearing. It was the silver sword. I knew that it meant something, and – I don't know, I had a really bad feeling about it. I got a horse and rode here as quickly as I could."

"I feel as though I should know what that silver sword means," said Ovid, squirming back up the pillows in an effort to sit up properly. "How did you know to come to the Temple?"

"When I realised you were missing, I sent anyone who could walk to check out all the temples in the town as a priority," said Avitius. "And the only one with a closed and barred door was Fortuna. My man ran to collect as many of us as he could find and we found you and some naked witches all dancing around."

He paused and added, "And the old woman, the priestess of Fortuna – she died in the midst of it all." He could see the question in Ovid's eyes, and added, "She collapsed while one of my men was trying to restrain her. He wasn't gentle, but the doctor thinks her heart gave out. One witch we don't need to worry about."

"Witches," said Ovid. He shivered. "I can't quite believe it but they were going to strangle me as an offering to Hecate." He shook his head and winced. "But I don't know why."

"Well, that is interesting, as you will soon hear," said Avitius. "But basically, you were in the hands of our murderers, responsible for all four killings, cat, horse, Antiope and Cynthia. And one of those three murderers is the woman from the marketplace."

"Your silver sword wearing woman, said Ovid. "What in the name of all the gods does that remind me of?"

"Don't try to remember yet," said Avitius. "The doctor thinks you might have memory lapses, because of the head wound."

"I never dreamed those killings could be done by women," said Ovid.

"Same here," Avitius stared at the wall across the room. "Not even our year in the Commission for Prisons and Executions prepared us for this, did it?"

"And Baucis... Where are they now?"

"Locked up in Headquarters with a guard of the least superstitious men I could find," said Avitius. "The rumour that they are witches went round the town as fast as a chain of signal fires. Nobody will be sad when they're dead and gone."

"What happens now – to them, I mean?"

"The Archon, assisted by the Town Council will try them, not that that will take long," said Avitius. "Then they will be executed. The Town Council has decided that it will be a nice touch to ask the Governor to sentence them." He didn't add that according to Menis, the Town Council had insisted on this so that any curse would lie firmly on Rome and not them.

"Have they said anything about why they did it?" Ovid asked.

"Oh yes," said Avitius. "It was like unstopping a bottle of vinegar and watching it all pour out." He shook his head. "A lot of bitterness."

"Bitterness about me?" Ovid could not stop the squawk in his voice.

"No, not just you." Avitius looked at him strangely. "It's a mixture. These women are obsessed in a way I've never encountered. They are convinced they follow the will of the goddess Hecate in driving the Romans from Tomis. Even though two of them are Roman."

"Baucis is Roman of course. And this Sabina woman?" Ovid remembered the Latin spoken by the leader. "I can believe it actually. She spoke Latin to me, really good Latin."

"Well, she still hates us apparently, and in addition, she hates you. You are everything Rome stands for, but you are also sent here as a punishment, so she saw you almost as a willing sacrifice."

Ovid must have frowned because Avitius apologised. "I'm sorry. But I think I have to try and use their own words, so that you see. In fact, it might be an idea if you actually talk to them at some point." He ended this last sentence on an upward, questioning note, and Ovid, though he felt his heart beat faster at the thought, did not immediately cry out his instinctive denial. The truth was that he wanted to see that woman, the leader. And he wanted to ask about his poem, the *Fasti*. Had she used that poem in her scheme, had she wanted him to be dragged into all this?

So, he breathed steadily and said, "The leader, Sabina, yes. But I can't stomach seeing Baucis again. Sorry."

POETIC JUSTICE

And then Cotela came in and made him drink more soup, and Avitius left saying that he would be back.

Ovid fell asleep as soon as he had had enough soup – or what Cotela thought was enough. When he woke briefly in the night, he was touched to see Apolauste sitting next to the bed, her head bowed down to her chest. As he stirred, a shadow came forward and Cotela whispered. "Is everything well, sir?"

"My head aches," whispered Ovid.

Cotela was there at his side in an instant and forced a horrible, woody-tasting drink down him which she assured him would do him good. Ovid told her to put honey in it next time, but it soothed his aching head and he managed to sleep again.

***

The next day, Doctor Rascanius from Avitius' Headquarters visited while Ovid was awake and entertained him with a list of everything wrong with him. To Ovid's annoyance the medic seemed much more concerned with his urine than with his headaches, which he dismissed with the memorable line, "Everything inside your skull got scrambled." The wound at the back of his head where he had been hit when he first entered the Temple of Fortuna was pronounced excellent. Everything else, according to the doctor, was insignificant. "Scrapes and bruises won't kill you," Ovid was told. He immediately resolved to have an all over wash as soon as he could and check the damage for himself. He wondered when he could persuade his keepers to let him hobble to the baths.

Avitius visited in the afternoon to find Ovid sitting up in bed and demanding proper food and some wine.

"What's the news?" Ovid asked as soon as he saw Avitius.

Avitius raised an eyebrow and made himself comfortable in the visitor's chair. He nodded at Cotela on the other side of the bed and asked if she had had any sleep.

"Yes, go and sleep," said Ovid. "While I have a visitor to look after me."

Cotela ignored him as she recited a list of things Ovid was not allowed to do and warned Avitius that there would be trouble if she found out that he had disobeyed her. She gathered up a few empty plates and cups and swept out, and Ovid looked relieved to see her go. He lay back on his pillows and said, "Ye gods I'm tired. I do nothing but sleep but still I'm tired. In a moment I must tell you something important. I forgot yesterday, I must not forget again."

"Has the doctor been?"

"Yes," said Ovid. "No bedside manner but what he says makes sense. I have to sleep until I get over whatever was in their weird drink, then gentle exercise and massage for my aches and pains, and lots of willow-bark tea for my headache. No wine and only bland food."

Avitius decided he had better not laugh. Instead, he asked, "Did he say what was in the drink?"

"No, just guessed that it was something poisonous that gave me hallucinations. He thinks maybe a very small dose of belladonna. Apparently my eyes gave it away. All part of their little ritual before they sacrificed me to Hecate," said Ovid, marvelling at how utterly strange the words sounded here in a room so ordinary.

Avitius remembered his first sight of Ovid's face as he caught him and gently lowered him to the floor. In the midst of the chaos, the yells and struggles as his men captured the three women, Ovid had stared up at him with eyes that never blinked, pupils so large that they were holes in the poet's skull.

"Can I ask a favour?" Ovid asked.

"You can ask," said Avitius cautiously. He wasn't giving Ovid any chance to exploit this situation.

"I need to wash but I'm not supposed to leave the room," said Ovid. "I can't ask Cotela. If you could give me a hand…?"

And thus, Avitius found himself organising a basin of hot water with cloths and towels, washing down the parts that poetry could not reach. He felt no embarrassment or awkwardness. Ovid was no different to a small child and needed the same care. Avitius dropped a clean tunic over his friend's head, watched him settle back into sleep and enjoyed a short doze in the chair himself. He had not slept well recently.

When he awoke with a crick in his neck, he remembered that Ovid had said he had something important to tell and wondered whether he should wake his friend or not. The chair was quite comfortable, despite the ache from sleeping in it, so after a stretch,

Avitius settled back down and wondered what made a woman behave like that.

"The silver sword," said Ovid suddenly, breaking into Avitius' musings and making him jump.

"I thought you were still asleep," complained Avitius. "Do you mean the charm we found at Cynthia's place."

"Do you still have it?"

It was still in Avitius' pouch. He got it out and Ovid pointed at it.

"I sent you a note, but Geminus anticipated you being a lot further north, and sent it to Nicopolis, I think. That is something quite special, that silver sword, my friend."

"And you are clearly feeling much better even than when I came in a couple of hours ago," said Avitius. "Go on, tell your story."

"My wonderful mother-in-law found it out for me," said Ovid. "That pendant is given to members of the Praetorian spy service working abroad. It's their identification, so they know who to trust. What do you think of that?"

Avitius made some rapid recalculations and came up with something quite disturbing.

"Are we to take it that the girl in the marketplace, Sabina, is a Praetorian agent?"

"My mother-in-law suspected that you were," said Ovid. "It makes sense I suppose, but then she doesn't know you."

"Definitely not important enough to be noticed by the Praetorians," said Avitius, knowing for certain that his name was on a list back in Rome – a list of ex-centurions still working for the government, possibly useful in emergencies.

"I wouldn't be so sure," said Ovid. "Seius Strabo is a very efficient prefect of the Praetorian Guard. But I'd be amazed if their agent here was a woman,"

Avitius looked at him and shook his head. "No," he said. "You're wrong. You of all people know about women. You know enough to write all that stuff in your poetry. You've written about Medea, haven't you?" He tactfully did not mention Ovid's recent experience at the hands of murderous women.

Ovid flapped a hand irritably.

"I have no delusions about women's intelligence or ruthlessness. I'm just surprised that the Praetorians would be enlightened enough to employ women."

"Maybe they don't," said Avitius. "Maybe she got the pendant through some underhand way. It just seems unlikely. The whole thing seems fantastic when you have lay it all out in a report to Rome as I do, on behalf of the absent Governor. What do I do, by the way? Leave it out of the report or add that she's a Praetorian agent? Do I tell the Governor?"

"Jupiter, don't mention it at all, to anyone," Ovid said with such firmness that Avitius felt heartened.

"Do you have nothing else about Baucis? Or Philemon?" This was the Ovid of recent days, tired, in pain, weak.

"I've sent a courier down the coast to see if he can find Philemon's ship putting in at any of the cities," said Avitius. "It's a long shot because with clear weather they may not put in at all or be too fast. Baucis has said nothing since we took the two of them, apart from a few rants about what Hecate is going to do to us."

"I wonder why she hated me so much," said Ovid. Avitius had no answer.

"You know — all this — it would make a great poem," said Ovid, beginning to tire again, his words slipping into one another.

Avitius shook his head and said, "Don't you dare make poetry out of this."

Then he called Cotela and went back to Headquarters, to spend the rest of the day fretting over his report.

POETIC JUSTICE

Chapter 38

June 14

Tomis was trying to get back to normal and failing. People were edgy, whispering in corners but not yet ready to say what they were really feeling — that they were afraid.

Ovid had not attended the trial of course. He slept as much as he could, knowing that Avitius would come and tell him what he needed to know. No doubt he would reintroduce the suggestion that Ovid meet with the women. Ovid thought Avitius himself had not got satisfactory answers, but would he really have any more luck? And he still could not bear the thought of seeing Baucis.

"Hello," he said when he awoke and found Avitius sitting at his side, eyes closed, mouth open, snoring very slightly. Avitius gave a snort and sat bolt upright.

"How are you feeling?" he asked.

"Do you know," said Ovid, "you are one of those horrible people who goes from asleep to awake in a heartbeat? So annoying for the rest of us."

"Ah, you make rapid progress," said Avitius. "Are you allowed wine yet?"

"No," said Ovid. "The jug is over there. Menis smuggled it in, well-watered unfortunately. I'm sure a single cup of the real stuff would speed my recovery on immeasurably."

"Three days ago, you had a cracked skull and were seeing invisible horses," said Avitius. "You are amazing. Or Cotela has done a deal with the gods."

"Aesculapius has a shrine somewhere in Tomis and she and Apolauste have been with an offering every day," said Ovid. "I for one would not dare to refuse any prayer they made if I were the god of healing." He paused and said more seriously, "I still get very tired. But I have been thinking about what you said, the women. I still don't think I can see Baucis but how about you and I talk to the young one, the one in charge?"

"Sabina," said Avitius. "She gave her place of birth as Sulmo."

"No," said Ovid immediately. "She can't come from my birthplace. I refuse to believe that."

"I agree," said Avitius. "She is trying to reach out to you, to make another connection with you, I wish I knew why."

He went over to the table and poured two cups of the drink that was definitely all water with a splash of wine. Handing one cup to Ovid he was pleased to see the improvement, but his friend was still looking ill. The weight had fallen off his bones, and it wasn't as though Ovid had much spare to begin.

Ovid drank and sighed. "Wonderful despite the water, thank you," he said. "Well, let's see this Sabina soon — when is Caecina due back?"

"I'd expect to see him day after tomorrow," said Avitius. "He isn't hurrying of course, not a great thing to return to, having to sentence three women to death. But the town needs this to happen. The anxiety and gossip about them being witches is very unsettling."

"Funny," said Ovid, "that when we thought we had a madman murdering women on a full moon, we didn't really have that much of a problem. But now we know that three witches were involved, the fact that the culprits are dead or safely behind bars means nothing, and people are more scared."

"Well, witches are scary," said Avitius reasonably.

"And you want me to meet one," said Ovid.

"Tomorrow?"

Ovid had no hesitation. "Yes, let's get it over. I'll have to walk very slowly to Headquarters I'm afraid."

"I'll sort out something," said Avitius. He rose. "And thank you. I know you're only doing it to help me, so I can present the Governor with an explanation. Anyway, I appreciate it."

Ovid waved an insouciant hand. "Anything for you, dearest Avitius."

Chapter 39

June 15

Ovid managed to wash himself without any help that day, and even got dressed. It was tiring but not exhausting. His head ached less today as well. When Avitius arrived to pick him up he had eaten and felt optimistic about his eventual recovery. He knew that ahead there would be days when his miserable side took over, but for now, he could tell himself that he would get through.

Avitius had, to Ovid's surprise, got hold of a litter and four slaves to carry it. Ovid had never seen such a thing in Tomis and could not help laughing until his body ached its protest. Avitius helped him climb in and walked alongside as they trundled their stately way to Headquarters.

"Go on," said Ovid. "Who did you have to kill – sorry, bribe — to get hold of this?"

Avitius said with just a hint of pride, "This is the Governor's official transport which he never uses. Sulla lent me the slaves."

"And which poor soldier had to get it out of storage and clean it up as a punishment for some nefarious crime?"

Avitius grinned. "We have two ne'er-do-wells on the rota at the moment who are always providing me with free labour. Their centurion despairs."

At Headquarters, they were shown into a small square room containing a table and three chairs. One of the chairs was placed against the wall: Ovid and Avitius sat on the other two facing it with a small table between them. Already laid out on the table were the obligatory plate of olives, jugs of wine and water with two glossy red cups. Someone was making a point.

"Nice," said Ovid as he sat down and picked up a cup. "Look at the hunting dogs running around the top — very well done. Is this the Governor's best ware?"

"Second-best," said Avitius. "He keeps the glass stuff for visiting kings and potentates."

And the door opened.

Ovid saw a young woman in a plain but clean tunic. Her long dark hair fell down her back and she showed no sign of having been ill-treated in her captivity. Of course not, he thought, not under Avitius. She sat on the chair opposite them, and a soldier stood on either side of her. Her deep brown eyes, slightly tilted at the outer edge were beautiful, but before he could gaze too long, she narrowed them and spat on the floor in his direction.

"What did I ever do to you?" he asked.

She put on a look of haughty surprise.

"You exist," she said.

Avitius leaned forward.

"You have admitted at your trial to killing two women and attempting to kill my friend here," he said. "Did you also kill a cat behind the Temple of Jupiter in January and a horse at the River View Inn?"

"Yes," she said.

"Why?" asked Avitius.

She looked at them both contemptuously.

"Rome is not welcome here," she said. "The Goddess does not want you here, so I looked for an opportunity to harm the standing of Rome in this town. My sisters and I offered the animals and the women to Hecate as part of a great charm that would have been completed if we had succeeded in sacrificing you, poet. The Romans would have been driven out of Tomis, and the will of the Goddess would have been accomplished."

"If only we believed you," said Avitius.

"Why did you use my poems though — to choose when you would carry out your murders?" Ovid asked.

She shrugged. "We were going to use the full moon at first but when I got a copy of your calendar poem I saw a way to discredit Rome," she said. "You are the most famous Roman here, so if I made people link the deaths with you, it would look bad for Rome."

"How did you get hold of the poem?" asked Avitius.

She gazed straight at him. "Baucis, of course," she said. Ovid stirred but Avitius did not want an interruption yet. He held out the silver sword charm to Sabina, out of reach but clear.

POETIC JUSTICE

"Is this yours?"

She looked at the charm and said nothing, but Ovid was watching her hands and saw a movement, as the thumb of one hand pressed into the palm of the other.

"That means something to her," thought Ovid. "But she won't tell us about it because it links her to the Praetorians. Why not just say so? They'll deny it of course, distance themselves from her as quickly as possible after this fiasco. Do they have some sort of hold over her?"

"There is something I don't understand," he said suddenly, as though he and she were having a casual conversation, maybe in a bar, as she poured his drink and told him what was on the menu. "You are a Roman, aren't you? You have said so when asking for an appeal to the Governor. Why do you hate Rome so much?"

"Not I," she said. "The goddess. She hates you. All of you. You have to leave Tomis. Then you will leave the Black Sea, leave the East, retreat back to your brutal western lands and stay there. This is the Goddess' realm and she will take it back."

This was said in ringing tones and she looked animated for the first time, colour in her cheeks and a smile almost breaking through.

"And what about Baucis?" said Ovid. "What does she think of all that?"

Sabina looked at him pityingly. "Baucis received her instructions from the Great Goddess herself on Samothrace," she said. "You were there. You did not notice."

"The goddess spoke to me on Samothrace," said Ovid. "I did not know she spoke to Baucis as well."

"Of course you did not know," said Sabina and her contempt was sharp, making little bumps rise on Ovid's skin. "You did not know because you never thought to ask. You never ask other people, do you? You never understand anything outside your own head. Baucis and Philemon have been carrying out the orders of the gods ever since and you were oblivious."

Avitius leapt in with an artificial cough and got out a wax tablet and stylus.

"Dear me," he said. "Well, a few points to clear up. When and where were you born?"

"The consulship of Arruntius and Marcellus, in Volsinii, in Etruria," she said readily.

"Why did you tell the court you were from Sulmo?" asked Avitius, as he scribbled.

She really smiled then. "I knew it would irritate the poet," she said. "I wanted him to come to me, and see, here he is."

"How did you know I come from Sulmo?" Ovid said curious.

She looked at him with contempt. "Everyone knows you come from Sulmo."

"She's right there," said Avitius. Why was he so cool, why wasn't this woman getting to him? Ovid was all at once exhausted.

"What do you want from me?" he said. "I am tired. I am ill. I want to go home, not sit here watching you act out your own tragedy."

She looked furious for a few moments then smoothed her expression, looking at the floor.

"Behold," said Ovid to Avitius, "now she is thinking."

That stung Sabina and she tried to leap to her feet, thrust down immediately by both soldiers. She took several breaths and then said to Ovid, "Ask me who I am."

Avitius cast his eyes to the heavens but Ovid just said, "Who are you, Sabina?"

She held his gaze as she replied, "I am Sabina, daughter of Corinna."

"Corinna?" Ovid looked at Avitius. Avitius shrugged and said, "You always said it was a pretty name." He leaned forward to get Sabina's attention and said kindly, "What are you trying to say?"

"My mother was called Corinna," said Sabina. "She was living in Rome when she killed my father. But you know all about that, don't you?"

Ovid heard a long breath expelled from Avitius but he could not look away from Sabina as she recited:

Her Parrot, a bird of echoes
from the eastern lands of India,
is dead.

"You're Corinna's daughter?" whispered Ovid. "She was pregnant with you when she left Rome?"

"Sometimes I wondered if you were my father," she said. "My mother though assured me that you never slept with her, and why would she lie when she had told me everything else? But she said that you wanted her. She laughed at that. She said it meant you didn't ask too many awkward questions. She was grateful enough to read everything you ever wrote. I have all your works." She leaned forward and whispered, "I'm your biggest fan," and burst out laughing.

Ovid turned to Avitius. Avitius nodded and gestured to the two soldiers.

"Take her back, lads," he said. "And this interview — you heard nothing, right?"

The soldiers each barked a sharp, "Sir!" as they hauled Sabina to her feet and pushed her towards the door. She was still smiling.

"She's going to have a line to exit on ready," thought Ovid. "I must say something, do something."

But she beat him to it of course.

"Your poems are horse dung," she yelled as she was dragged from the room.

In the sudden silence that followed her words, Avitius and Ovid looked at one another and burst out laughing, though Ovid shook with relief that she was gone.

***

Ovid was exhausted but insisted on one drink at The Lyre of Apollo. Avitius had guessed that they would end up there and so when the litter dropped them off, Macer and Vitia were waiting. Macer shook Ovid's hand very gently and guided him to his usual table, and Vitia said briskly, "Good to see you up and about. I've got some soup if you're hungry."

"No soup," said Ovid firmly. "Bread, cheese and olive oil, please. It is good to be here."

The normality of his welcome, the small talk of deciding on food and drink was soothing. Macer and Vitia studiously left them alone once served, and Ovid found he ate with appetite and enjoyment.

"Corinna's daughter! What a charmer she was," he observed once he was full. "Why wouldn't she talk about the silver sword do you think? Who is she protecting? And my poetry is not horse dung."

"I know but let's focus on the important things — if she is a spy for the Praetorians it would explain why she won't talk about how she got your poem," said Avitius. "They probably have some hold over her."

"I expect Baucis and Philemon stole the poem on the journey," said Ovid. "I don't know how I'm going to break it to Fabia about them. They've been with the family for years, you know. They were freed in my father's will." He gazed into his wine, then suddenly looked at Avitius. "I don't understand one thing though. My poem vanished long before Baucis could have had her message from the gods on Samothrace. Why did she and Philemon steal it?"

Avitius shook his head. "Maybe you are mistaken over the timing."

"I'm not," and Ovid sounded tired and grumpy. Avitius willed him to drink up.

"Eat your cheese," he said. "And let's just be grateful that Sabina the witch is going to her grave."

"She's appealing to the Governor, won't that delay things?"

Avitius shook his head. "She is not appealing the penalty itself. She is hoping for a swift death," he said. "She doesn't want to be crucified, who does?"

Crucifixion had not occurred to Ovid. He shuddered. "She can't be crucified. Neither can Baucis. They are Roman citizens."

"He won't crucify them, but he will want it done quickly," said Avitius with confidence. "He barely notices Tomis, remember — he looks at the whole province, and considers what his reports look like in Rome. To him this is a minor local matter, which he dealt with when the locals couldn't. He is probably right."

Ovid thought that Caecina seemed to have kept himself carefully clear of the whole affair but said nothing.

"I was surprised she told us where she actually was born," said Avitius. "But she had the whole speech planned, didn't she? She just wanted to have a go at you again. It was like watching a madwoman. Strange after so many years where she has kept it together, building up a fake life here in Tomis."

"She genuinely thought that once she had recited my own poem back to me, we would accept everything she said, didn't she?" said Ovid. "Do you believe her?"

"Who knows with a half crazy, wholly evil bitch like that?" said Avitius. "Drink up, I need to get you back before Cotela sends out search parties."

"But — if Sabina is Corinna's daughter…" said Ovid unhappily.

"She isn't. And even if she were, it doesn't matter," said Avitius. "You owe her nothing."

Chapter 40

June 17

Caecina Severus had been warned by Avitius so after one sharp look at Ovid he made no comment, though any idea he might have had about going easy on the women would have survived no further. Ovid had lost a shocking amount of weight since Caecina had seen him last, and his hair was now almost completely white. The grooves from nose to corners of the mouth were deep and did not vanish as his facial expression changed, not even when he smiled. Not that he smiled very often. His usual expression now seemed to be one of slight puzzlement, with frowning brows. He looked as if he had covered his thumbs with lamp soot and pressed a smudge underneath each eye.

They were in the courtyard of the Headquarters building, a small dais had been set up with a chair for Caecina, and several benches put out in a rough semicircle facing the dais. Men were already taking their places, the Town Council of course, several of Caecina's officials, the priest of Jupiter, Sulla the businessman and Hermes who nodded at Ovid. Avitius stood behind the Governor so Ovid went over to sit next to Hermes.

"I don't want to be here," muttered Hermes, "but I owe it to Ani. At least Gorgo and the girls think so."

Ovid made no reply and settled down, carefully noting the men around him, who either steadfastly looked ahead or nodded, embarrassed. A large official sat in front of him, and he felt quite reassured by the knowledge that he was mostly hidden.

When the women came in, escorted by several soldiers, he looked at the floor and concentrated on his breathing. He thought of the wine he had just been served by the Governor and decided it was from somewhere in Asia Minor. But even that made his treacherous mind go straight to the drugged wine he had drunk in the Temple of Fortuna, and so he decided he had to look.

The two women stood in front of the Governor with their backs to him but he could recognise them. How strange to see Baucis with her hair let down. It must be that the women were not allowed

POETIC JUSTICE

hair pins in their prison. He felt embarrassed as though he had walked in on her getting dressed, and lowered his gaze to his sandals,

The proceedings were brief. Caecina read out the charges and the guilty verdict, then went straight on to pronounce a sentence of death on each woman. He added that as they were Roman citizens he would give them a swift execution by strangling. Sentence would be carried out at dawn the next day in the prison. At this, the women stirred, and Sabina took a step forward.

"Hecate is the lady of earth, sky and sea," she said. "We would prefer to be thrown from the cliffs into the sea."

Ovid looked up. What was she doing?

"Denied," said Caecina shortly.

Ovid did not try to see the women's faces as they were taken away. He just felt a sense of relief. Stiffly, he got to his feet and looked for Avitius to take him home. He needed to get home.

Once Ovid was installed in his study, with Cotela fetching food and drink, Avitius handed over a small cloth bag.

"I thought you should have this," he said. "I can't keep it anywhere it might be seen, it might create difficulties. Why would I have the secret sign of the Praetorians? You have it. Hide it away of course, but you never know – it might bring you luck."

***

After a nap, Ovid sat at his desk, the sheaf of papyrus in front of him. He did not feel like working on *The Fasti* any more but it was too good to throw away. A stray line caught his eye:

God is in us: we warm to his touch.

Yes, far too good. He had to think of his posterity. Nobody was going to remember this sad string of deaths in Tomis, but his poetry would be immortal.

"Time to write myself back to Rome," he said to himself. He rolled up the sheaf of *The Fasti*, tied it with red book ribbon, and stowed it in one of his book niches. As he did so he was annoyed to see that his hand was shaking. He turned abruptly, threw himself into his chair and took a fresh sheet of papyrus. Carefully he dipped his pen into the ink pot and with a flourish wrote:

The Sorrows of Ovid – continued

Chapter 41

Byzantium, June 27
FESTIVAL OF THE LARES

Sejanus conducted a simple ceremony on his own in front of the guardian household gods in the house he was borrowing. The three bronze statues stood in a niche in the wall, with a tripod underneath containing a small brazier. The fire was lit and he dropped three careful splashes of wine, not enough to dampen the flames, before burning three pinches of incense.

This done, he sat at the desk and tackled the pile of messages that had accumulated while he had visited a selection of Black Sea towns. As ever, he concentrated fully, only slowing as he read the account of the trial and execution of some witches in the town of Tomis. He frowned a little as he realised how Sabina had disobeyed him, and mentally noted that he would need someone reliable to replace her in the new province. The loss of Baucis made him pause for just a few moments, and the death of the old priestess Tyche barely registered.

A gentle cough at the door broke his thoughts and he looked up at the middle-aged man hovering. Just off the ship, Sejanus guessed, with a bag over his shoulder, and in need of a shave. He stood and smiled at the newcomer.

"I was wondering when you would arrive," he said. "Welcome, Philemon."

POETIC JUSTICE

Author's note

Thank you for reading this book, and I hope you were as intrigued as I have always been by one of its central questions - why the poet Ovid was suddenly banished by the Emperor in 8 CE. The only clues the poet gives us was that it was because of his "poem and mistake". There will be more about this in further titles in the series.

Ovid was born on the 21 March 43 BCE, into a nicely well-off family who gave him an excellent education. In his youth, Ovid did serve on a couple of commissions, and one of them may well have been the Commission for Prisons and Executions, and some patrolling around Rome may have been involved. I think the job of an historical novel is to take the "maybe" and run with it.

All the poems and festivals mentioned in this book are real, and I use my own translations. Tomis was a real town – now the Romanian city of Constanța – and many of the Romans mentioned, such as Caecina Severus, Fabia and Sejanus did exist. However, many people and places are completely fictional, including Avitius and his family, and the bars like Hermes' Place.

The island of Samothrace did hold a magnificent sanctuary to the Great Gods, and the statue of Nike described by Ovid may be seen in the Louvre today. It's rather lovely.

For short stories, articles and more information about the world in which I set my novels, please visit my website at https://fionaforsythauthor.co.uk .

Acknowledgements and thanks are due to: Jacquie Rogers, Stuart Leeming and SmartCookieVA .

And finally – Ronald Syme was arguably the greatest ancient historian of the last century, and his books were, as ever, magnificently helpful.

Printed in Great Britain
by Amazon